Fear & Phantoms

A Victorian Murder Mystery

Carol Hedges

Little G Books

Cover Artwork and Design by RoseWolf Design

Cover Photograph by Jane Wright

This edition by Little G Books (August 2018)

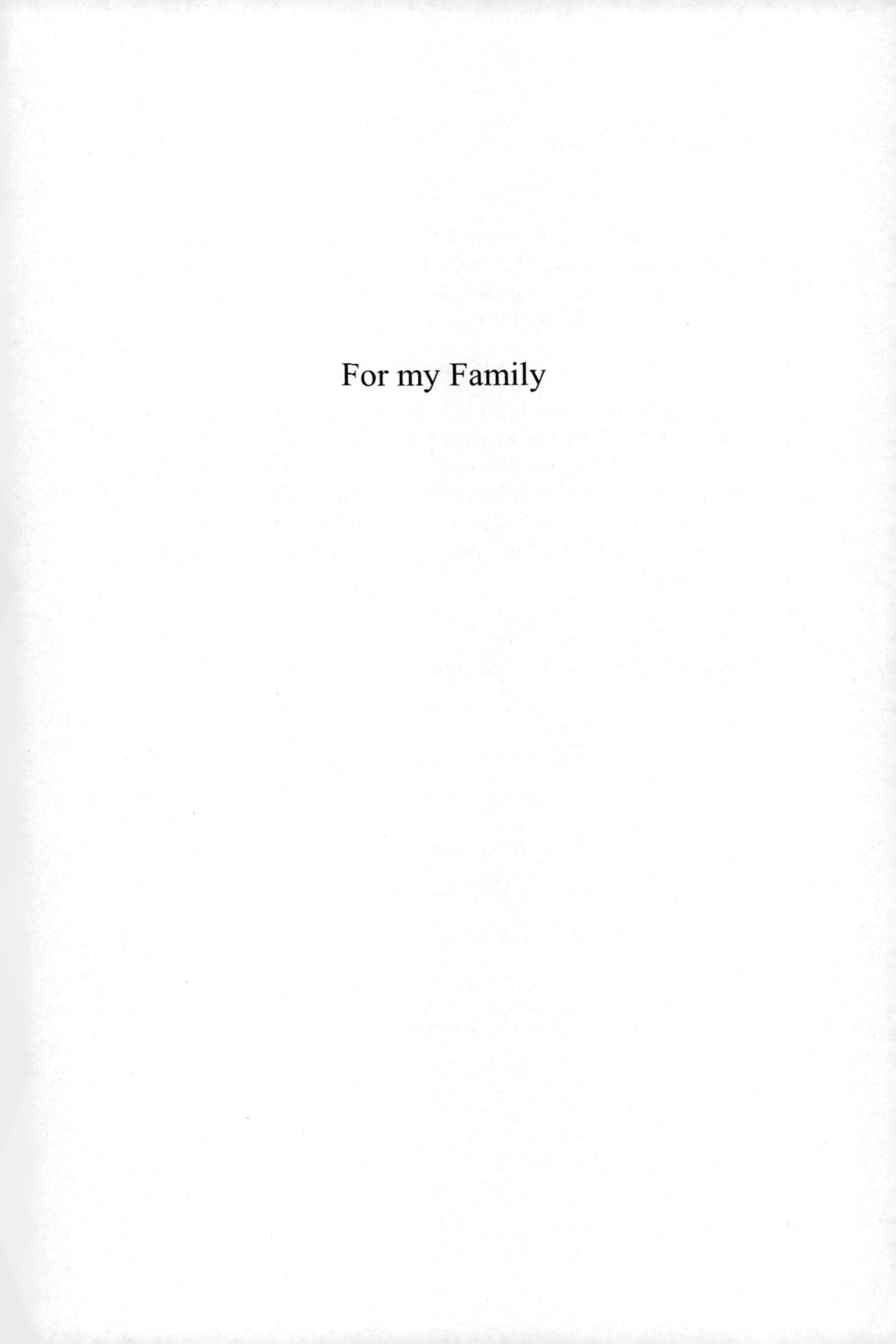

For my Family

About the Author

Carol Hedges is the successful British author of 17 books for teenagers and adults. Her writing has received much critical acclaim, and her novel Jigsaw was shortlisted for the Angus Book Award and longlisted for the Carnegie Medal.

Carol was born in Hertfordshire, and after university, where she gained a BA (Hons.) in English Literature & Archaeology, she trained as a children's librarian. She worked for the London Borough of Camden for many years subsequently re-training as a secondary school teacher when her daughter was born. Carol still lives and writes in Hertfordshire. She is a local activist and green campaigner.

Fear & Phantoms is the sixth adult novel in this series.

The Victorian Detectives series

Diamonds & Dust

Honour & Obey

Death & Dominion

Rack & Ruin

Wonders & Wickedness

Fear & Phantoms

Acknowledgments

Many thanks Gina Dickerson of RoseWolf Design, for the superb cover. To the following people, who always encourage and support me: Terry, Shelley, the two Sues, Ros, Barb, Rosie, Val, Jo, Anne, Brenda and Sheila, my editors, not forgetting numerous friends on Twitter and Facebook ... many thanks.

Most of all, I owe a debt that is un-payable to all those wonderful Victorian authors whose work I have shamelessly plundered, paraphrased and pastiched. Without them, this book would never have been written. I thank them, albeit posthumously.

Fear & Phantoms

A Victorian Murder Mystery

“I am dead, thou livest; report me and my cause aright.”

Hamlet Act 5 Scene 2

London, 1865. A night in early January. The snow, which started falling silently in a lacy haze earlier in the day, is now coming thick as down, and has reached a depth of three inches. It mutes the sounds of horse and carriage, the plod of human footsteps. At this hour, the hum of life is stilled, the shops dark; the bars and gin palaces have long thrust out their crowds to slip and slide their way home.

It is 2.00 in the morning, an hour that is both early and late. Winter stalks the streets. Look more closely. A man, muffled up against the bitter cold, is making his way cautiously along the Strand. He walks circumspectly, picking his way through newly-fallen snow, pausing between the faint glow of the street lamps to check his way forward.

He is a recent arrival in Babylondon, drawn by the prospect of golden streets and golden life-chances. Earlier, he has dined, cheaply, then slipped into one of the many private gambling clubs that litter the back streets, where the nobility and no-ability stake their money on the throw of the dice, the spin of the roulette wheel.

There, he drank wine the colour of old blood, held his nerve, played his cards with verve, and Lady Luck smiled upon him. Now, a large bone-white moon is his only companion as he reaches the top of the Strand and prepares to cross the road.

The man steps off the kerb, loses his footing, staggers a few steps, then slips and falls backwards, cutting his head open on a sharp edge of pavement. He attempts to rise, but he is unexpectedly prevented by a strong hand that grasps him by the shoulder, pushing him back down.

For a brief moment, the man stares up at the flakes crossing the light of the street-lamp, then straight into the eyes of his assailant. Recognition dawns.

"But … no, you are …" he murmurs.

Then his head falls back, his eyes close and he lies still.

Snow continues to fall, whiting out the street, resculpting statues, folding and unfolding, teasing the eye with glimpses of spires and towers. At such a time, on such a night, nobody is around to see what looks like a street robbery. 2.00am is a world unto itself. The assailant bends over his victim. A few seconds later, he straightens up, and disappears into the snowy night, leaving the man crumpled in a heap on the ground, blood from the deep cut on his head petalling the snow with crimson.

Eventually dawn arrives, bringing with it the army of street-sweepers, who shovel up the snow, piling it into white mountains alongside the kerb. The first carts roll into the city, their wheels muffled. The carters walk alongside, guiding the horses as their hooves splutter on the slippery ground, their breath gushing from their nostrils in clouds of steamy vapour.

Hey! Ho! A cry goes up, the shout echoes round the street. One of the horses has fallen, and now it lies full length upon the roadway, its flanks heaving, hooves kicking up the snow like white foam. The carter leans upon its neck, trying to calm the beast, while a green river of cabbages pours over the sides of the cart.

Men rush to help. More rush to help themselves. One particular scavenger, a cabbage under each arm, leaps up the nearest pile of snow with the nimble agility of a Swiss mountain goat. Suddenly, his foot catches upon something sticking out at an awkward angle, and he is sent sprawling. As he falls, the man reaches out, his fingers searching for the object that tripped him in a desperate attempt to stay his progress. Next second, his eyes widen in horror as he realises what exactly it is that he has grasped hold of.

****

Helena Trigg's eyes open on a confusing world. For a few minutes, she lies in bed wondering why the morning light is so bright and the roads so silent and still. Then, curiosity sends her shivering to the window, where she sees a city that yesterday was black with its winter coat of soot and dirt, has been suddenly changed while she slept into a silver city of almost unbelievable beauty.

The rooftops are newly thatched in white, each street-lamp is crowned with a pure white nightcap of snow. It is as if the whole city has softened, and been transferred overnight to some Polar region, where it glitters and sparkles like a giant white wedding cake.

Wrapping her shawl more closely around her slight frame, Helena Trigg opens her bedroom door and knocks gently upon the door opposite to wake her brother Lambert. When there is no reply, she cracks open the door and peeps round. Her brother's room is empty. His clothes are not on the chair at the foot of his bed, and the bed covers are tidy. He must've woken and set off already. His journey to the city bank is longer, so it made sense to start earlier.

Helena Trigg returns to her own room to make preparations for her day. She lights the fire, boils the kettle, and makes herself a cup of tea. She cuts some bread from the slightly dry loaf. Then she sits in the rocking-chair, a souvenir from the home she and her brother left several years ago, and enjoys a few moments of peace.

It will be a difficult journey to her place of employment ~ the snow lies thickly in the streets, and her boots need mending. But needs must, so she dresses in her work blouse, long dark skirt and black knitted stockings.

Piling her hair into a net, she pins on her bonnet, buttons her navy wool coat and dons the worn leather boots. As she descends the stairs, she checks in her purse, just in case the odd sixpence might be lurking there. No luck. So, no omnibus ride this morning. Thank goodness her wages will be paid at the end of the week. Her little store of provisions is running low. And the rent on their rooms is also due, though Lambert's wages will take care of that.

By the time Helena Trigg reaches her workplace: a smart new office building off the City Road, her face and feet are numb, her hands are frozen and the feathers in her bonnet are drooping with cold. She mounts the stairs and lets herself in with her office key. She is the first to arrive, so after admiring the frost patterns on the inside of the windows, she makes up the fire in both outer and inner offices, takes the cover off her high wooden desk, and sets out her pens and inkwell.

As she settles herself behind the desk, blowing on her fingers to get some warmth back into them, she reminds herself how lucky she is to have this job, lucky to have a kind employer, lucky to be earning her own money, and most of all, lucky to be sharing her life with her beloved twin brother Lambert, who, since the death of their parents, is the most important person to her. Helena Trigg opens the black leather-bound ledger, blows on the tips of her fingers once more, and prepares to join battle with the army of figures within.

****

It is a truth universally acknowledged (by all Scotland Yard officers) that a detective inspector in possession of a great mystery must also be in want of a mug of coffee. And, as if on cue, here is Detective Sergeant Jack Cully of Scotland Yard's detective division, carefully carrying a mug of the fragrant beverage to Detective Inspector Stride's office. He is taking his time because the heat of the mug is warming his cold hands nicely.

As Cully enters the paper-strewn office, Stride glances up from the report he is reading.

"New suit?" Cully remarks.

Stride rolls his eyes. "The wife. Decided the old one was getting too shabby. Threw it out. I ask you, a perfectly good suit ~ it still had years of wear in it. I don't understand women."

"Women always feel it's their job to try and improve us, I think."

"Then it's our job to resist improvement," Stride says crisply. "By the way, there's been another sighting."

Cully sets the mug down carefully upon a pile of documents.

"Where, this time?" he inquires.

"The same place. Up-line tunnel just before Baker Street Station. Second workmen's train of the morning. Seen by ..." Stride peers at the report, "Mr Bob Ferris (17) apprentice carpenter, Mrs Venetia Ablethorpe (33) no given occupation, Mr Simeon O'Blue (21) navigator, Mr

Dolphus Cooke (31) omnibus driver, and so on and so on. Twenty-eight names in all. Every single one claiming to have seen it. How many times is that now?"

"Four," Cully says. "Five, if you count the man who claimed he saw her at Paddington Station flying towards the ceiling, although I think we can discount his statement, on the evidence of drink taken a few hours previously."

Stride gestures towards the morning copy of *The Inquirer*, which has been placed on his desk earlier. The headline reads:

The Madonna of the Metropolitan Railway!
Mysterious Vision Baffles Railway Officials!

Underneath is a drawing of a woman in a long white dress. She appears to be hanging suspended in empty air, rather like a human balloon. Light radiates from her head, and a group of stunned people are staring up at her, mouths agape. In the background, a train can just be seen emerging from a tunnel.

"Ah. Slight journalistic licence," Cully says drily. "She's never appeared at an actual station, always in the tunnel."

"That's not really the point, is it?" Stride says testily. "The press has gone and given her ~ it ~ whatever is going on, a name. Worst possible thing. Remember *'The Slasher'*? As soon as the press starts turning some criminal into a hero, our job becomes a hundred times harder."

"Do you think she is a criminal?"

"I don't think she is anything at all. She doesn't exist, except in the minds of a few gullible working people with vivid imaginations," Stride says tartly.

“Not all the sightings have been by working people, though,” Cully reminds him. “How about that professor from University College?”

In response, Stride buries his nose in his coffee mug.

“Do you want me to cut along to Baker Street Station and talk to one of the officials again?” Cully asks.

“Warn them, you mean,” Stride grunts. “I expect once word gets around ~ and now that rag has put it on the front page, it will spread like wildfire, the station will be awash with tourists, busybodies, religious maniacs and gawping sightseers.”

“At least no crime has been committed.”

“As yet …” Stride adds laconically. “Best warn them, though. Where there are crowds, there are criminals. And members of the press, which is to all intents and purposes the same thing,” he adds disgustedly.

“On my way,” Cully says.

There was a licensed refreshment room on the station platform. It served, as he recalled, rather good sandwiches.

****

Rather good sandwiches, and much more, are currently being enjoyed by Acton Teddler, a badly-dressed, bow-legged, cloth-capped, straggle-moustached individual, known locally as a conniving opportunistic scrounger, or as he prefers it, shrewd business entrepreneur.

It was he who, atop the snow mountain, suffered the tumble that led to the astonishing discovery. Now, here he is again, some hours later, ensconced at a corner table in the King's Arms, regaling all and sundry with the tale, in return for ale and sustenance.

"At first, I didn't realise wot I was a-grasping hold of," he says, in a throaty whisper. "Then I looked dahn, and there it was: an arm, sticking out. A hooman arm. All blue, and cold as the snow what it was a-poking out of."

His (current) audience gasp in appreciative horror. Teddler pauses, coughs. "Thirsty work, all this describing," he remarks, nodding to nobody in particular. The hint is taken, the order is given, and another glass of ale materialises. He takes a large slurp.

"I thought, there but for the grace of God," he remarks piously, rolling his eyes upwards to the smoky bar ceiling. A plate of mutton chops and potato passes by. He watches its progress. Sighs. A similar plate is swiftly placed on the table. Teddler takes up his knife and fork and saws at a chop in a suitably martyred manner.

Perceiving they have now reached the lunchtime interval, the audience drifts away. By the time Acton Teddler has scraped up the last of the gravy and licked it noisily from his knife, the seats on the other side of his table are vacant. He glances round the bar, and his glance encounters that of a gentleman with a flashy suit and a knowing look. The gent saunters over.

"Greetings, squire," he says, seating himself opposite the replete entrepreneur. "This is your lucky day."

Teddler nods his agreement. It certainly is. He may be two cabbages down (a nimble-footed street urchin made off with them), but in the food-and-drink stakes, and the centre-of-attention stakes, he is undoubtedly a winner. And if he plays his cards right, he is hoping to continue his winning streak for a while longer.

"I 'spects you've come to hear my tragic story?" he remarks, eyeing his empty glass hopefully.

In response, the man pulls a business card holder from an inside pocket and hands him a card. It reads: *Mr Richard Dandy, Chief Reporter on* ***The Inquirer*** *(The ONLY newspaper to speak for The Common Man!)*

"I am prepared to offer you a once-in-a-lifetime opportunity, my good man," Dandy says, tapping the side of his nose with an ink-stained forefinger.

"Oh yeah?" the good man replies.

"How would you like to see your name and your picture in London's biggest daily newspaper?"

Teddler screws up his eyes and tugs at a greasy forelock, signs that he is thinking hard. Meanwhile Dandy sits back, folding his arms and smiling in a shark-who-has-spotted-a flailing-swimmer way.

"Ain't much of a reader," Teddler confesses, eventually.

"Maybe not, maybe not, but consider the effect upon those who ARE. You walk into any public house carrying a copy of *The Inquirer*, with your story inside, and, well, there'd be a rush to the bar to buy you a drink for your heroic gesture."

"There would?"

"There would. I can assure you. Un. Doubtedly. Now, squire, time as they say, is money, so let us repair to some quiet place, where you can tell me all about what happened. In your own words, which I shall write down in this notebook."

"Why can't we stay here?" the performer of a heroic gesture asks, loth to leave the current fount-head of free meat and drink.

"We could stay here, squire. Yes. But I reckon the police will be arriving shortly. And somebody in the crowd out there is bound to mention you and where you may be found."

(For once, Dandy is not the purveyor of fake news: Inspector Lachlan Greig is even now bearing down upon the crime scene, two police constables in his wake.)

At the mention of the word 'police', Acton Teddler wipes his mouth on the limp sleeve of his jacket and gets up hurriedly.

"Orl right then, maybe I will go along of you after all."

Dandy grins, then, taking the future media star by the elbow, he steers him towards the back entrance.

"No need to show ourselves out there. Follow me, squire: I know a nice little bar where nobody knows your name."

Scarcely have press and prey moved on, than Greig and his men arrive to take stock of the situation. The body has been extracted from its final bed of ice, and is now covered, for decency's sake, by a cloth. The crowd of onlookers, gawpers, innocent bystanders, cabbage pilferers and citizens who just happened to be passing, await the arrival of authority.

Greig makes a rapid visual assessment. Then he gets out his notebook and writes down the position of the body, its relation to its surroundings and makes a quick sketch of what lies before him. He lifts the cloth, breathes in sharply, then lowers it again.

"Does anybody know who the young laddie was, or where he came from?" he asks.

The crowd shakes its collective head. Greig eyes them narrowly.

"I was told the discovery was made after a wagon of cabbages went down in the snow," he says. "I hope nobody here has been helping themselves to the contents. That would be stealing."

Certain sections of the crowd suddenly find cogent reasons to look extremely innocent and hide various bags, baskets and objects of a cabbage-shaped nature behind their backs.

"Who found the laddie?" Greig asks.

After a bit of communal discussion, a name is reluctantly volunteered, along with the destination of the King's Arms. Greig motions to the two constables.

"Tom, stay here and wait for the wagon. Harry, you come with me. Let's see what this Mr Acton Teddler has to tell us."

Greig sets off in pursuit of his quarry, but by the time he reaches the King's Head, he will find that the bird he seeks has flown. By the time he has returned to the crime scene, he will also find that the body has been removed to the police mortuary, and the crowd of useful citizens, who might conceivably have told him where Teddler lives, has removed itself elsewhere.

****

Meanwhile, Detective Sergeant Jack Cully has arrived at the white Italianate building that is Baker Street Station. Its little minarets and arched windows always remind him irresistibly of a bath and wash-house. Entering the door, he finds a youthful ticket seller dividing his attention between issuing tickets and a large slice of bread and butter.

Cully leans into the aperture and announces his presence. The youthful ticket seller swallows down his latest mouthful and directs him to the broad stone staircase leading down to the platforms. Cully descends, leaving the cold morning air outside, but becoming aware of an even greater chill, mixed with the pungent smell of smoke.

Reaching the platform, he also becomes aware of a group of people standing close together at the far end of the platform. They seem to be staring fixedly in the direction of the tunnel. He walks towards them, but is hailed by the station manager, who hurries over.

"That was quick, sir!" he says.

"It was?"

"We only sent the boy a short time ago."

"I see," Cully says, not seeing. "What seems to be the matter here?"

The manager gestures towards the small group.

"They are the matter. Been here since first light. A-singing and a-praying and a-preaching. Handing out leaflets. Bothering the passengers. I've asked them to move along, twice, but they ain't moving. That's why I sent the boy."

Cully walks towards the group, who have now broken into some sort of hymn tune. They are led by a strikingly tall man of almost skeletal thinness. He has a heavy black beard, clerical collar and the deep-set glittering eyes of a religious fanatic.

Vague memories stir. Cully recalls the time when he and Sergeant Evans (as he was then) did the rounds of various religious groups in the course of an investigation they were conducting. Jack Cully is certain that he encountered this man then. He cannot remember which particular strange sect he belonged to. He fears he is about to find out.

The small group are still belting out their hymn, (which seems to involve rather a lot of 'smiting'). Cully taps the man on his black clerical shoulder.

"Excuse me, sir. I am Detective Sergeant Jack Cully, of the Metropolitan Police," he says. "Your continued presence on this railway station platform is causing a nuisance to passengers. There have been complaints to the railway staff, and they have complained to us. I must therefore request that you desist from your activities and leave."

The man spins round, his eyes boring darkly into Cully's.

"And I am Brother Amos, leader of the True Bethel Bible Believing Brethren, and WE are about the Lord's work, and answer to no earthly authority," he hisses.

Ah yes ~ Cully remembers him now. Forty minutes they spent shivering in the cold run-down hovel that passed for a church, while Brother Amos lectured them on obscure bits of the minor prophets that proved that the final showdown between God and Satan would definitely take place in Camden Town.

Cully is just contemplating his next move, when a train comes puffing out of the dark tunnel, its twin lamps glowing like fiery eyes. It pulls up at the platform, the guard shouting 'Baker-*Street* … Bak-*er-Streeet!'* as the doors are flung open.

In an instant, the group stop singing and launch themselves upon the exiting passengers, pressing leaflets into their hands. The station manager materializes out of nowhere.

"See my problem?" he murmurs.

Cully sees it all too clearly.

“Look officer, I don’t mind religion, in its proper place. Not that I’m what you’d call a religious man myself ~ leave that sort of thing to the wife, but ever since that whatever-she-is appeared, it’s been nothing but trouble. Seen the shrine, have you?”

He gestures towards the tunnel. Cully follows his pointing finger. At the other end of the platform, just in front of the down line tunnel, he sees a cloth-covered box with a gold framed picture of the Virgin Mary. Candles and flowers surround her.

“The little bits of paper on sticks are prayers,” the station manager tells him. “They keep blowing all over the place every time a train comes in.”

“How long has it been there?”

“Since yesterday. Dunno who put it up. Nobody saw them. I was thinking of clearing it away, but then I thought ... well … don’t want to upset people, do I?”

Jack Cully doesn’t see why not. His job description means he has spent most of his working life ‘upsetting people’. He pulls a wry face. Suddenly, the station manager grasps his elbow.

“Oh no! What are they doing now?” he exclaims.

As the train pulls out, the True Bible Believing Bethelites walk purposefully to the far end of the platform, Brother Amos at their head. Reaching the little shrine, he pauses, then, raising his voice, he exclaims, “Lo! Is it not written: *Thou shalt not worship idols*? Tear down this vile shrine, brothers and sisters! Tear it down, I say!”

“He can’t do that ~ can he?” The station master gasps, as the little shrine is roughly dismantled and tossed or kicked over the edge of the platform.

Mentally paging through the police handbook, Cully ponders his next move. Technically, the shrine isn't railway property, so he can't charge them with destroying it. But the group are preventing people from going about their lawful business by blocking the platform, and they are accosting them as they alight from the carriages.

"Maybe I'll give them another stern verbal warning," he says.

"Too late," the station master replies, gloomily.

While they have been watching the destruction of the shrine, another train has entered the station. Even as Cully is getting out his notebook, the iconoclasts scramble aboard, slam the carriage door behind them, and are born away into the malodorous tunnel. Cully curses under his breath. The station master contemplates the ruined shrine. He shakes his head sadly.

"Some of those prayers were for sick kiddies," he says.

"Let me know if they come back. I'll try to bring a few constables with me next time," Cully says, thinking how ironic that the engine carrying off the group was called Pluto. He is pretty sure the significance would be lost on Brother Amos.

He warns the station manager about the article in *The Inquirer*. Then, after refreshing himself at the station bar, he sets off back to Scotland Yard. While Cully is battling the ice-bound slipperiness of the London streets, and the erratic progress of its foot passengers as a result, the body of the murdered man will arrive at the police morgue.

****

Helena Trigg has spent a long and tiring day at the quill-face. When she finally replaces the cover on her desk and makes her way downstairs, snow still lies in the streets, so by the time she reaches her lodgings, having negotiated the crizzled cart ruts and horse-footings, her boots are soaked through and her feet have lost all feeling.

Helena Trigg opens the front door. She carries two hot mutton pies, purchased at a local pastry-cooks, for her and Lambert's supper. Her brother will appreciate some hot food, as he will also have had a long walk back from the bank where he is the chief clerk.

Helena mounts the stairs. She is looking forward to her supper, then to spending the evening catching up with Lambert's news. She enters their little sitting room to discover that the fire is unlit and Lambert is not present. Puzzled, she hangs up her bonnet and mantle and knocks on his bedroom door. There is no reply.

While Helena is trying to make sense of this, she hears a cough on the landing outside her door. Without hesitating, she runs to the door and flings it open, but her loving greeting dies when, instead of her brother, she is faced with her elderly landlord, who gives her a letter addressed to her brother, and a disapproving look.

Helena takes the letter into the living room, propping it against a vase on the mantel-piece. She lights the fire, and the two gas lamps on either side of the mantelpiece, then sits in the shabby armchair that is 'hers' and eats one of the still-warm pies.

Where is Lambert? That is the question. Gradually, as the evening wears on, the letter becomes the focus of her attention. It bears the official seal of the London & County Bank where he works. Someone has written: **Very Important** on the envelope, just above Lambert's name.

Finally, Helena can stand it no longer. She picks up the letter, slits it open with the butter-knife, and reads the contents. For a moment, she cannot understand what is written. Surely there has been some sort of mistake? She re-reads the missive a couple of times, her mind whirling.

Time passes. Helena Trigg sits motionless, staring at nothing, the letter lying on her lap. The candle sputters. The fire dies. She waits for Lambert to return, to explain, to laugh, to say it is all a silly joke. Finally, when all the light and warmth has gone from the room, and no brother has returned, she buries her broken face in her hands and gives way to a paroxysm of sobbing.

****

Night falls, bringing with it more snow, which starts falling, soft as silence. The hum of city life gradually ceases; the shops darken, and the gaudy public houses and music halls thrust their squalid clientele onto the streets. Some, who have spent their last shilling, will walk these streets all night. Some will try to find a bed under a tarpaulin, or in the niche of a bridge.

Look more closely. Shoeless children crouch on door-steps, having not made enough from their day's begging to afford a night's shelter from the cold. A few bedraggled Magdalens wait at street corners, shivering in their finery, in the hope of catching a late drunkard as he goes shouting homewards.

Here and there, where the flagstones have been taken up to mend a broken gas main, grotesque shapes of men and women gather round glowing braziers. They stretch out mottled blue hands towards the red-hot charcoal, or smoke clay pipes. Nobody speaks. Each is alone, rendered mute by their own misery.

Pale with want, homeless, friendless, destitute and withered, these night wanderers might once have been the pets and protegées of London, the admired of the Argyle. Gilded youth and maidens, now come to dust and degradation. Empty-pocketed and sodden-faced, they stand waiting for the first grey streaks of dawn to gild the sky and the first breakfast-stalls to arrive.

****

Night thins. The city sharpens itself in the first light and comes back to life. Helena Trigg wakes and sits up. There is frost on the inside of her window. She feels sick and tired. Bone-achingly tired. Her face is stiff and raw from weeping. She rises, and once again goes into her brother's bedroom. He is still not there. She stands upon the threshold, thinking how much Lambert's presence had filled the place, how empty it is now without him.

Helena prepares to face the world. She dresses, piling on as many warm clothes as she can, then forces herself to eat the remaining cold mutton pie, washed down with tepid water. She must keep her strength up if she is to get through the day. Cramming on her bonnet and coat, she slips the letter into her pocket, and sets off to consult the one person in London who might be able to advise her on the correct course of action to pursue.

The offices of J. King & Co. are located on the top floor of a brand-new block. In the current absence of the proprietor, who has taken a few days off, the chief clerk, Trafalgar Moggs has been left in charge. Here he is now, seated behind his desk in the inner office, his straw-coloured hair askew, a quill pen tucked behind each ear. He is checking off the sales figures in a brass-bound ledger and nodding thoughtfully.

A sound in the front office brings him hurrying out from his sanctuary. The young clerk has just arrived for work and is setting out her pens and inkwell on the high wooden desk by the window.

"Ah, a very good morning to you, Miss Trigg," Moggs says, smiling.

The young clerk tries to return the greeting in the same spirit, but her pale, woebegone face paints a different picture. Moggs is instantly solicitous.

"Why, Miss Trigg? What is the matter? Do you have a headache? Here, sit down, let me fetch you a glass of water," he says, pulling out her high stool from under her desk.

Helena Trigg hoists herself onto her stool, then buries her face in her arms with a groan. Much alarmed by this turn of events, Moggs stands by, waiting for her to gain control of her emotions. After a few minutes, she raises her head, her cheeks wet with tears.

"I am so sorry, Mr Moggs. I have tried to be brave, really, but it is very hard, in the circumstances. Very hard indeed."

Moggs pulls up the second stool, and perches on the edge of it. Marriage to Portia Mullygrub has taught him many useful lessons about dealing with the fairer sex. Patience being right at the top of a very long list.

So, he waits patiently for the clerk to get control of herself. Eventually, Helena Trigg reaches the sniff-and-eye-mopping stage, at which point, she produces the official envelope from the bank, and silently hands it across the desk.

"Please read this, Mr Moggs. My brother Lambert has not been home for two nights. Now this letter from his bank has arrived. I do not know where Lambert is, nor do I understand what has happened, and what I should do."

Trafalgar Moggs extracts the letter and reads it in silence. Then,

"It says here that your brother must attend an early meeting this morning, as there are *'certain very serious irregularities connected to his dealings with a bank client'*. Has he ever spoken to you about this?"

She shakes her head. "Never."

Moggs chews thoughtfully at the end of one of the quill pens.

"And you say your brother has not been home for two nights ~ presumably he has not been at work either, or they wouldn't have written to him. So, in his absence, and given the importance of the matter, and the accusations made, I think you should attend the meeting yourself."

Helena stares at him. This was not one of the many options running feverishly through her mind. Moggs continues calmly.

"I see the London & County Bank is based in Lombard Street ~ that is not too far. You should be able to walk there in good time. Do you have a notebook and pencil in your bag? Good. Make sure you take careful notes of what is said at the meeting. When you return, we will discuss it, and decide what to do next."

She rises, smiling through her tears. "Thank you, Mr Moggs. I knew I could count on you for wise advice. And you are right: I do need to find out what Lambert is accused of ~ and make sure his employer understands that it must be some terrible mistake. My brother is an honest man. He would never contemplate anything irregular. I know that for a fact."

"Then go and make sure the bank knows it also."

Helena Trigg ties her bonnet strings. "I will. I am sure once I have explained everything to the meeting, they will see that there has been an error somewhere. I shall return as quickly as I can." She folds the letter and tucks it into her bag.

Helena Trigg leaves the offices of J. King & Co. and sets off determinedly in the direction of Lombard Street, promising herself that she will work the time she owes at the end of the day. She is quite certain she will feel much happier once she has proved that Lambert is not, nor could ever be, at fault. A terrible mistake has been made. It is now up to her to rectify the situation.

****

While we wait the arrival of Helena Trigg at her brother's bank, let us pause and consider Lombard Street, centre of the London banking and finance business since the fourteenth century.

Heaped in riches, the Great Fire of 1666 destroyed it, but gold rebuilt it, gold maintained it and gold sustains it even now. Lombard Street is the golden heart that keeps the global arteries of global trade circulating. Every road leads to Rome, says the proverb; in contrast, every commercial road leads to a bank.

And those doing the circulation are the cashiers and clerks, all 170,000 of them, who flock into the City square mile. Every day, between nine and ten o'clock, omnibuses meet at the Bank, disgorging clerks by the hundreds. They come by swift, grimy little steamboats from Chelsea and Vauxhall, spruce clerks in their black suits and top hats, swarming like ants along Upper and Lower Thames Street. Some also arrive by the humbler conveyances known as 'Shanks's mare' or the 'Marrowbone stage'.

A City clerkship is a sought-after position. Competition is fierce, and success depends upon cash or contacts. Lucky for Lambert Trigg that his late mother had a brother in a senior position in a private joint-stock bank, and he managed to secure one of the coveted jobs for his nephew. And coveted it is! Stand outside London & County Bank and look up. See the splendid work of the new City architects.

A monumental edifice, the brick and pillared building bespeaks the bank's wealth, respectability and reliability. Step across the marbled entrance: here are the bank clerks, ranged in long rows, writing, casting-up accounts, weighing gold and silver coins, and paying them away over the counter like so many brass buttons.

In front of each clerk is a bar of dark mahogany, a cash box, a bill-file and the day-book, a little table, a pair of scales and a small fraction of the public, pushing to get a *locus standi* as close to the action as they can. Listen to the rattle of gold as the clerks push it across the tables with their little brass shovels.

Here is an old man, waiting to pay or be paid. He checks his large silver watch and stares fixedly at the customer in front of him. She is a young woman with a small child, who reaches out with his small pink starfish fingers and crows with delight as the bright coins are weighed, then passed across the table. She scoops them up gratefully, squirreling them away into a pocket. As she stands up to leave, and the old man takes her place, the entrance door opens, and Helena Trigg enters.

She glances around the busy room, her gaze lingering upon one particular counter, currently unoccupied. This is where her brother Lambert, the chief cashier, customarily sits. Helena stares fixedly at it for some minutes, as if her looking could magic up the occupant. Then she approaches one of the other clerks, temporarily customer-less, and whispers her business.

The clerk rises, indicating that she should take a seat and wait. Helena folds her hands in her lap. The light from the ceiling falls upon her slender girlish figure, bathing her in a pale glow. Several customers eye her curiously, but she does not notice. Eventually, the clerk returns and informs her that Mr Nathan E. Billiter, the bank manager, will see her shortly.

Thus, in due time, Helena Trigg is escorted by two junior clerks, one on each side, (like a prisoner going to face the guillotine, she thinks) across the banking floor to a big oak door. One of the clerks raps smartly upon the door. The other turns the polished brass door knob, and Helena Trigg enters the inner sanctum of the London & County bank.

The inner sanctum is panelled in dark wood. A dark wooden floor leads from the door to a mahogany desk, with a raised edge at the front. On the desk is a silver letter-rack, two round inkwells, a selection of pens, a blotter, a small rack of wax seals and a green-shaded brass lamp.

Behind the desk sits Mr Nathan Billiter, black suited, with a starched white collar and stern expression. He is a plump and paunchy man, with a slightly pursed under-lip from a habit of counting money inwardly. Behind him, are the dark wooden shelves containing the enormous leather-bound account ledgers, several inches thick and stamped in gold.

Mr Billiter is writing a letter. He writes a flowing copperplate hand. He does not look up or acknowledge Helena's arrival, leaving her to stand in front of the desk like a naughty schoolgirl (which she is not).

She attempts a gentle cough. Mr Billiter continues writing. Only when he has signed his name with a flourish, applied the blotter, and tossed the letter into a metal tray, does he deign to lift his head. He regards her with an expression of perplexity. He tugs the end of his moustache. Fishes a gold watch from his waistcoat pocket and glances at it.

"Yes, young woman? What is it? You wished to see me, I believe? Is it a bank matter or a personal one? I am on my way to a very important meeting and can therefore only spare you a couple of minutes."

"It is about that meeting that I have come," Helena says, drawing the letter from her bag and handing it to him. Brow furrowed, Mr Billiter stares down at it.

"This is a private letter, addressed to an employee of this bank. Do you mind telling me your connection to the matter?"

"Lambert Trigg is my brother."

His head snaps up.

"Then can you tell me where, in the name of God, your wretched brother is now?"

She shakes her head.

"I do not know where he is. He has not been home for two nights. I have heard nothing from him at all. That is why I came. The letter says there has been some irregularity, so I thought ..."

Mr Billiter fixes her with an icy stare.

"Do you have ANY IDEA, young woman, what sort of trouble your precious brother is in?"

Helena lifts her chin.

"No, I have not. But I am sure whatever it is, Lambert is quite, quite innocent," she declares. "Whatever irregularities have occurred, I am here to answer for my brother and to explain matters as best as I can."

Mr Billiter purses his lips.

"I doubt that very much. These are financial issues dealing with banking practice ~ they are highly complicated and therefore beyond the mental comprehension of a woman."

Helena folds her arms defiantly.

"I am a financial clerk in a commercial city business, sir. I deal with money matters every working day. I am sure I have a very good grasp of how things are done."

He gives her a long, hard look. Helena returns it. She does not lower her gaze. Fear and indignation keep her eyes fixed upon his face. Eventually, Mr Billiter looks away.

"In that case, you had better sit down, young woman. And prepare yourself for a shock," he says, motioning her towards a seat.

****

Meanwhile, Detective Inspector Stride is also in a state of shock, though in his case it comes from his worst nemesis, in the form of *The Inquirer,* and its chief reporter Richard Dandy. The morning edition has a banner headline proclaiming: **Abominable DEATH of**

SNOWMAN in London Streets!! Does ANYBODY CARE?

There follows an interview with someone called Acton Teddler (surely not, thinks Stride) who claims to have found the body and goes into gruesome detail using descriptions worthy of a third-rate melodrama. Most of it has to be anatomically impossible, Stride opines.

Nevertheless, the newspaper cannot resist its usual dig at Scotland Yard, the Metropolitan Police and the civic authorities, all of whom are responsible for the state of the pavements, the lack of street cleaners and the unfortunate tendency of people to expire in inclement weather.

Muttering imprecations, Stride stabs viciously at the offending article with a pencil, until a quiet cough brings him back to reality. He glances up. Jack Cully is standing on the other side of the desk, arms folded. He has an amused expression on his face. Yet again, Stride marvels at his sergeant's uncanny ability to materialise on his side of the door before he hears him knock.

"See this, Jack," Stride gestures towards the offending journal. "He's only gone and done it again: The 'Snowman' indeed! And where did they get that picture? And who is Acton Teddler, and how come he isn't speaking to us?"

"Indeed," Cully murmurs, nodding.

"Death is not some street side-show," Stride snorts. "It's not an entertainment for the passing mob. This poor man must have parents somewhere, maybe a wife and family. What will they think when they read this tripe!"

"Quite."

Stride balls up the offending page and throws it across the room, where it doesn't end up in the waste basket.

There is a pause.

"If you are ready, Robertson has requested our presence," Cully says.

"Oh God, this day is just getting better and better, isn't it?" Stride groans.

There are parts of his job that Detective Inspector Stride quite enjoys: that moment of quiet triumph when the threads of a case form themselves into a credible picture that can be seen and understood; the sight of an empty desk after he has dealt with a load of files and unnecessary paperwork.

On the other hand, there are aspects of his job that he really loathes. Dealing with members of the fourth estate is one. Telling people their loved ones have been murdered is another. But visiting the police mortuary and sparring verbally with Robertson, the saturnine police surgeon probably tops them all. His only consolation is that Detective Sergeant Cully, who usually accompanies him, is almost as queasy as he is.

Stride pushes himself to a stand and reaches for his coat and muffler.

"Better get it over with, then," he mutters.

The two detectives make their way out of the main building by the back door, crossing the snow encrusted courtyard that leads to the cold, whitewashed mortuary. They descend the three steps and open the wooden door.

Robertson glances up from the metal dissecting table, his eyes alive with that peculiarly intense enthusiasm that Stride finds so baffling. As far as he is concerned, the nearest he prefers to be to a dead body is not at all.

"Ah, gentlemen," the police surgeon remarks with lugubrious relish, "here we all are, eh ~ looking once more upon an example of man's inhumanity to man. So, what do we have today?"

He whips back the sheet covering the body.

"Now then, where shall we begin?"

Stride tries a quick sideway look at the corpse, but it makes no difference. He feels his head begin to swim and a peculiar clammy sensation forms in the palms of his hands and down his spine.

"Why don't you save time and just tell us?" he growls.

Robertson regards him with benign amusement.

"Still finding it troublesome, detective inspector? *Timor mortuis conturbat me*, as you might say."

Stride is pretty sure he wouldn't. Even if he knew what it meant in the first place.

"Let me explain what we have here," the police surgeon continues. "Young man, well nourished, not a manual labourer judging by the state of his hands and clothes. Drink had been taken, but that was not the cause of his demise. It appears, upon initial examination, that he fell, cracked open his head, and then froze to death on our streets."

"Froze to death," Cully repeats, shaking his head.

"At the outset, this was indeed my opinion, given the pallor of the skin. The effect of cold upon the circulation is to drive the blood from the surface to the interior of the body, as you no doubt know. There were other characteristics that I also observed: an over-distention of the heart, anaemia of the viscera, the florid hue of the blood. Also, the effect of the wind on the night of the death would have contributed to his demise: even a slight breeze can lower the temperature in a very striking way.

"But something about the nature of his death rang a distant tocsin, as it were. You probably won't recall the case of Molly Hardwick, some eight years ago? No? Let me enlighten you: Molly Hardwick was a maid in a gentleman's residence. She was found early one morning frozen to death in the street. Accidental death was the initial conclusion. It was a bitterly cold night, snow lying on the ground, as now, and the girl was known to be partial to a tipple or two.

"When the medical officer in the case made a few further examinations, he found a stab wound to the base of the skull, previously missed due to the girl's long hair. Such a wound was unlikely to have been the result of a fall, nor could it have been self-inflicted. And so, the death of the young woman was deemed to be homicidal in nature after all.

"I therefore decided to make a similar minute and thorough examination of the head and neck area of the young gentleman you see lying before you, and lo! I found a small puncture wound, just under the chin and hidden by the gentleman's beard."

"You are saying that this man was stabbed and left to die?"

"If the wound was inflicted *pre-mortem*, that would appear to be the case. The position of the wound also suggests that the assailant must have stood very close to the deceased ~ make of that what you will."

"Do you have his clothing and personal possessions?" Stride asks.

The police surgeon gestures towards a pile of garments on a counter.

"I do indeed, detective inspector, but I think they will be of little assistance to you. He appears to have been 'picked clean' as the common street parlance has it. The only personal possession I discovered upon the body was this," the police surgeon goes over to the pile of clothes, lifts up the overcoat and dips into a side pocket. "Here you are, detective inspector. Make of it what you will."

"A playing card?" Stride frowns. He turns it over. "The ace of spades."

"How odd. Why a playing card?" Cully muses.

The police surgeon shrugs. "That is for you to find out, detective sergeant. As you know, I always maintain a strict distinction between the functions of the pathologist and the investigating officer."

He reaches into his medical instrument case and extracts a ferociously curved wooden-handled blade.

"If you have no further inquiries of an anatomical nature, I must get on with my work, which is now to make an examination of the internal organs. You are, it goes without saying, welcome to remain and observe it. No? Sure? Then I shall bid you both good day."

"He really enjoys our discomfort, doesn't he?" Stride says, as they pick their way across the treacherously iced courtyard leading to the main building.

"Indeed, he does. So where do we go from here?" Cully asks.

"I suggest you go and ask Leonard to do a drawing, then have a couple of constables run it and a description round to the main police offices. Once we know the identity of our mysterious man, we can start to piece together why someone wanted to do away with him."

Stride opens the door to the main building, which is nearly as cold as the courtyard.

"Meanwhile, I shall do some serious thinking around our mysterious playing card. Possibly over lunch. There is a message here, Jack. I don't know what it is yet, but I intend to puzzle it out."

****

A short while later, Helena Trigg, now fully appraised of the activities of her absent brother, makes her way back to her place of employment. She feels strangely lighter, as if she has been shedding matter, losing herself. As if she is filling up with cold air, or the gently falling snow. And yet despite this lightness, she is not rising, rather she is sinking down, descending into darkness.

She watches the faces that pass her by, and wonders what greeds, what desires or furies drive them. Snow melts, leaving pot-holes filled with muddy water and covered with thin sheets of ice, waiting to be shattered by boots. All around, icicles crash down from gutters and the eaves of roofs. She is travelling on an inner journey, approaching the edge of the horizon. Eventually, she will fall off.

Meanwhile, having got rid of his unexpected visitor, Mr Billiter makes his way to the bank's boardroom, where the trustees of the London and County Bank await his presence. He has imparted the information of the misdemeanours of his clerk to the best of his abilities, though he is pretty convinced that he has been wasting his time, because despite the assertions of the young woman to whom said information was conveyed, he does not believe she would be in possession of the necessary mental acuity needed to understand the matter fully. She may be one of those 'modern girls', but she is still the owner of an inferior female mind, and the ramifications of the banking business would be totally beyond her limited comprehension.

Billiter pauses outside the imposing teak door that leads to the boardroom, taking a moment to regain his composure and assume the suitable demeanour required by the occasion. On this side of the door, Billiter is master. On the other side of the door, he is the servant. He runs a nervous finger around a starched collar that seems suddenly too tight, tugs at a waistcoat that suddenly feels more like a straitjacket and opens the door.

Facing him is the big heavy boardroom table, with the current chairman, Sir Ichabod Temperance, seated at its head in a high-backed chair. On either side of him, the current shareholders sit, sober of suit and unyielding of expression. Portraits of the bank's original founders and shareholders, be-wigged and equally forbidding, hang on two sides of the walls.

An audible silence falls as Billiter makes his way to his place at the foot of the table. The only sound is the creak of his boots. The temperature in the room drops by a couple of degrees as he lays the day-book before him, continuing to fall as he fumbles through its closely-written pages.

"Ah, Billiter. We have been awaiting your arrival with some impatience," Temperance says. Icicles hang off his words.

"I apologise to the meeting. I was unavoidably delayed," Billiter murmurs, keeping his gaze firmly fixed upon the ledger.

"We would have thought a meeting of such importance would outweigh anything else," Temperance observes.

Billiter clears his throat. Opens his mouth to explain. Is brushed aside.

"So, gentlemen, as we are now all gathered, let us begin this extraordinary meeting in the usual way," Temperance says briskly.

The shareholders bow their heads. As Billiter's head is already bowed, he remains *in situ*, letting the words of the prayer wash over him. If he were a man of prayer, which he is not, his orison would definitely be of the *'Oh God, please in your great mercy, get me out of here'* kind.

"And now," Temperance says, when the last 'amen' has been uttered, "Let us turn to the matter in hand. As I understand it, a discrepancy has been discovered in the day-book of the chief cashier. A discrepancy of some magnitude, I have to inform the meeting, amounting in total, I believe, to the sum of £100,405 6s. 7d."

There is a swift indrawing of horrified breath.

"How long has this been going on? My God, it could bring down the bank!" a shareholder exclaims.

"It's an outrage! Sack the man! Drag him before the courts! And deport him to the colonies!" another shareholder cries.

Temperance lifts a restraining hand. "Gentlemen, be calm, I beg you. Mr Billiter is here to explain the matter to us in precise and exact detail, which he will shortly do. We shall then consider our response and the actions we wish to take. We will not act hastily nor rashly, discretion being ever our watchword."

He favours the hapless manager with a steely glare.

"The meeting now awaits your explanation, Mr Billiter," he says, folding his arms.

Billiter licks his lips nervously, then launches into his explanation.

"It would appear that the cashier in question, Mr Lambert Trigg, has been paying out large sums of money upon a regular basis to a client who does not exist. Let me explain. Some four months ago, an account was opened in the name of Mr Godwin Fitzwarren, who applied to the bank with a letter of credit from the Paris branch of Rothschild's Bank. He claimed to be a civil engineer, British but based in Paris and working with the French government on the French railways. Now he had returned to London, having secured several big contracts from railway companies here, and backing from the government.

"He wrote that he needed funding to start his business enterprise in this country. The letters guaranteed his credit worthiness. The bank opened an account for Mr Fitzwarren, putting it in the hands of Mr Lambert Trigg to manage. Mr Fitzwarren then proceeded to withdraw large sums of money regularly, each time presenting Mr Trigg with bills of exchange from the Paris bank.

It was only when the bills were sent to the Rothschild's Bank in Paris for redeeming at the end of the customary three-month period that the fraud was discovered. The Paris bank confirmed that it had never written the initial letter of credit, never issued the bills, had no record of any such bills, and could only assume the whole thing was a complete forgery.

"I immediately suspended the account and sent two men round to the address given in the letter of approach. It did not exist. Nor had anybody there heard of Mr Godwin Fitzwarren."

"But surely your cashier must've been suspicious when so many bills were being presented?" one of the shareholders remarks.

"In the only interview I had with him, he told me that the gentleman in question told him he needed the finance to buy stock and parts. The cashier informed me that the bill forms were all written on blue paper, identical to those issued by Rothschild's Bank: they are very distinctive. He swore that he had no suspicion that they were forged."

"And why isn't the young man here to give an account of himself?"

Billiter bites his bottom lip.

"He has been absent from his desk for two days. I have now ascertained that he hasn't been home since the interview."

"So, he's legged it, clearly suggesting that he knew all too well who this Fitzwarren was, and that he was in on the business all the time," the shareholder remarks acidly.

"It would appear so," Billiter admits unhappily.

"Leaving behind debts of … how much did you say again?"

"£100,405 6s. 7d." Billiter shifts in his seat.

Silence falls. The shareholders stare. The portraits glower. The temperature drops.

"So, gentlemen: with the permission of the meeting, this is what I suggest we do," Temperance says, raising a hand to forestall any comments. "We will issue a whole new tranche of bank shares, hinting that we are about to conclude an important merger with a rival bank. We will use the capital from the sales to shore up our reserves. Unless anybody else has a different solution, of course?"

He pauses, glancing meaningfully round the table. Heads are shaken glumly. Nobody has.

"I also suggest we put in some of our own money ~ just to keep the day to day business afloat. A temporary measure, I am sure. Meanwhile," he says, pausing until every shareholder is making eye contact, "we will take extreme care to keep this matter out of the public domain. Not a word of what we have discovered must go beyond these walls. Let us remember that some of our customers are baronets and members of Parliament ~ Lords even. If the loss gets out, even the slightest suspicion of a loss, it could precipitate a run on the bank. I do not have to remind you what happened when there was a run on the Limerick and Tipperary Bank, do I?"

He does not. A shudder runs around the table. The shareholders nod their agreement to his suggestion.

"In that case, I call this extraordinary meeting of the shareholders to a close. And remember, gentlemen: Not. A. Word. To Anybody. Outside. This Room. Not your wives, your servants, your business acquaintances, the men you encounter at your clubs. The matter stays here. It must do, for all our sakes. Is that clearly understood?"

It is. The shareholders rise. Billiter rises also, but Temperance waves him back to his seat.

"Not you, Billiter. No, indeed. Not you. We have unfinished business here."

The shareholders troop out of the boardroom in silence, each casting a malign look at the hapless manager as they leave. Billiter keeps his head down and tries not to remember his parting conversation with Lambert Trigg's sister.

He had impressed upon her, using his sternest tone (the one he reserved for berating the junior clerks) that the preservation of the bank's good name was paramount, and warned her in the strictest manner possible not to make any further investigations that might cause a slur upon its reputation.

To his astonishment however, the uppity young woman had failed to be suitably chastised. Instead, she had replied, in a distinctly defiant tone of voice: *'I shall do whatever it takes to clear my dear brother's name from this false accusation.'* Then she had risen abruptly from her seat and stalked out, her head held high.

Billiter tells himself that it was just a silly female reaction. After all, what could she do? She is a young woman with no knowledge of the world. He had hurried after her, meaning to dismiss her with a stinging rebuke for her boldness, but she'd managed to quit the bank premises before he could do so.

****

Let us pause at this point. A few hours earlier, at just about the time that Helena Trigg was hurrying out of the London and County Bank, a handsome young woman with inquisitive deep blue eyes and hair the colour of untamed treacle, arrives at Farringdon Street Station ticket office, where she requests 'a single to Baker Street Station, if you please', in a firm, bright voice.

She hands over the money, receives her ticket, then descends the broad stone staircase, arriving at the wide wooden platform, which feels like a soft carpet to her feet in comparison with the rough pavement above.

The young woman's name is Lucy Landseer, and now she stands upon the platform itself, trying to contain her excitement as she awaits the arrival of the down line train to Farringdon. It is her first encounter with the Metropolitan Railway.

Up until now, her peregrinations through London have taken place above ground, on omnibuses, via the odd hansom cab, but mainly upon her own two feet. This morning, she is going to sample the delights of this novel way of travel for herself.

After sampling them, she will return to her lodgings and write about her experience in a lightly witty manner. When she has satisfied herself that her article contains the requisite amount of light and wit and not too many inky blots, she will sally forth and deliver it to her editor. After that, she will return to her room and get on with her novel.

Lucy Landseer is the epitome of the Modern Girl about Town ~ this is actually the title of a series of articles she is writing for *London Life*. She also writes short stories for several women's magazines. And essays on various topics. All her output appears under the pseudonym of the *Silver Quill*.

As she waits for the train to arrive, she thinks back to the response to her first story, tentatively submitted to *All the Year Round,* with fingers crossed. It had elicited an unexpected but encouraging letter from the celebrated proprietor: *'Your writing shows great promise. There needs, however, to be a love scene. The public like love-scenes. I should suggest a thoroughly happy ending. The public like happy endings,'* he'd written.

But what, Lucy Landseer asks herself, had she known of love scenes and happy endings back then? She was barely seventeen, the daughter of a country rector, one of eleven motherless children, all scrambling up in a rambling house. As the youngest, her education was left pretty much to her own devices.

Back then, she was like a pirate, pillaging her father's vast library, squirreling books upstairs to her tiny box-bedroom, devouring her treasures by candlelight while the rest of the family slept, and the house creaked and groaned its way through the hours of night like a great galleon. She stuffed her mind with Greek and Latin, geography, mathematics and philosophy, always half-understood, barely grasped, but all entrancing in their baffling complexities.

Lucy's reply to the question: What is love, could not echo that of Silvius, in Shakespeare's play '*As You Like it*'.

'It is to be all made of sighs and tears;
It is to be all made of faith and service;
It is to be all made of fantasy,
All made of passion and all made of wishes.'

But time passes; it knows no better, and here she is three years later, in the greatest city on earth. She has lodgings in one of the hostels run by the Young Women's Christian Association, which is providing her with *'a home life based on Christian principles and at a moderate charge'* as the little booklet in her bedside table drawer informs her.

The moderate charge also includes the sort of uninteresting, badly-cooked food to which the daughter of a country clergyman is perfectly accustomed. On the plus side, the hostel has a lending library: rather bland in content, but she is steadily working her way through it.

Lucy is also studying at the British Museum and attending the Lectures to Ladies at Bedford College (currently being given by a rather dashing young lecturer from Cambridge University) for, after much persuasion, she has funding from her father for a whole year. At the end of the year, she must either demonstrate to him that she can earn her living by writing or return to the rectory and become a governess to her numerous nieces and nephews.

Lucy Landseer has already decided that she is never ever going to return to the rectory. Her life-journey is elsewhere. It is here, in this noisesome, odorous, overcrowded city that she has made her dwelling place. Whether it will include love is, as yet, unclear, but in London, she has found its beginning.

Avid for experience, she has been walking the streets, exploring the highways and byways, peering into shops and lighted windows. In fact, she has turned herself into that most unusual of young women: a flậneuse.

The train arrives in a huff and puff of smoke. People jump down and people jump in, and off it goes, swift as an arrow. Lucy feels an icy shiver of delight run down her young spine as the train plunges into the first tunnel. She is actually passing under the city, touching its very foundations.

Perhaps, in some bygone times, doublet-and-hosed noblemen stood near here and fought a duel with each other for the hand of a fair maiden. Maybe the great William Shakespeare quaffed a flagon of ale at a nearby public house before going home to write his plays.

She makes a note of this for future reference.

She also notes down the presence of gas-lights, giving an almost homely feeling to the carriage, although the draft through the window apertures makes the burners flicker somewhat. The carriage is nicely fitted with leathered seats, and the smell of steam, about which she has read considerable adverse criticism, is malodorous but tolerable. Several gentlemen in the carriage are smoking, but she has become used to this and it bothers her no longer.

The train (she saw that it was called *Cerberus* ~ perhaps something can be made of this?) puffs into stations, their names called upon the air as if they were comestibles on a market stall. Passengers disembark and passengers board.

Lucy observes them all, giving some of them fictitious names, and making up little stories for her article: here is Miss Spillikins, a pale bony spinster of fifty years, flat-chested, long-nosed, her personal charms fled with the years. She dresses modestly, in the last of her finery and ekes out a penurious and lonely life in a backroom in some small court. She is on her way to the Dame school, where she will attempt to din the rudiments of reading and writing into the heads of frowzy unwashed children, who laugh at her behind her back.

Next to her sits Mr Demimonde, whose horseshoe patterned cravat, garish waistcoat and horses head tie pin mark him out as a lover of the turf. He is meeting up with some pals for a day's sport, culminating in a night at a cheap music hall, where he will quaff (she really likes the word '*quaff*') ginger ale, and roar out the latest bawdy songs at the top of his voice.

Her train of thought (sic) is suddenly interrupted by a large red-faced lady on the opposite seat. She wears a highly horticultural bonnet and a muff which resembles an electrified cat, and now remarks in a loud voice, to anybody who might be listening that *'Er Em'ly 'as bin travellin' back and forth for a week, but she nivver yet saw nothing of the Virgin Mary.'*

Intrigued, Lucy puts away her notebook and bends an ear to the conversation that ensues. Here is something new. She has read of the strange apparition with, it must be said, some degree of scepticism. After a moment's pause, Miss Spillikins murmurs quietly that she has never seen it either, nor does she actually believe in its existence.

"Ho, do you not?" the horticultural one remarks, adding words to the effect that just because one don't believe in something, doesn't mean it don't exist, like marriage and the government, which exist, but in which she personally puts little faith.

The argument is batted to and fro for a while. The train stops at Portland Street Station to let on new passengers. Amongst them is a plain but well-dressed woman with a young girl of about ten years who holds her hand.

They make their way to the far end of the carriage and sit down. The train pulls out of the station and enters the tunnel leading to Baker Street Station with a shriek, which is suddenly echoed by an even louder shriek that seems to come from somewhere much closer to hand than the engine.

"I saw her! I saw her!"

The girl is pointing out of the window.

"There was a lady! She was all in white! I saw her! She was flying in the air!"

Everybody crowds to the back of the carriage and peers out of the windows, but the engine smoke obscures everything. The girl continues her litany, watched with approval by the woman who accompanies her. Miss Spillikins purses her thin lips. The horticultural bonnet crosses herself.

"Ow! Holey Muvver of Gawd, pry for us sinners," she chants.

The train enters Baker Street Station and draws up to the platform. People spill out of the carriage, and rush to the tunnel end. They are joined by passengers from other carriages, who pick up on what has happened, so that by the time the train departs, most of its former occupants are now gathered in front of the down line tunnel.

Lucy goes with them ~ here is a story worthy of the *Silver Quill's* attention. She slips through the crowd, listening to the excited and rapturous chitter-chatter, making mental notes of who says and does what. Eventually, she reaches the little shrine, now enlarged by three wooden boxes and covered with a red bobble cloth.

Horticultural Bonnet, grasps her sleeve.

"Did yer see her?" she asks, "I fink I caught sight of summat."

Lucy shakes her head.

"I saw nothing."

"And ter fink She appeared to an innercent little child! Ow how blessed she was! Where is the li'l mite? I wants to shake her preshus li'l hand."

Yes, where is she indeed? Lucy Landseer scans the crowd of people peering expectantly into the dark smoky tunnel, but rather to her surprise, given their prominence in the initial sighting, both woman and child are nowhere to be seen.

****

Meanwhile Helena Trigg is returning to her place of work after her meeting with the manager of the London and County bank. Everything seems suddenly to take longer and require so much more effort. She pushes on, breath coming out of lungs, muscles working against muscles. She is in the midst of people. Yet she feels as alone as she has ever been.

The ground catches up with her: she stumbles and nearly falls. She is aware of curious glances from passers-by. She wants to cry out that she is not drunk; she is in shock. Deep, deep shock. Somebody makes a remark behind her back and sniggers. She doesn't look round. Part of her wants to. She doesn't let it.

Helena climbs the stairs. Her hands fumble with her bonnet-strings. Her coat feels like a dead weight on her shoulders. She pushes open the door. The outer office is empty. The door to the inner office closed.

She hoists herself onto the high wooden stool, opens the ledger, and dips her pen into the inkwell. The comfort of figures, the immutability of numbers, this is what she needs to calm her quaking heart and lift her flagging spirits. She will immerse herself in her work and try to put the last few hours out of her mind, albeit temporarily.

Unbeknown to Helena, however, there is an important conversation taking place in her employer's office. The two participants, senior clerk Trafalgar Moggs, and the owner of the business, Miss Josephine King, are discussing the young clerk's predicament, and trying to come up with helpful suggestions.

"It seems to me that we have a dilemma," Josephine says. "We might aid Miss Trigg's financial position by increasing her hours ~ there is certainly much to do with the new orders coming in. But then we would decrease the time she could spend looking for her brother."

"I am not sure how she'd even begin to search for him," Moggs says, pulling absentmindedly at a strand of his straw-coloured hair. "London is such a vast place, everyone treading on each other and crowding together. And then there is the matter of her sex ~ a single young lady cannot exactly go to taverns or music halls, or other places of low repute, can she?"

Josephine regards him with amusement.

"Do you think that is where her brother might be, Mr Moggs? Perhaps we should send you or William to inquire?"

Moggs pulls a face. "I do not think my dear wife Portia would appreciate that, Miss King. She already finds it a strain to keep house, what with the children coming so thick and fast that I can barely take account of them!"

"Then what do you suggest? For we cannot let her continue alone in her quest."

Moggs takes a moment before replying. "I think the time may be right to approach the proper authorities. With Miss Trigg's agreement, a letter of introduction could be sent to Detective Sergeant Cully at Scotland Yard, asking for his help. It is a delicate matter, and we have always found him to be discreet and tactful, have we not?"

"Indeed, we have. My friend Lilith Marks cannot praise him enough. I believe that several of her cakes have already found their way to his home, for without his help, she would never have been reunited with her daughter Essie. Yes, Mr Moggs, that is an excellent suggestion. Let us call Miss Trigg into the office, and put it to her. If she agrees, I'll write the letter at once. It should be in the detective sergeant's hands by this afternoon at the latest."

****

Mid-day finds Detective Inspector Stride sitting on his own in a wooden booth in Sally's Chop House, a dark, low-ceilinged place off Fleet Street. It is Stride's favourite watering-hole though sadly he is not Sally's favourite customer, having rather too much policeman and rather too little man-in-the-street about him. People, however innocent, do not like to be reminded of the forces of law and order, especially when they are enjoying a hot lunch.

Stride forks up pieces of baked potato, watched at a discreet distance by Sally, an enormous man with a bulbous broken nose and a gravy-stained apron. In the not too-distant past, Sally was a villain of some inadequacy, but as a result of a misunderstanding involving a close relative, a pawnbroker and a canteen of cutlery, he decided to give up his life of crime for a career in catering and opened the Chop House.

Stride lays his knife and fork on his plate and digs in his pocket. He places the ace of spades playing card picture-side up on the table.

"What d'you make of this, Sally?"

Sally edges cautiously closer. The trouble with policemen, especially this one, is that he can never be sure if they are just passing the time of day, or about to embark upon some retrospective investigation that might lead to unforeseen consequences of a magisterial nature.

"Looks like a playing card to me, Mr Stride," he ventures.

"But what does it MEAN, Sally?"

Sally rolls his eyes in an 'in-all-the-chop-houses-in-all-the-cities-you-had-to-walk-into-mine' sort of way.

"You need to have a whole pack, or you won't get much of a game?" he suggests.

"The. Ace. Of. Spades," Stride says patiently. "What does one think when one sees the ace of spades?"

As this is way above Sally's job description, which consists of serving plates of hot dinners from animals of dubious provenance, taking payment, and checking the spoons haven't been pocketed, he merely shrugs.

"'Nother plate of chops, Mr Stride?" he suggests. "Help the thinking along a bit?"

Stride sighs and pushes himself to a stand. He repockets the card and pays for his meal.

"No, thank you, Sally. I must get on."

"Well, you have a very pleasant day then, Mr Stride," Sally says earnestly, relief plastering his features. "Good luck with all the thinking. And I hope you find the rest of your pack of cards."

Sally heads for the till. Stride heads for the street. He makes his way gingerly along the still slippery pavements until he reaches Scotland Yard. As he barrels through the front door, the desk constable looks up and gestures with his head towards the Anxious Bench ~ the rough wooden seat for those waiting to hear news of their nearest and dearest.

Stride follows the gesture. A pale young woman sits on her own at one end of the bench. She is staring at the floor, her hands clasped tightly in her lap. She gives the appearance of trying to take up as little space as possible. As Stride approaches, she glances up eagerly.

"Oh, Detective Sergeant Cully? I have been waiting to see you. I have a letter," she fumbles in her bag, "ah, here it is. I was told you'd be able to help me."

Shaking his head, Stride takes the letter.

"I'm sorry, young lady, my sergeant isn't in today. I'm Detective Inspector Stride. May I read this letter and see if I can assist you?"

The young woman studies his countenance solemnly for a few seconds, as if trying to decide whether she can trust him from the lines in his face. Then she sighs resignedly.

"Yes, you may. My name is Helena Trigg. The letter is from my employer. She was intending to send it, but given the nature and urgency, I have brought it myself."

Stride opens the letter, raising his eyebrows as he reads the signature at the bottom of the page.

"Ah. I see. Your employer, you say. Well, well. If you care to accompany me to my office, we could discuss this matter in private, Miss Trigg. Or you can wait for my colleague. Detective Sergeant Cully will return tomorrow."

The young woman hesitates. She subjects him to another long searching look. Then she nods quickly.

"I understand, thank you, and I am happy to talk to you, detective inspector."

Stride leads the way to his paper-strewn office, dusts off a chair and positions her in it. Then he attacks the smoky fire with a poker, moves a pile of documents from the centre of his desk to an outlying region, and sits down. He reads the letter. Then, cupping his chin in his hands, he waits patiently for the young woman to tell him her trouble.

****

The Victorian postal service is the wonder of the age. It was hailed by its founder, Rowland Hill as 'a powerful engine of civilization', and from the passing of the Penny Postage Act, a communications revolution has taken place. There are between ten and twelve deliveries daily in most big cities; the first is at 7.00 am, the last at 8.30 pm.

From the busy intricacies of the central Post Office at St Martin's-Le-Grand, countless millions of letters, parcels and packages issue forth with a military efficiency. A veritable Niagara of language pour through the sorting rooms, to be deposited via the letter-carriers through the letterboxes of rich and poor alike.

Here is one of those letter-carriers now, trudging through the snowy streets, his postbag slung over his red-coated shoulders. It is late afternoon and the gas-lighters are beginning their rounds. He steps gingerly along the pavement, rendered even more treacherous by local boys, who have been making slides ever since the first fall of snow (there have been many letters of complaint to *The Times* about this lawless behaviour).

The letter-carrier arrives at his next destination. He reaches into his bag and thrusts a letter through the slit in the door. It is one of those houses divided into rooms for rent. Slightly shabby, and could do with a lick of paint, but he's seen far worse. It still has its lion-headed knocker, and spear-headed railings. The letter is immediately taken up by the elderly landlord. It is for the female tenant on the first floor. Its contents will come as a great shock.

****

Detective Inspector Leo Stride prides himself on being a modern man. It is an opinion not universally shared by the rest of Scotland Yard, especially the younger constables, who privately regard many of his views as fit only for exhibition in the British Museum (Ancient Antiquities Department).

However, the concept of a 'female accounting clerk' working in a city office is straining the elastic of his credulity almost to breaking point. Nevertheless, Stride is a professional, and thus has listened to Helena's account of her brother's disappearance, made copious notes, and reassured her that the finest minds in Scotland Yard would now bend themselves to solving the mystery.

He accompanies Helena Trigg to the front entrance, and shows her out into the street, passing Inspector Lachlan Greig coming in. Greig eyes Stride's companion with interest. When Stride has bid Helena farewell, he finds his colleague waiting for him. Greig nods towards the door and the departed Helena.

"A fine lassie. What brought her here?"

Briefly, Stride outlines Helena's story. Greig nods a few times, then says,

"Interesting. Maybe we should call her back to take a look at that poor young man in the mortuary? From what you say, her brother went missing at about the same time as he was killed. What do you think?"

Stride stares at him for a long moment, while outlying bits of his brain start making connections. Then he brings his fist down on his open palm.

"By God, Lachlan, you are right! Why didn't I think of that?"

Greig heads for the door.

"Do you know where she was going?"

"She said she was returning to her place of work."

Greig pauses.

"Ah. What a pity."

"No, I have the address. Follow me ~ if we are quick, we might just be able to catch her before she gets there."

Hatless and coatless, Stride plunges out into the freezing afternoon, where the weather is just hesitating between an iron frost and a drizzling thaw, unable to make up its mind which.

The two detectives hurry along streets where gas-lights flare, illuminating fine shop fronts teeming with cashmere shawls, ribbons, lace collars, linen cloth, and bales of silver spoons and forks. They proceed at a brisk pace past a jeweller's shop, the window glittering with heaps of baubles, trays of rings, clocks, tiny ladies' watches, bracelets and guard chains.

They do not stop to admonish the desolate ragged wretches who stand with noses pressed to the glass, staring wistfully at all the luxuries displayed within, any one item of which would fill their bellies and those of their hungry children, who wait hopefully at their side.

They cross the road, passing gin-palaces, with their columns and mirrors and ormolu candelabras, where a man might set down his three halfpence and drain his glass of blue ruin or short in the Geneva-laden, tobacco-scented atmosphere, before smacking his lips, wiping his mouth with his hand and passing on.

They hurry by more shops, cheap gin providers, followed by a mix of saloons, costermongers with barrows of bruised and winter-blasted fruit, pie-shops, fancy stationer's shops, cheap-jacks, sandwich board men, always scanning the pavement ahead and the opposite side, and finally, they spot the small figure of Helena Trigg, resolutely striding towards her place of work.

Greig steps quickly ahead, calls her name, then as she stops and turns, her eyes widening in astonishment, he takes her gently by the elbow and waits with her until Stride catches them up.

Instantly, a small belligerent crowd gathers round them, on the basis that a young woman detained by a tall man who looks like a member of the police, must be innocent and in immediate need of rescue. Only when Stride has threatened, Greig has appealed and Helena has reassured, does the crowd melt away, leaving the three of them to return to Scotland Yard.

When Helena Trigg and her brother were children, they used to play on a see-saw, built for them by a kind neighbour. She remembers the feeling of stomach-churning anticipation as she reached the top of the arc, hovered for a second, then plunged down towards the ground.

'Here we go up, up, up, and here we go down, down, down ...'

She remembers singing the centuries' old rhyme, the summer sun beating down on her head. She remembers the sweet smell of the wood, the feel of the plank between her legs. All these things are remembered, as she stands in the cold white-washed morgue, in front of the wooden table and waits for the police surgeon, whose name she has already forgotten, to pull back the cloth covering the body.

"Are you quite ready, young woman?" he asks.

Mutely, she nods, feeling the blood come beating up from her heart.

He lifts the cloth. She stares down. The air takes on a thickness; she cannot breathe. The walls start to cave in around her. Dimly, she hears someone saying,

"Catch her, Lachlan. She's going to fall."

These are the last things she hears, before darkness descends, taking her with it.

****

Let us swiftly change location. Here is a den of thieves. But not as one might imagine it. This is not some seedy dive down a back-alleyway, with smoke-blackened walls, sawdust on the floor and drink-stained tables. You will see no swarthy, low-foreheaded coves in greasy caps, wielding cudgels and followed by sullen bulldogs called Bruiser or Bully.

In contrast, black and white tessellated tiles lead up to a grand entrance, with a stucco porch and a painted front door with upper panels of fashionable acid-etched glass. This street contains elegant townhouses, many occupied by the cream of society. People here come and go in smart carriages with family crests, and liveried footmen on the box. They employ staff to serve and wait upon their every need.

At this particular address, the Hon. Tom Scallywagg, MP might drop in after a heavy session on the backbenches of the House. The eminent criminal lawyer Minimus Scrutor accepts invitations to dine here, and the fabulously wealthy Nabob of Khoratoum is a frequent visitor.

Enter the richly-curtained study. A fire burns brightly. Gold-framed paintings of various foreign scenes hang on the dark red flock wallpaper. Leather-bound books with elaborately hand-tooled spines are arranged in ordered rows in a mahogany bookcase.

Lounging in an easy chair, in front of the welcoming flames, his elegantly-shod feet to the blaze, we see the current owner of this house, a tall, dandyish figure in immaculate evening dress. He lifts a heavy crystal goblet of hot spiced wine, and sips appreciatively. His two companions, their attire also marking them out as people of influence, continue smoking cigars and perusing the financial pages of the newspapers.

Here are members of respectable professions; they bank at Coutts, share the same box at the opera as members of the aristocracy. Their quail eggs and Strasburg pies come from Fortnum. Their tailors are expensive and exclusive. They belong to the best clubs. They do not look like criminals. They look exactly like what they are: highly successful Victorian businessmen and professional members of the social elite. That is how these men have eluded the forces of law and order for so long and continue to do so.

"Gentlemen, let us speak of present matters," says the host, languidly throwing his cigar end into the fire. "First, our Man of Law: what news from the Inner Temple, Jacob?"

The individual thus addressed is a lean, black-clothed man, perhaps fifty years old. From a distance, he has a benign appearance of a philanthropist, having a bald head, pale sunken cheeks, and high-domed forehead. Closer acquaintance however, reveals a pair of thin parched lips, a long hawk-like nose, grizzled side-whiskers and a sharp chin.

It also reveals something malevolent about the deep-set eyes. Truth to tell, his whole countenance bears the remote gimlet expression of one who views the whole of mankind as standing in the dock before him and judges them guilty as charged. When he speaks, his voice has the dry, ironic tone of a hangman.

"All is in hand. My connections with the criminal world have proved yet again aidant and remedial to our purposes. My network of accomplices is secure. Whatever funds we need can be obtained, by one means or another."

"I salute you!" The house owner lifts his glass and tips it in the lawyer's direction. "Now, how goes it in the sporting world?"

The reply comes from a plump middle-aged man in a well-cut tweed suit that strains across his ample stomach. His expression and demeanour bespeak a man of the turf, one who moves from Melton Mowbray to Newmarket, as the season changes. He lifts a copy of the *Sporting Times*.

"I've opened five more betting shops. And I have a contact in the new telegraph office who sends us the results as soon as they come through, before even the *Pink 'Un* gets them.

Each shop has got a set of very respectable looking gents, don'tcherknow, who hang about telling all and sundry that they are experts and know what horses are a dead cert to win. They then pretend to place huge bets on them. The punters believe them of course, and follow their example, and then lose their entire stake."

"And indeed, 'tis the way of the world, is it not? For us to win, others must always lose. Is that not the case?"

"The balance of probability would agree, Adonis," the lawyer says, inclining his head.

Of the three, he is the most revered by his fellows, for he is a man who will stop at nothing and suffer not the smallest qualm of conscience.

Yet both his companions know that, in another life, his advocacy is eagerly sought by those who will pay the earth to get the scales of justice to tip in their favour, and his cases are regularly reported in the legal and national papers.

"Yes, it is indeed the case, my friends," the lawyer continues smoothly. "But be assured, the scales of win or lose will always tip in our favour. The cards will never fall against us. And my ingenuity is no match for the witless plodders of Scotland Yard. Everyone who threatens the success of our joint enterprise pays the price, sooner or later, of that you may rest assured."

There is a pause after he has spoken, his companions seeming to weigh up his words, in the light of their own contribution to the aforementioned joint enterprise. Then 'mine host' laughs, throws his cigar into the fire and pushes himself to a stand.

"Yes indeed. And now, dinner awaits us, my friends. I have a private room booked at Simpson's and a bill of fare that will delight even the most jaded palate. My carriage is at the door. Let us sally forth without delay, while the night is still young. And after dinner, to the Italian opera house to hear the great Mantolini sing, followed by our usual night at the gaming tables. Come, an evening of enjoyment lies before us."

****

No lavish bill of fare awaits Helena Trigg, who is even now approaching her lodgings. It has been a day like no other, she reflects, as she reaches the gate. This morning, she was told that Lambert, dear honest Lambert was a thief. Then she visited Scotland Yard, a place she has never been to, and spoke to a member of the detective police.

And then …. oh, then ~ Helena grips the green iron railings, she saw .... and after seeing what she saw, she had fainted. In public and in front of complete strangers. The shame of it brings a hot flush of colour flooding to her cheeks. It was the anticipation, and the shock: she had never seen a dead body before.

When her parents had died, Helena had been out of the country, visiting old family friends who were now domiciled abroad in France. Winter storms had delayed her return to England, and by the time she'd reached the village, both her parents' funerals had been held.

It was the sight of that poor tragic face, staring up at her, a lock of fair hair falling upon the smooth unlined forehead. So young … such horror ~ the image was burned upon her brain and she knew it would haunt her for many weeks to come.

But it wasn't Lambert.

Helena enters the house. Scarcely has she crossed the threshold, when the door to the ground floor parlour opens to reveal her landlord, Mr Mutesius, wearing his fur cap, long green brocade gown and shuffling slippers. His white hair straggles down in lank strands onto his bony shoulders.

In the background hovers Mrs Mutesius, with her faded old-fashioned morning bonnet, false front of curls and her rusty black gown. She peers anxiously over her husband's shoulder. Peering anxiously is Mrs Mutesius' default expression. Helena has never seen her look anything different in all the time she and Lambert have lived here.

Mr Mutesius clears his throat. Helena waits, thinking of the rent money that is due tomorrow and mentally working on her stalling strategy.

"Here is a letter for you, Miss Trigg," Mr Mutesius says in his strange high-pitched voice. "It came today. I have been waiting for you to arrive to deliver it personally into your hands."

He turns, hisses, "Clarrie ~ the letter! The letter!" Then he hands Helena a white envelope, slightly greasy at the edges.

Wonderingly, Helena takes it. Who could have written to her? She never receives letters. She stares at the handwriting on the envelope but does not recognise it at all. Meanwhile, the two Mutesius wait expectantly, their gaze, curious and hopeful, fixed upon the letter, (a gaze overlaid, in Mrs Mutesius' case, with anxiety).

"Thank you, I shall take it up to my room to read," Helena says firmly, heading for the uncarpeted wooden stairs.

She climbs. Behind her, she hears a brief whispered exchange, then the parlour door closes. She continues to climb. Reaching her landing, she draws the key from her bag and lets herself into the shared sitting room. It is as cold and dark and as unwelcoming as the grave.

Helena places the mysterious letter upon the table. Then she sets about finding a lucifer match to light the lamps. She fills the kettle from the china jug on the windowsill. Priorities. She needs to have something inside her before she tackles whatever lies inside the envelope. Better to receive bad news upon a reasonably full stomach.

She cuts a thick slice of bread and spreads it with pale yellow butter, scraping the last bits from the inside of the little glass butter dish and wiping the knife clean on the bread. Then she pours hot water onto a handful of tea-leaves and swirls them round in her cup.

Her supply of food is diminishing almost to extinction. And there is the small matter of the rent. One way and another, without Lambert's contribution, matters are deteriorating rapidly. She must shortly make some hard choices.

Helena settles herself in the rocking chair and reaches for the letter. She slits open the envelope with the butter knife and reaches inside to draw out the contents. For a moment, she sits stunned, not believing what she holds in her hand. Two £10 notes!

She searches inside the envelope, but there is no accompanying letter, no indication from whence came these unexpected riches. What does it mean? Is it a sign that Lambert is alive and well, and thinking of the sister he left alone in London? Or something more sinister?

Helena Trigg puts the money back in the envelope, and takes it over to the mantelpiece, slotting it behind the little china shepherdess that belonged to her mama. Then, she eats her meagre supper. She now has the wherewithal to pay her rent and buy coals and food for a couple more weeks.

She decides not to think about 'afterwards'. Instead, she will focus upon finding out what happened to Lambert and proving that he is innocent of the terrible charges levelled against him. She does not know how she will do this, but she knows that whatever the consequences, she must try.

That night, and for several nights to come, Helena Trigg lies awake, listening for the familiar footstep on the stair, waiting to hear her brother's voice, his laugh. In her dreams, they walk the flowered meadows of home, hand in hand, phantom children, ghostly siblings who were always together, always happy in each other's company.

In the silence, she breathes in darkness, drinking it down like bitter medicine.

****

Meanwhile Jack Frost still holds the city in his icy hand. Cobwebs are pendulous with frosted silver instead of dust. Gigantic icicles hang in jagged rows from gutters, like the teeth of some prehistoric monster. Pavements are regularly blocked by great falls of snow descending from overhanging roofs.

Whatever the hour, day or night, the doors of the city workhouses are besieged by poor unfortunates who find themselves houseless and hungry, while others, the industrious poor disdain the relief of alms, and quietly suffer the cruel indignities of inadequate clothing and semi-starvation.

This season of extreme cold is a melancholy and sickly time of year. Medical men are active day and night, as are coffin-makers and undertakers. The parish cart passes you by as regularly as the local omnibus. The bills of mortality rise, and many a sad heart and weary head pray for the coming of a gentle south wind that shall snap the iron chains that bind the city.

Look more closely. Here, in a cold garret room with scarcely any furniture, except for a cracked china washstand and a low truckle bed, a man lies upon a greasy mattress under a mouse-coloured blanket. There is a clotted gash along his throat. The boards by the bed are stained with blood, as is his black frock-coat. There is dried blood upon his shirt. It is clear from the rigidity of his features and blue-tinted skin, that he has been dead for some days.

Morning light filters though the grime-clouded window, bouncing off a broken mirror. The wallpaper is a mural of stains. The face of the corpse bears a look of frozen horror. His unseeing eyes are staring at the ceiling. His fists are clenched, as if warding off the Pale Horseman.

Inspector Lachlan Greig stands in the doorway surveying the melancholy scene. On the landing behind him stand a constable and the landlady, who is wringing her hands, and working her mouth into strange shapes. Behind her, the rest of the lodgers crowd up the staircase, availing themselves of the privilege of propinquity.

"What was his name?" Greig asks her.

"Ow sir, Mr P'liceman," the landlady bursts out, "I nivver knowed who he was. He jist arrived a week ago and said he needed a place to lay his head for a while. He seemed respecktable in his dress and way of speech. He paid me a week's rent, and that was the larst I saw of him until just now, when I knocked on the door coz one of the other lodgers said they'd heard strange sounds a-comin' from his room a while back. I jist stuck my 'ed round the door to see if he was orl right, and there the pore young man woz, a-weltering in his own gore. A-slain by his own hand, as you see him lyin' there before yore very eyes."

Motioning to the constable to guard the door, Greig steps further into the room and approaches the bed. *What do I see*? he asks himself. He stares thoughtfully down at the body, mentally making an inventory of its position, the various articles of clothing, the worn but serviceable black leather shoes arranged neatly under the chair.

What do I not see? he queries. He stares more fixedly, searching with his eyes for a razor, or a knife. Then something snags his attention. Grieg bends closer and gently prises open the dead man's fist. Straightening up, he beckons to the constable to join him.

"Stay by the door, constable, and don't let anybody enter the room. You were right to call me in. There has been foul play here, tricked up to look like suicide," he says quietly.

Ignoring the landlady's repeated protestations about keeping an 'orderly house', Greig elbows his way down the frowsty stairs and out into the street, where the usual attendant mob are gathered on the pavement, waiting for the body to be brought out. They are being held at bay by two more constables.

"Do not let anyone in or out until I return with Detective Inspector Stride," he says.

"Oi, Scotty, care to give us the lowdown on what's happening in there?" a familiar and much-loathed voice yells from the back of the crowd. Greig's expression hardens. How Richard Dandy, chief nuisance on *The Inquirer* manages to attend every important murder in the city is a mystery. A mystery which, sadly, he and his colleagues have never managed to solve.

"That's Inspector Greig to you, Mr Dandy," he replies, irritation making his accent even more pronounced. "My origins are my own affair. And I have absolutely nothing to say to you at this time."

Grinning evilly, Dandy elbows his way through the crowd.

"D'you hear that everybody? The boys in blue are so short of men they're now employing FOREIGNERS. For which you, the man in the street, are paying. C'mon Inspector, a few words …?"

"Go away, Mr Dandy. Is that few enough for you?"

Dandy Dick pretends to write this down, while remarking loudly to nobody in particular,

"Interesting, isn't it though. People die every day ~ yet here you are. One has to ask why?"

The crowd goes into nod-and-mutter mode. A grievance, especially a free one, is always welcome as light relief from the hum-drum nature of everyday life.

"He's right. When the baker down our road died, nobody came to investigate," a voice in the crowd agrees. "Shop closed down the next day. Got to go miles to buy a loaf of bread now."

"The old soldjer who used to beg outside the Plough and Harrow ~ he went recently, never saw a policeman asking why."

Dandy gestures towards the mutterers and malcontents. "See, the man in the street agrees with me. They are asking why too."

"Well they can ask as much as they want. They are not going to be told anything, and neither are you," Greig replies. He doubles back to the door. "Nobody in, nobody out and none of you are to speak to that man or any of his tribe. Understood?"

The constables nod. Greig flashes them a warning look, then departs for Scotland Yard. What he has just seen inside the house requires the attention of Detective Inspector Stride. Greig was on his way to somewhere else, when he was diverted here by a local officer. Now, he must be on his way once more. An important meeting is shortly going to take place. Though at this moment, only he knows about it.

****

Nathan Billiter, manager of the London & County Bank, finds himself upon what might be called the horns of a dilemma. He has told the bank shareholders that discretion is his watchword. Or something to that effect. He promised them that no inkling of the fraud perpetrated upon the bank by one of its clerks and his accomplice would ever leak out into the public arena.

And so far, it hasn't.

But now, here he is, being fetched from his inner sanctum because a member of Scotland Yard's detective division has turned up unexpectedly, wishing to talk to him about a 'private matter concerning the bank and one of its employees'.

He suspects that there can only be one reason why this unfortunate state of affairs has happened: the young woman ~ the sister of Trigg. He underestimated her, and now he is about to pay the price for his misjudgement.

Billiter has never crossed paths with a detective before and is unsure of his position. Guineas, sovereigns, and shouting at the junior staff, these are his areas of expertise. He wishes he had the benefit of a lawyer, so that he might know what he could, and what he should not say.

Meanwhile, he makes his way onto the banking floor, where all the clerks have their heads down and are pretending to be scrupulously busy in a way that indicates they are covertly listening and secretly agog with excitement.

The detective, a tall man with striking sandy hair and moustache, introduces himself. He has a Scottish accent and the sort of demeanour that indicates he won't tolerate fools gladly. He hands Billiter an envelope containing two £10 notes.

"This envelope was received last night by a young woman whose brother has recently gone missing. He is employed by your bank as the chief clerk. His name is Lambert Trigg. I see you recognise the name. That is good. His sister has asked us to help her find him, or at least, discover what has happened to him. Can you please take a wee look at the writing on the envelope and confirm that it is not in his hand?"

Billiter confirms it, adding that Mr Trigg is no longer in the employment of the bank.

"Do you recognise it as the hand of anybody else here?"

Billiter does not.

"The notes inside the envelope, now. Is there any way you could say if they came from this bank ~ maybe by checking the numbers against notes issued by your clerks?"

Billiter explains why this is impossible.

The detective glances round the incredibly busy clerks.

"Was Mr Lambert Trigg friendly with anybody in particular working here on the banking floor, while he was in the employ of the bank itself?" he asks, raising his voice so that the question is heard by all the bent heads.

Billiter cannot say for sure, but he doubts it. This is a place of business after all.

At which point, one of the clerks raises his head from the ledger he is furiously inscribing and gives the detective a quick, meaningful glance. Inspector Greig, for it is he, nods thoughtfully, while pretending he hasn't seen it.

"You have been most helpful, sir," he says smoothly and mendaciously. "If you can remember anything else that you think might help us in our investigation, here is my card. Please do not hesitate to contact me."

He turns on his heel and strides towards the exit. No eyes follow him. Every clerk seems absorbed in his work. Billiter glances round, looks down at the card, surreptitiously tears it in two, and lets it drop to the floor as he returns to his office.

A brief silence follows him out. Then the normal sounds of daily business resume. A clerk rises, crosses the floor, and picks up the two pieces of card. Pocketing them, he returns to his place and silently continues writing up his day-book.

****

Meanwhile Detective Inspector Stride is interviewing lodgers, and discovering far more than he wants to know, or is able to credibly believe, about their lives. The house in which the stranger lost his life is full of sober hard-working, God-fearing, upright citizens. Apparently.

None of them would dream of spending a night drinking at the local hostelry (whose name they all know, including the names of the owner and the two barmaids), though interestingly, none is able to give him the name of the local church or its vicar.

On the night in question, everybody was in their rooms, engaged in lawful pursuits of a useful and improving nature. What they all agree, however, is that they heard the front door open and slam shut at shortly past midnight (ground floor lodger). Then there was the sound of several sets of footsteps running up the stairs (first floor lodger). There were voices expostulating, then the door to the attic was wrenched open (top floor lodger).

A scream and a bump were heard, followed by something that sounded like a heavy object being dragged across the floor. Then footsteps descended, and the front door opened and closed once more. Nobody poked their head out of their room to see what was going on, and nobody went to see if they could help, because, well, it wasn't any of their business, was it?

Stride could well believe this. London was full of people who might know what their neighbour had for dinner every day, but not know his name, nor the names of his children. They might only be separated by a brick and a half, but never trouble themselves about the course of their neighbours' lives.

A man might be brought home dead, or be discovered dead, and the only concern of his landlady would be the procurement of the next tenant. (The sign 'Lodgins' has already gone up in the front window of this house). *Magna civitas, magna solitudo*. It's the sole Latin epigram he knows, thanks to the police surgeon, who quotes it copiously. Probably because it resonates with them both.

Stride has just finished interviewing the final lodger when Jack Cully arrives, accompanied by the men who will transport the dead man to the police mortuary. Stride draws him to one side.

"Greig found this in the dead man's hand," he says quietly.

He hands Cully a playing card.

"Ah. Our ace of spades. Again," Cully says. "Apparently, it's known as the 'Death Card' amongst players ~ it's the spade, you see. They're used to dig graves. And death comes for us all in the end; there being no escape."

Stride stares at him. His fellow officer never ceases to amaze him.

"My father-in-law used to be a bit of a gambler when he was young," Cully explains. "We got talking after the funeral. He knows a lot about the history of cards. And card games ~ did you know, for instance ..."

Stride interrupts him, "So these deaths are both linked in some way? Damn it Jack! One death is bad enough. Now we've got another identical to it. I hate multiple murders." He brandishes the playing card. "What is he saying? And who is he saying it to? I hate multiple murders with coded messages even more."

"You always say that people who kill more than once will always end up making a mistake; they can't help it," Cully says.

"I say a lot of things," Stride replies gloomily. "Right, Jack. We're done here. Let's go back to the Yard and see if anybody has turned up to identify our first body. Meanwhile, we'll put out a death notice for the second one. Hopefully, we can then find out what they had in common which might throw some light on why they were murdered. And then we must stop whoever is out there, before he kills again.

****

It is a few hours later. Stride has removed himself from his report-strewn desk to his favourite watering hole, where, over a plate of mutton stew and dumplings, he is still minutely studying the two ace of spades playing cards to see if he can divine anything useful from them. He is sure there must be something.

Stride knows the two main reasons why a man commits murder: sex and money. The oldest motives in the world, and still the most powerful. So, which is it here, he wonders as he moves the cards round the table for the umpteenth time, like a 'Find the Lady' pavement trickster.

He recalls other cases of multiple murders, all committed by a single individual. There was the Case of the Wantage Poisoner, the Case of the Barrister's Missing Monocle and the Case of the Slasher. In each case there was an identifiable pattern and a definite motive.

Sally, the eponymous proprietor of Sally's Chop House, re-fills his glass on the basis that the sooner this customer eats up, the sooner he will depart. Stride's facial acrobatics, coupled with his air of focused detectiving, are making other customers shift uncomfortably in their seats.

"I see you found yourself another playing card, Mr Stride," Sally says. "Few more and you'll be able to build a nice house."

Stride glances up.

"Did you know the ace of spades was a death card, Sally?" he asks.

"Couldn't possibly say one way or t'other," Sally replies vaguely, having learned from past mistakes that it is always best not to admit to anything that could be taken down and used in evidence at a future date.

"And here are two of them," Stride muses.

"Good thing you only die once then, innit."

Sally removes Stride's chipped plate and coughs in a meaningful manner.

"Anything else I can get you, Mr Stride?"

There will be a pattern, Stride thinks gloomily. There always is. Not because the murderer plans it, but because all human beings are creatures of habit. The trouble is, it may take another death, maybe more deaths, before the pattern emerges.

Another cough from Sally brings him back from his cogitations. He digs into his coat pocket and deposits a few coins into the man's huge hands. Thanking Sally, he dons his hat and makes his way out into the street, much to the proprietor's relief and that of his customers.

****

Having finished her lunch ~ a dainty plate of sandwiches and a small cup of coffee purchased and eaten in one of the elegant little tea-rooms that dot the West End with the sole purpose of refreshing the female shopper, Lucy Landseer, *aka* the *Silver Quill,* steps out boldly.

She has just delivered her latest article, entitled 'Jack Frost at Our Terrace' in which she described the problems of freezing water-pipes, personal sponges that turn into pumice and towels as stiff as boards. She'd also described the early morning appearance of 'snow-birds': small street boys who would clear away the snow for a few coppers. It was a light and amusing piece, and approved by her editor.

Lucy Landseer is now a free woman for the afternoon. London, with all its fascinating quirks and curious unexplored corners lies before here. And there is one rather large 'corner' that is drawing her back.

Ever since she travelled on the underground railway, the strange ghostly apparition that she almost nearly saw, has snagged her imagination. Lucy cannot get it out of her mind. She has been researching everything she can find out about the Madonna of the Metropolitan Line, and as a result, has decided to write her own piece, which she is quite sure will be far more inspiring than the hyperbolic over-written stuff she has waded though.

She makes her way to Baker Street Station, the primary location of the visions, and purchases a platform ticket. It is her intention to walk up and down the platform, describing the various sights and sounds.

She is also going to re-visit the little shrine, maybe talk to people gathered there. With luck, one of them might have seen the apparition, and be prepared to share their experience with her. If not, she will fall back on her vivid imagination and writerly talent. After all, it is no more than Mr Sala and Mr Dickens do, she reminds herself.

As the clock strikes three, Lucy Landseer descends the stone steps that lead to the broad wooden platform, forty feet below the earth's surface. The air is not as cold as up above, but despite that, there is a chill to it, rather like entering a cathedral on a warm day, she thinks. Though cathedrals do not usually smell of railway train steam.

Gaining the platform, she surveys the crowds waiting for a train to arrive. They seem to belong to a cross-section of people, defying the earlier predictions that people would never voluntarily choose to go underground unless they were manual workers or criminals. Mind you, she reminds herself as she heads towards the far end of the platform, they have the added incentive of the beauteous Madonna to draw them down.

Lucy reaches the shrine. It is now taking up even more space and has been furnished with six votive candles, all burning brightly. It also seems to have also acquired a constable with broad shoulders and folded arms. He regards her approach with a stern expression. Lucy favours him with her sweetest smile. The one that used to wring all sorts of concessions out of her Papa.

"I'm sorry, miss, but you can't linger here," the constable says. "Orders of the station master. I must ask you to move along the platform."

Lucy demurs.

"But officer, I mean no harm. I have heard about the wonderful holy apparition, and being in the neighbourhood, merely thought to see for myself what is taking place."

"Nothing is taking place," a male voice behind her says.

Lucy turns. The voice emanates from a man in his mid-thirties. He is clean-shaven but for a pair of side whiskers, and wears a well brushed, though equally well-worn woollen overcoat and a brightly knitted red scarf. His eyes are kind, but there is a weariness at the back of them. Lucy turns on the charm.

"Oh, I can see that for myself, sir. I just hoped ... perhaps …"

"To see something that doesn't exist? To take part in some mass hallucination? Do you not have better ways of spending your time, young lady? Are there not department stores a-plenty, and tea-rooms to patronise?"

Lucy twinkles at him. "There are, sir, but I am not of such a mind to waste my time in these pursuits. I am a serious writer and a studier of mankind."

The corners of the man's mouth twitch. Lucy is just warming to her theme, when a train enters the station. The man steps forward, turning his back upon her. He waits for the train to stop, then opens the end carriage door.

Lucy watches as he lifts out a little girl, and helps a woman carrying a large basket to descend. As she steps down, Lucy can see she is expecting another child. The little girl runs straight towards the shrine, her eyes dancing.

"Look Mama! Is it Christmas again?"

The mother smiles indulgently.

"No, Violet, it will not be Christmas for a long, long time now. Come, we have deliveries to make. If you are good, there may be a sugar bun for you later."

The man takes the heavy basket from the woman's arm, then steers his family through the throng of passengers towards the exit. Lucy watches them walk away. All at once she spies two individuals she remembers from her previous train journey: the girl and the respectably dressed woman are just stepping on board the train, which is about to depart.

Lucy makes a snap decision. Signalling to the guard, who has just raised his flag, to wait, she hurtles in a reckless and most unladylike manner down the platform, scrambling aboard the carriage they have just entered.

She takes a seat at the end, from whence she can observe the two passengers without necessarily drawing attention to herself in the process. They sit opposite each other, not exchanging any glances, nor conveying the slightest hint that they are connected.

The train enters the thick darkness of a tunnel, feebly lit from above via a row of skylights. It reaches Edgware Road Station. The woman and child get out, followed by Lucy. To her surprise, they remain on the platform. She edges closer. Some words are exchanged between them, but she cannot make out what is being said.

A train going in the opposite direction arrives, and they board it. Now, Lucy is highly intrigued. What is going on? Feeling more like a detective than a writer, she follows them, placing herself in an inconspicuous seat.

The train chuffs back towards Baker Street. And then it happens: the girl suddenly cries out, pointing towards the window. The woman, acting as if she has never met the girl, leans towards her, asking loudly what she has seen, then sits back, one hand to her bosom, her eyes wide, as if in shock.

The passengers, already alert to the possibility, ask whether she has seen the Madonna, and upon being informed it is so, immediately divide into two camps: those who suggest the girl is suffering from some illness ('green sickness' being the most likely explanation, offered by a man who says he is a doctor and an expert in the hysterical sufferings of young girls), and those who think they may well have seen something also.

The train deposits its passengers at Baker Street Station. The 'believers' immediately make their way along the platform, some heading towards the shrine, announcing excitedly to those waiting on the platform and those getting off the train that the vision has made another appearance. The sceptics head for the steps leading up to street and sanity.

Lucy follows the woman and the girl as they make their way out too, slipping unnoticed through the crowd, their heads down so as not to attract any public notice. Arriving at street level, the pair cross the road and make their way along Baker Street, pausing every now and then to glance into a shop window, for all the world as if they were just two normal individuals out for an afternoon stroll.

Lucy stays on the opposite side of the street, never letting them out of her sight for a second. This is thrilling! It is like a story by Mrs Braddon, with herself, Lucy Landseer, as the heroine. She is just working out whether the woman could be an evil governess who is controlling the girl for the purposes of marrying, and subsequently inheriting, her father's great fortune, when a hansom passes between her and her quarries and when it has gone, there is no sign of the couple on the opposite pavement.

Lucy grits her teeth, cursing her overactive writer's imagination. While she has been building literary castles in the air, her prey has escaped. She studies the buildings opposite and decides that only one of them could practically be the destination of the woman and the girl. But now it is too late to take her investigation further.

The local church clock has just struck the hour, and she must hurry home, gobble down the hostel's dull but adequate cooking, and then set out for Bedford College, where she has a lecture to attend, and an essay to hand in.

She casts a final look at the building, making a mental note of the street number. For she will be back, she promises herself. Oh yes, this is far too good a story to let drop. Lucy Landseer, writer and undercover private detective, is on the case.

****

As Lucy Landseer sets off in the direction of her lodgings, Inspector Lachlan Greig arrives outside the London & County Bank. He is just in time, for as the clock finishes striking four, a chaotic commotion of clerks rush through the doors, and set off up Cheapside, each carrying their billbooks, containing bank letters with the same message of 'three months after date, please pay to order' which they will deposit into the nearest letter-boxes.

Amongst them is the young clerk Greig noticed earlier. The bank enjoys a high reputation, and the spruce clerks reflect this in their smart black with buff waistcoats and dandy-looking umbrellas.

Greig waits for the clerks to come back, knowing that once the bank closes to the public, they will spend the last few hours of their day transferring all the day's transactions from their individual daybooks into the bank's ledgers.

As the chattering clerks approach the bank, he steps out onto the pavement, scanning the returning faces until he sees the man he is after. The clerk recognises him in return. He slows, letting his fellows charge ahead. When they are alone, he says,

"It is my turn to read the day's business for the clerks to copy. It will take an hour or so. After I have finished, I may call in at the Ship Aground before going home. If I find you there, we shall have some supper, for they do a reasonable meat pie, and over supper, I will tell you all I know about my friend Lambert Trigg. That is why you're here, isn't it Mr Scotland Yard detective?"

Greig's eyes widen. He had tried, on his previous visit, to keep his actual identity to himself. He had thought he'd succeeded.

"Oh, you need not look surprised," the clerk smiles wryly. "Not much escapes the clerks, though Billiter likes to think otherwise. We may not have a voice, but we have eyes. And minds. We know what conversations take place in offices and boardrooms and who attends them. And now I shall return to my work."

He gives Greig a friendly nod and re-enters the bank.

The Ship Aground (formerly the Traveller's Rest) was once a coaching inn. But since the growth of the City with its banks and business houses, past coachfulness, in the form of coloured prints of coaches arriving, coaches in bright sunshine, coaches departing in snow, in fog, and ostlers with sturdy coach horses, have now been replaced by present coachlessness, in the form of pictures of galleons, steamers, and various sailboats struggling in wild seas.

The barmaids have tempest-toss'd hair under their mob caps. The pewter tankards behind the bar hang at an angle that might induce feelings of sea-sickness in the land-lubber. The air in the bar hints at an ongoing battle between cooked food and drains. The clientele consists mainly of cashiers and clerks from the various city mercantile and financial houses.

Greig settles himself in a side booth to await the arrival of Trigg's colleague. While he waits, the pub fills with young men in black frock coats and tall hats. They throng the bar, talking loudly, joshing with the two barmaids, who seem to know many of them by name. They toss back sixpenny glasses of sherry, then pack into the various booths, where they are brought plates of steaming food.

Eventually, Greig's contact walks in, to be hailed from various quarters. He glances quickly round, then heads for Greig's booth, where he snaps his fingers, signalling to a passing waiter.

"Two beef and potato pies, and two pints of best beer," he says, glancing at Greig to check this is acceptable. While they wait for their food, the clerk engages in friendly banter with various clerks from other houses, using terms that Greig doesn't understand, but guesses that they refer to the various financial processes common to all of them.

Supper arrives, and both men consume it with relish. When the last of the gravy has been scraped up and the plates cleared, the young clerk (his name, he tells Greig is Jonny Crace) lights up a pipe and leans back on the wooden bench.

"And now, let us turn to the business in hand," he says. "But before we do, I have to know one thing: have you been brought into this on behalf of Billiter and the bank shareholders? Because if that is the case, then I have nothing to say to you."

Greig explains carefully about Helena Trigg's visit to Scotland Yard, her determination to clear her brother's name, and her subsequent request that Scotland Yard should render her any assistance it could. Which is why he, Greig, paid a visit to the bank, and why he is here now. The clerk listens intently, nodding every now and then. When Greig has finished, Jonny Crace takes a few puffs of his pipe, then sets it down.

"Lambert and I go back many years," he says. "We were at school together. When he came to London to work for the bank, his uncle was kind enough to write a letter asking them to consider me for a post also. Lambert rapidly rose to be the chief cashier at the bank ~ a position of great trust. I was his junior, at his side and in his confidence about most things.

"Since he disappeared, I have thought a great deal about it, and I am pretty sure the change I noticed in him started at the end of October, and coincided with the arrival of a certain new customer called Mr Godwin

Fitzwarren ~ a name that might be familiar to you, if you have spoken to Lambert's sister?"

"He was the man who defrauded the bank out of a fortune by opening an account and handing over fake bills of exchange?"

"The very man. Lambert was given his letter of introduction and asked to set up banking arrangements on his behalf, and to deal with him personally. He was told to treat him with the utmost courtesy. I don't know what story the man spun in the letter, but it was swallowed hook, line and sinker by our manager."

"But not by his chief cashier, I'm guessing?"

Crace shakes his head. "No indeed. Lambert prided himself on being a quick study, and he told me, later, he could tell from the off that there was something not quite right about Fitzwarren. The man was a little too polished, a little too genuine to be genuine, if you follow me. '*Like glass pretending to be diamonds*' is how Lambert put it to me.

"But he had his orders from Billiter, so he obeyed them. He accepted Fitzwarren's bills and paid out the money. And then three months later came the message from the Rothchilds' Paris banking house that the bills were forgeries, the man wasn't a customer of theirs and they were not going to honour his debts.

"Lambert opened that letter ~ as chief cashier he also dealt with all the correspondence coming into the bank. I saw him stagger back, as if he'd received a mortal blow. I was serving a customer at the time, but as soon as I could, I went over to his desk. He was just sitting there, shaking, and white as a corpse, the letter in his hand. He showed it to me. *'It's the end of me, Jonny,'* he said. *'They'll blame me, then they'll sack me. Oh, my poor sister ~ my poor Helena. That I should bring such disgrace down upon us both.'*"

"But surely now, it was not his fault?" Greig protested.

"He was the one who was put in charge of the account. He accepted the bills. He paid out the money," Crace said. "I advised him to take some time to think it over and get his story straight in his mind before going to Billiter with the letter. He said he would. But a few hours later I noticed that his place was empty. He had packed up his writing tools and cleared his desk. The letter was all that remained. And I have not seen nor heard from my good friend Lambert Trigg since."

"Where do you think he has gone?"

The clerk plays pensively with the stem of his pipe.

"Lambert confided to me just before all this happened, that there was something about this particular man that sent shivers down his spine. He said every time Mr Fitzwarren approached his desk, he felt the hairs on the back of his neck stand up like spikes and he was sure the temperature dropped a couple of degrees. Of course, I laughed at him, but he persisted. He believed he was in the presence of real evil. If you want my opinion, Lambert is lying low somewhere, and will do so until the man is caught and put behind bars."

"If that was his opinion, he should have stayed and helped the police to catch the man then. Running away could look like the action of a coward," Greig says tartly.

"If he stayed, all the blame would be heaped upon Lambert. His life, and that of his sister, wouldn't be worth a halfpenny piece. Do you think our bank will be the only one to be defrauded? I doubt it. But none of our shareholders will speak out in public, for fear that the bank might fall. They would rather see a competitor go to the wall, and their clerks lose their places. That's the sort of cowards they are. Lambert has done the right thing, and I won't have his name brought into disrepute by you or anyone else!"

The young clerk's eyes burn with anger. Greig puts out a placatory hand.

"Easy, man, easy now. I mean no disrespect. We are on the same side here. I want to catch this Fitzwarren as much as you want him caught. If you could furnish me with a description, that'd be a great help."

Crace gives Inspector Greig as much of a description as he can recollect. Greig writes it all down. Then he pushes himself to a stand.

"Thank you, Mr Crace. For your time and for your assistance. We will meet again, I hope. Next time in happier circumstances."

He tips his hat and walks out of the pub. Night has settled in, and the lamp-lighter is doing his evening rounds. The whole area is full of round-shouldered pale-complexioned clerks making their way home. An evening chill has descended. Greig pulls his muffler closer about his neck before going to find himself a cab.

****

The night is cold, but clear. Stars twinkle above in the infinite velvety blackness of sky. It is 2.00 am and the city sleeps. Listen. Here are the slow footsteps of a night constable as he patrols the silent streets. He puffs out his breath and claps his arms round his body for warmth.

More sounds. A stray dog lifts its muzzle and howls its hunger to the uncaring moon. A late cab clatters over cobbles. Someone staggers and crashes to the ground, cursing their ill fortune in an unknown tongue. A gas-lamp flickers and buzzes overhead.

This is the dead hour, when despair shifts inside, half-awake to its own strength; a time of occluded memory, when those who cannot rest, despite a day's exertion, rise and walk about the city, in an attempt to fill the empty hours between night and the approach of dawn.

Thus, a man will turn out of bed, put on his day clothes and quietly slip out of his own front door. He will walk all night, without the slightest sense of exertion, covering street after deserted street. All seem the same to him; they are dead and uniform, like bodies without souls. The city is so lonely at night that he will sometimes fall asleep to the monotonous sound of his own feet.

There is a dumbness that fills the numberless rows of houses, with their long lines of lamps; the empty avenues, the voiceless silence of the streets, where only the solitary tread of the night walker echoes between the walls, bringing to life the past, and conjuring up the presence of the dead, who come so fearfully and oppressively to mind at night, sending the imagination of the solitary night walker wandering for ever onwards and onwards.

Caught between sleeping and waking, a man may cross London Bridge, seeing the little spots of light from the bridge lamps reflected in the dark water, like so many demonic eyes. He is the urban undead, condemned to walk under the star-peppered sky. He paces out the hours, meeting only the ghost of a watchman carrying a corpse candle, or a lamplighter leaving a little track of smoke as he passes with his red-hot link.

Night crouches upon pavements, broods darkly and heavily in nooks and corners. At night, London is the city of the dead; it is echoic with former shadows.

Generations of past inhabitants fill the streets, follow the night walker as he paces relentlessly the passing hours. He has no sense of danger, only the awful awareness that one can walk and walk until night pales into dawn, and then a further dawn without coming to an end of the great city.

****

It is eight o'clock on a bad morning, following a bad night. The streets are slushy, muddy and miserable; nowhere more so than one particular street behind Drury Lane theatre. This street has seen better days, and better weather, but time and slush make all seem desolate, and the once-fine houses are now divided and sub-divided, the ground floors transmogrified into mouldy little shops full of damp oranges, odd cakes of fancy soap, stringy fowls hanging on hooks, dusty loaves, shoe brushes and blacking bottles.

Here, all the fronts are soot-blackened, all the windows dingy, the area steps broken, the railings hideous. Here, gaunt young women carry out needlework at miserable prices, knowing that an inability to pay the two-penny rent of a lodging will lead to utter destitution. Men slouch in doorways, or fall stupefied out of gin-shops. Dogs lament, cats quarrel and children shout.

In the midst of the street, sandwiched between the marine-store that sells paint in unlikely colours, old tools, and buckets that leak, and Bridget's rag-and-bone shop with its clothes and rags, odd remnants of finery and lace trimmings, is a small shop that at first glance, seems to have no viable reason to exist, especially in a run-down backwater like this.

Behind the wooden shutters, just now being taken down by a shambling, awkward, tow-haired, out-at-elbow lad known locally as the boy Muggly, is an empty window. Or at least, a window with nothing in it but some pieces of mouldering leather, a few old branches and what look like a couple of dead crows.

Glance upwards to the sign over the shop door, however, and enlightenment dawns. This is the emporium of Mr Trinkler, Upholsterer & Preserver of Small Animals & Birds. Let other hands work in gold, pearls or silver, Mr Trinkler prefers the corpses of defunct animals (and the odd piano stool).

Enter the shop, and you are presented with shelf after shelf of glass cases, full of birds and beasts in a variety of strange and unlikely poses. Here are two kittens in lace collars, blue silk britches and tiny jackets. They have slates in their paws, and small leather satchels on their backs, as if setting out for school. Their tiny green-glass eyes stare furiously out of their furry faces, as if resentful of the need to get something for which they have no long-term use whatsoever.

Here, a couple of squirrels in tail-coats play at croquet. There, some parrots with breasts and plumage far brighter than anything found in nature (courtesy of some small pots of paint purchased from next-door), perch on a small branch, poised between fall and flight.

Approach the wooden counter, where an animal, possibly once of the canine persuasion, sits in a guarding pose, one paw raised warningly. Behind the counter are the glass bottles and jars containing the tools of the taxidermists' trade: arsenic, and white soap, along with camphor and salt of tartar and lime, for Mr Trinkler belongs to the old school and likes to use traditional methods of preservation for his tableaux and dioramas.

In the back room are trays of specimens: cats, rats, foxes, mice, crows, and a pair of egg-yellow feathered canaries, currently lying on the worktable as they are in the throes of being stuffed and mounted. Mr Trinkler has high hopes of them.

The boy Muggly, having taken down the shutters, now fetches a broom from the inner recesses of the shop and begins to sweep it out, ready for the day's business, for despite its humble setting and obscure location, the demand for traditionally stuffed birds and beasts as a decorative art-form brings a steady stream of customers into the shop.

Here is one now. A tall, spare individual in a well-tailored black suit and an expensive beaver top-hat pauses upon the threshold. He wears a dark woollen overcoat and carries an ebony walking stick with a silver handle. His face is part-hidden under hat-brim and muffler, only a hawk-like nose and a pair of grizzled side-whiskers are visible.

He enters the shop and rings the small brass counter bell sharply to summon Trinkler from the back. Alas, only the boy Muggly is currently in attendance. He shambles out from the work room, where he has been stealthily consuming a stale treacle tart bought from the dusty bakery four doors down. Upon seeing who has arrived, he stops dead in his tracks, chokes on his current mouthful, and breaks into a fit of coughing.

"He isn't here," he says, when he is finally able to articulate.

The man gives Muggly a withering glance.

"He isn't here, honoured sir. Pray continue ..." he says, a phrase which, in Muggly's terrified mind translates as 'prey ... continue'. He gives a little whine, drawing into himself like a whipped dog.

"He went down the docks early, Mr Honourable Sir. There's an Indiaman come in overnight and he wanted to see if the sailors had any birds for sale. Sir, Mr Honourable," he stammers, his eyes firmly on the ill-swept floor.

The man tuts his irritation. His gaze sweeps round the shop (making a better job of it than Muggly did).

"Tell him when he returns that I have need of his services. He knows where to contact me. Tell him it is the usual business, but urgent this time, and I will pay the usual rate. Do you understand all that, stupid boy?" he asks, poking Muggly rhythmically in the chest with the end of his walking stick to emphasize each word.

Muggly nods vigorously. Of course, he doesn't understand; just the presence of the man has sent his brain into a tailspin, but anything to get rid of this customer. The man gives him a further contemptuous sneer, then strides quickly to the door, flinging it wide open. There is a crash, a small scream, followed by the sound of a string of piping curses.

Muggly runs to the door. Sitting on the step is a scrawny wiry girl with a very large tin bucket, now on its side and spilling water into the street. She shakes her fist at the departing figure.

"Oi, mister! look wot you done!" she yells. "An' now I ain't got no water to clean no more."

Muggly picks up the bucket and takes it into the shop. The girl rises and follows him, twisting her black straggly curls round her soapy fingers. She crosses the threshold with the caution of a street-cat, her small half child, half woman face screwed up in anticipation of impending trouble.

"I hate that man, Muggly," she says. "I dunno what it is about him, but summat ain't right. Why does he keep coming around to the shop? I nivver seen him buy anything."

Muggly shrugs. "Mr Trinkler does some sort of business for him. Dunno what it is."

"Well, whatever it is, it won't be good news," the girl says, "You wanna keep your head down, Muggly."

Muggly rolls his eyes in agreement.

"You wait here, Pin, I'll get you some water from out the back," he tells her.

Pin (so called because her sister is a sweated needlewoman for a Jewish tailor) folds her arms under her grubby pinafore. Her black eyes, shrewd and bright, dart round the shop, taking in the glass cases with their various animal contents.

By the time Muggly returns, with a full bucket, Pin has discovered a group of tiny kittens in frilled bibs and tuckers. They are having a tea-party in their minute prison. She has her snub nose pressed to the glass and is crooning endearments to them.

"I had a kitten once, only it ran out into the road and a cab squashed it flat," she observes.

"We get a lot of animals that way," Muggly tells her laconically. He hands her the bucket. "Are you hungry, Pin?"

"I'm always hungry, Muggly. Ain't had nothing but water to eat since day before yesterday. Nellie's got to finish her order and take it over to Moses to get paid. Then we can buy something to eat."

Silently, Muggly hands her a piece of his treacle tart.

Pin's eyes light up. She grabs the tart and wolfs it down.

"Thanks, Muggly. That was prime!" she says, wiping her mouth on her sleeve. "Pity it weren't a meat-pie, but better than nuthing, eh?"

Pin spits on her palms, picks up the bucket, and wrestles it out of the shop.

"See you later, Muggly," she calls jauntily over her shoulder. "Don't do anyfink I wouldn't do."

Muggly returns to his tasks. There are cabinets and cases to dust. While he works, he ponders about what Pin said, trying to work out in his mind what she meant, and what are the things she might not do.

He ponders about it for a long time, not being a front runner in the uptake stakes, and he is still pondering about it when Mr Trinkler returns to the shop with a bag of squawking, protesting parrots, and proceeds to shout at him for not completing his tasks properly, and then sends him packing with a kick in the pants for his pains.

Muggly is still pondering at full strength a day later, which is when he remembers he was supposed to deliver a message to Mr Trinkler. Which he now can't do, because he was told to get out of the shop and never come back.

****

Let us transfer to a different location. Here is a twelve-roomed house in Cecil Street. It has blue damask curtains in the first-floor windows, red in the parlour, and a sign that proclaims: *Apartments Furnished* ~ for however full a house may be, there always seems room for one more inhabitant.

This is not your typical run-down noxious-smelling poor lodging house, where unfortunate souls who've scraped together a few pence from a day's hard labour may bed down in rows in wooden cots on mouldy bug-ridden straw mattresses. This is a substantial residence, where the lodgers, though not quite as substantial as the houses, still belong to a respectable class, or are men with small inheritances and large aspirations. In other words, they are in well-paid employment, and always set forth in the morning with clean linen, brushed top-hats and overcoats, and carry with them rolled umbrellas of impeccable provenance.

The landlady of the desirable residence, a widow, takes pride in telling each new lodger that 'she was not always in these circumstances, believe me', and that 'her late husband's executors have treated her shamefully'. She has various accounts with the local tradesmen, and it is a pleasure to watch her dimpling smiles as she cajoles them to let her 'just run up another shilling on my account until rent-day'.

Now, when the dinner plates have all been cleared away by Lizzy-Lou, the pretty servant maid, pipes are lit and talk turns to events of their various working day. Fred Trent, bank clerk, and lover of fancy waistcoats and hair-oil, takes up the evening paper to search for scandalous stories. (Young Trent has his eye on Lizzy-Lou, though owing to the smartness of her tongue, and speed of her fists, this is the only part of his anatomy to come into any direct contact with her, so far).

"Here's something rum," he remarks, after a few minutes' page-rustling.

His dinner companions look up. Usually when Fred finds 'something rum' it involves shenanigans of a highly salacious nature involving male members of the aristocracy and ladies who are not aristocratic in the slightest. Or vice versa.

Given that none of them are courting at present, nor are likely to be, given the long hours they toil at their desks, which means infrequent appearances at social gatherings where ladies might be present, other people's erotic encounters are the nearest they get to the female sex.

"Remember how I told you we were one down at the office, since Will Brewster had decided to take himself off without a by-your-leave? Well, it says here in the newspaper that a body's been found in some tenement somewhere, and if it don't sound exactly like him, then I'm a Dutchman."

As Trent is clearly not from the Low Country, this statement is received with interest.

"How do you know it is him?" one of the lodgers asks.

"It says here there was a brand-new pair of yellow leather gloves found in his coat pocket. And a dog's head cravat-pin. I know for a fact that he bought a pair of yellow gloves because I was there with him at the time. Fancied a pair myself, but I didn't have the necessary tin on me at the time. And he had a cravat-pin the same as the murdered man. I say ~ this is hot stuff! The detective police are asking for help in identifying the man."

"Is there a reward?" one of the lodgers asks brightly.

Trent scans the article. "Doesn't say. But there's bound to be something. Stands to reason."

"I've never seen a murdered man," the same lodger remarks thoughtfully. The rest concur. They have never seen one either. Nor want to. They eye Trent speculatively, as if, by association, he has suddenly become part of the crime.

"Better cut along tomorrow and help them, then," another lodger advises.

Trent nods. "I think I shall. Got nothing to lose, have I?" Then he stands up, folds the newspaper and places it in his pocket.

"If you'll excuse me, gents all, an early night calls. Must be up betimes tomorrow to get down to Scotland Yard before I start work."

Trent makes his way upstairs, passing Lizzy-Lou on the first-floor landing, but so engrossed is he with the importance of his prospective visit, that he merely nods her a greeting as he lets himself into his room, which is probably just as well, as the comely housemaid is carrying a brimming chamber pot in one hand.

****

It has rained overnight. Now a cold, damp, clammy wet wraps the city like a moist greatcoat. Rain continues to come down thickly and obstinately, choking the streets' throats with a fine mist. Gutters brawl, waterspouts are full, and water cascades and drips from every overhang and projecting ledge.

Morning finds Detective Inspector Stride walking to work in the rain, trying to avoid the umbrellas that pass and re-pass, throwing off little waterfall sprinklings, and spinning round and round like so many tops as they knock against each other on the crowded footway. He tucks his chin down on to his chest and steps out briskly.

Detective Inspector Stride is currently a man investigating a case with no motive, no suspect, and no clues to either. As a consequence, he is suffering from doubts, which is never a good thing in an investigation. Doubts are like cold water, and you don't want cold water when you are trying to solve a double murder.

Yesterday was spent poring over the police surgeon's reports, the coroners' reports, and even, such is his current plight, the reports in the national newspapers. But all his work has yielded little more than the ongoing idea that truth is a relative and flexible concept.

Yesterday he had interviewed Mr Acton Teddler, a highly unsavoury character exhibiting all the proclivities of an experienced pillager. He was the man who'd found the body of the first victim. He had been finally run to ground by Inspector Greig. But the interview only served to increase his gloom and his mistrust of humanity in general.

Stride's long experience in the police force tells him that men who kill more than once possess a kind of self-destructive passion that ends up betraying them. All he has to do, ideally, is bide his time, then play his cards right. However, he only has two cards, and he doesn't yet know the rules of the game being played.

He has arrived at work early, as he is finding sleep equally illusory. As he walked through the stirring streets, the early morning damp reflected upon wet pavements, house-tops and lamp-posts, clinging to him like an invisible cloak. Small street children were crying with the cold, and the usual crossing-boy stamped his feet and blew on his fingers, complaining to all and sundry that he felt 'as cold as a frog'.

Stride's consumption of strong black coffee is unexpectedly interrupted by the desk constable, who informs him that there is a gentleman out front who wants to see a detective about something important.

"So, fetch Jack Cully," he growls without looking up from the mass of paperwork.

"Not arrived yet," the constable replies.

Sighing, while mentally cursing the way members of the public believe they can just walk in off the street any old time of the day and waste his time, Stride follows the constable to the outer office, where a smartly-dressed young man, whose general demeanour proclaims him to be a member of the City clerkdom, leans on the desk, glancing about him with interest.

Stride notices that the man's eyes keep flicking towards the various 'Dead Body Found' bills pinned to a noticeboard, as if he is irresistibly drawn to their gruesome descriptions of the latest murder victims. He steps forward.

"Detective Inspector Leo Stride," he says politely. "How may I be of assistance?"

The young man points at the board.

"My name is Fred Trent, sir. I am a junior bank clerk at Heywood & Company, and I think that I may be able to help you identify one of those men."

Stride stares at him in disbelieving silence for a minute or so. Then says,

"Right. Right. I see. Very well, if you'd like to accompany me, Mr Trent, I shall take you across to the police mortuary at once, and let's see what you can do."

A short while later, after the ashen-faced bank clerk has been shown back out into the street (minus his breakfast), Stride and Cully convene in the former's office.

"A pattern, Jack. That's what I always say: there's a pattern to these things, and by God, we're beginning to see it at last!" Stride thumps the desk with a fist, causing various folders and reports to slide onto the floor.

"Bank clerks. They must be the murderer's target. Lambert Trigg and William Brewster both worked in a bank. I'm betting that man the newspapers called *The Snowman* worked in a bank also. Similar age. And the same playing card was left at the scene of his murder, wasn't it?"

"Pity we couldn't keep him any longer," Cully remarks.

For alas, the body of the first victim, having lain in the mortuary unclaimed for the requisite amount of time, has now been taken to a place of burial, and quietly disposed of.

"Why should anyone decide to kill bank clerks though?" Cully continues. "I'd have thought of all people, they were the most inoffensive."

"Lambert Trigg's bank was being systematically defrauded by a customer calling himself Fitzwarren," Stride says, tapping the desk with a pencil. "Suppose this individual is playing the same trick on other banks?"

"But hunting down the cashier? ~ he must be deranged in the head."

Stride shakes his head. "He is clearly obsessed, Jack. Obsessed with the oldest passion in the world and I'm not referring to the passion of the heart. It's money I'm talking about. Gold and silver. For which a man will lie, steal and kill. And when we're talking about more money than you and I will ever see in our lifetime, why would he not want to secure his anonymity by any means available?"

"And the playing cards?"

"Ah, yes, the ace of spades. It is his signature. The mark of his crime." Stride rises from his seat. "He is arrogant enough to claim his work. As if he is proud of what he has done and wants people to admire it. But we are on to him now. We have worked out his *modus operandi*, as Robertson might say. And now we will pay a visit to the manager of the Heywood & Co. Bank.

"We'll ask to see Brewster's day-book. And inquire whether they have recently accepted a new customer who's been withdrawing large amounts of money. And we're not going to be fobbed off with excuses of privacy and confidential information. Life and death, that's what we're dealing with here, and life is more important than money!"

****

Stride's words would have found an answering accord in the heart of Helena Trigg. Along with the similar sentiment that 'blood is thicker than water'. For Helena has recently come to an important decision. Much as she appreciates the efforts of the detective division to help her, at the end of the day, Lambert is her brother and it is up to her to find him.

Helena has thought long and hard about how to do this, racking her brains in the long watches of the night. At last inspiration has come from an unlikely source: a newspaper left on a park bench. While eating her meagre lunch under a grey sky, she read the various stories of the day, then turned to the pages of advertisements, where, amongst the puffs for various pills and ointments, and gentlemen with property wishing to meet ladies, or vice versa, she discovered several advertisements asking for news about individuals who'd gone missing.

Helena had removed the relevant section, leaving the newspaper on the bench for another reader. Then she'd carried the pages back to her desk, placing them under the ledger while she'd got on with the afternoon's business. But even as she bent her head over her column of figures, the germ of an idea was slowly boring a hole in her brain.

As soon as she reached her lodgings, Helena had sat down at her dressing table and written her advertisement. Next day, carrying the result of her labour in her hand, and with an expression of determination upon her face, here she is making her way to the heart of London's 'newspaper land', Fleet Street.

Helena has selected two particular newspapers: *The Times* and the *Illustrated London News*, these being the ones most prominently displayed upon the news-stands she passes each day. Also, Lambert used to bring home any copies of them left in the bank by customers and read interesting snippets aloud to her in the evenings.

As she hands over her two envelopes at the front desks, together with the fee for placing her message, she utters a silent prayer that the right person will purchase one of the newspapers, turn to the advertisements and personal messages, and read her plea that: *Any information on the current whereabouts of Mr Lambert Trigg, former chief cashier at the London & County Bank, is to be sent to S, Box 22, where it will be gratefully received.'*

Helena has decided that a simple box number, and a message that does not mention an abandoned and desolate sister, are the most likely to elicit the information she seeks without drawing attention to her sex. She remembers Mr Moggs telling her the story of his landlady, who innocently answered an advertisement in a newspaper, and subsequently almost fell victim to a conman who tried to trick her out of her money.

Satisfied by the assurances that her advertisement will receive prompt attention and be in the papers as soon as space permits, Helena purchases a cup of coffee and a piece of bread and butter to fortify her on the walk to work.

As she makes her way to J. King & Co. to start her day, she reflects that her first overwhelming feelings of isolation and helplessness have slightly diminished. She is becoming accustomed to the solitude of her life, finding the silence of the evenings less oppressive.

Now, the feeling of glass inside her shattering only comes occasionally, when she wakes in the pale, cold dawn, and reflects how she will get older, and Lambert won't. But she is teaching herself to twist quickly away in order not to hurt herself further.

****

Meanwhile Stride and Cully arrive in Threadneedle Street and make their way past the vast white-columned building that houses the Bank of England, with its offices, nine open courts and spacious rotunda.

Crossing the road, they head down towards the lesser financial houses, but are brought to a halt by the sight of a line of carriages drawn up all along the pavement and a small but vociferous crowd of well-dressed individuals standing outside what they now see to be the building housing the private bank of Heywood & Co.

As this is not the usual rent-a-mob that shows up whenever word gets round that a body has been found, the two detectives approach it circumspectly, only to be hailed from the back by a familiar and much loathed individual, wearing his loud check suit and a jauntily-angled cap.

"Well look who it ain't! Wotcher gents both! The forces of law and order have turned up, my friends and fellow citizens. Now you'd better look to your laurels, if you don't want to spend the night in a police cell at Scotland Yard. Morning, Stride. Took your time."

Stride gives the owner of the suit a glare so stiff you could iron shirts on it.

"That's Detective Inspector Stride, *Mr* Dandy, as you well know. And why are you here?"

Richard Dandy sticks his thumbs into his waistcoat pocket and grins maddingly.

"Got wind there was going to be a run on the bank. Got it before you. As per. Came hot-foot down to see what's what. Hope you haven't saved the Police Benevolent Fund in there, Stride, coz I don't think the widows and orphans are going to thank you. Har, har."

Stride mutters an imprecation under his breath. Meanwhile Jack Cully works his way through the crowd until he reaches the front, where two men in city black and top hats are beating on the door of the bank with their umbrellas.

"What seems to be amiss?" he inquires politely.

The men gesture at the door, which is shut.

"The bank has stopped payment," one says.

"When? Why?"

"Insufficient funds, is all they'll say. What I say is, they have got £5,000 of my money in their vault, and I want it back," the other man says, as he recommences beating on the door while the crowd voices its various sums of money owed behind him.

Stride raps on the door, shouting as he does so, "I am Detective Inspector Leo Stride of Scotland Yard. Open this door."

"You won't get any joy," the first man remarks sourly. "We've been here ever since the bank opened ~ or was SUPPOSED to open."

After a brief pause, when nothing happens, the door is cautiously opened a few inches, and the scared white face of a junior cashier peers out. Stride pushes hard on the door and slides through the gap, followed by Cully, who closes the door firmly as the crowd surges forward. The cashier starts to protest but is silenced by a look.

"Where is the manager?" Stride demands.

The man swallows nervously. "He's in the boardroom, but he ain't coming out."

The detectives survey the silent banking floor. Behind their mahogany counters, the clerks and cashiers are cowering like soldiers under fire. Stride looks for Fred Trent, spots him, and beckons him over. The young clerk looks even paler than he did after viewing the body of his colleague.

"Oh sir, what can I say? When I got in to work this morning, they told me straightaway that the bank had failed overnight. We are all to be dismissed with no wages as soon as the auditors arrive to check the books."

"Take us to the boardroom," Stride commands.

Mutely, Fred Trent conducts them through an archway at the far end of the atrium and points towards a closed door.

"That's where Mr Frith is but you can't go in. He said he ..."

But Stride has already tried the handle, found the door locked, and is putting his shoulder to it. The door yields after a couple of attempts. On the other side, the detectives find a middle-aged man crumpled behind a desk, his expression a mask of utter horror. His face is ashen, and his cheeks unshaven, as if he has spent all night in this room.

He is surrounded by several enormous leather-bound ledgers strewn higgledy-piggledy on the desk itself. The ledgers are open at certain pages, marked with slips of paper. The man is attempting to load a small pistol. Cully steps over and lays a hand on it.

"This is not the way, sir," he says quietly.

The bank manager stares up at him, his eyes wild and disorientated.

"Who are you? You are not the auditors."

"We are members of the detective division of Scotland Yard, sir," Cully tells him, slowly edging the gun away from the manager.

The man groans, collapsing into the chair, his head in his hands.

"My God, that was quick ~ are you come to arrest me? Go ahead, then ~ arrest me! Oh, the disgrace! Poor Mina and Harry, how will they bear the disgrace?"

"Bear up, sir. We are not here to take you into custody," Stride says. "We'd just like to know the circumstances that have led to the bank going under. We think it may be relevant to another case we are investigating."

The manager shakes his head in bewildered confusion.

"Another case? Another case of what?"

"Let's start with these ledgers," Stride says smoothly. "I see you have marked them up ~ perhaps you can explain to us the significance?"

The manager tries to lift himself off the chair by pulling his hair with both hands.

"God rot him ~ may he rot in Hell for what he has done to the reputation of this bank!" he cries.

"Yes indeed. And the slips of paper?" Stride persists.

"Each one marks a transaction: a cheque presented at the desk. He had a cheque book, you see, drawn at Messrs Coutts & Co ~ you have heard of them? 59 Strand. An established banking-house, with a fine reputation. My staff never doubted his integrity, why should they? They cashed the cheques, and now Coutts & Co has sent them all back marked *'Not endorsed'* and the bank is ruined, for there are not enough funds to meet our customers' requirements."

"And the gentleman in question? What of him?"

"He has apparently absconded, and set us, his creditors at defiance."

"His name," Stride says. "Can you tell us his name?"

"Mr Abraham Atkinson. He said he was an American entrepreneur and a man of great wealth. But clearly, he was not who he said he was. Nor was the address he gave us real."

Stride and Cully exchange glances.

"One last thing: could any of your staff give us a description of this Mr Atkinson?"

The manager stares into the middle distance for a while. "I never met him. He always dealt with the same cashier, and I am pretty sure it was our chief cashier, Mr Brewster. He is absent on unpaid leave at the present time. Shall I get him to write to you when he returns?"

Stride's expression is set and grim. "That won't be necessary, sir. Sadly, I have to inform you that the body of your chief cashier currently lies in the police mortuary. We must pursue our investigation without Mr Brewster's aid. And now, I hear footsteps in the corridor: I expect your auditors are arriving, so we shall take our leave."

The manager gives him a stricken glance. Stride signals to Cully and together they leave the boardroom. Cully drops the pistol surreptitiously into his coat pocket as the manager starts frantically re-arranging the ledgers on the desk.

Studiously ignoring the pleas for information from the waiting crowd outside the bank the two detectives head back to Scotland Yard.

"And there you have it, Jack," Stride says. "I'm prepared to stake my reputation that we are dealing with the same man. Not that I believe he is the actual murderer. He is the brains of the business, so above such dirty work. No, he will employ others to track down and finish off those who might bring him to justice."

"If only the banks would communicate with each other, they could send round a warning letter and a description," Cully says, shaking his head.

"That'll be the day," Stride says. "There are eighty-five banks in the city, I counted them ~ some with several branches, and they all want to make money from or for their customers, which they do on their reputation and their good name. It's not in their interest to share anything. And that's how this individual is managing to defraud them of vast sums of money so successfully. I'd say serve them right, but for what we just witnessed back there. You saved that man's life, Jack. Well done."

But not *his* reputation, Cully thinks, sadly. Nor *his* good name, which must be worth more to him than all the money taken from all the vaults of every bank in the city.

It is said that give a rumour a twenty-four-hour start, and the truth will never catch up. By closure of the day's business, notice is issued in the City that Heywood and Company, a family bank of impeccable probity, and held in good reputation, is unable to meet its current debts and financial obligations and has therefore ceased trading.

Much later that night, the new barmaid at the Cat and Fiddle public house will step out into the side alleyway to empty a bowl of slops and will notice a dark shape curled up against the pub wall by a stack of barrels. Knowing that the landlord doesn't approve of vagrants and tramps, especially vagrants and tramps sleeping in the alleyway, she will get a broom and poke the offending sleeper, directing him loudly to 'be about his business'. It will take some time before she realises that, as far as this earthly realm is concerned, his business ceased some time ago.

****

It is the following morning, and here are Stride and Cully standing in the cold whitewashed police mortuary facing another dead body and their various private demons.

"Good morning, detective inspector and detective sergeant. Once again you find me *in media res*, as it were," Robertson, the police surgeon remarks happily, as he arranges a series of viciously-curved, steel-bladed medical instruments upon the bench.

Stride stares at the covered body. "Just tell us what we've got here."

The police surgeon whips the cloth off the top of the body.

"See for yourself, detective inspector."

"But … isn't that the manager of Heywood & Co. private bank?" Cully exclaims.

Stride stares silently at the poor tormented face of the deceased, and his eyes widen in dismay.

"You're right, Jack. It is that unfortunate man. And it looks as if he managed to carry out his threat after all. Well, well, what a tragedy. Suicide. Poison, I think by the look of him. A nasty painful way to die."

Robertson folds his arms and regards them balefully from under his bushy eyebrows.

"Oh really? If members of the detective division are now going to offer free and unsolicited opinions about the causes and methods of death, without possessing the relative medical qualifications, then I see I shall have to seek employment elsewhere."

Cully tells him about the previous day's meeting he and Stride had with the bank manager, and how he had to restrain him from blowing his brains out.

"He wanted to end his own life, and now it seems he has managed to carry out his wish," he says.

"Ah. I see. Well, I do not doubt your word detective sergeant, but it comes under the category of hearsay, which, as you both know, would not be admissible in a court of law as evidence, unless it forms part of the *res gestae*. I refer you in this matter to *Reg. v Crudd, March 22nd 1859*, and the summing up of Lord Chief Justice Cockburn."

God give me strength, Stride thinks, a sentiment entirely at odds with his devout atheist beliefs.

"So how did he die then?" he says tersely.

The police surgeon gives him a long meaningful stare.

"I am about to make a thorough examination of the body," he says. "I admit, there is always a *prima facie* probability in favour of suicide, especially in the middle-aged, but I shall furnish you with my *professional* findings in due course, as I always do."

"Was anything discovered in his pockets, or on his person when he was brought in?" Cully asks, in an effort to diffuse the tension, which is making the atmosphere of the police mortuary even colder than it already is.

Robertson indicates a bundle of clothes under the bench. "There are his belongings as they arrived. Please feel free to examine them for clues. You deal in clues, after all, do you not? You say you know the man, so I expect you will want to go and inform members of his family of his demise. I shall await their arrival to view and identify the deceased."

Cully riffles swiftly through the bank manager's few possessions. He glances up at Stride and shakes his head. The police surgeon looks meaningfully from the two detectives to the body on the table and then to the various empty jars by the window sink.

"Any further questions, detectives? Any further anatomical observations? No? Sure? Then I shall bid you both good-day. I assure you I shall furnish you with my full findings as quickly as I can."

Stride leads the way back to the main building.

"It was suicide, Jack, or I'm the Chancellor of England. You saw him. There was not a rip or a bloodstain on his clothes as far as I could see. And we may not have found a playing card on his body, but he is part of the same game. Damn it ~ now it'll be our duty to inform his wife and family. And they will have to sit through a coroner's inquest, and listen while some jury who never knew him, make a judgement about his state of mind."

"The newspapers will have a field day," Cully observes. "I expect they'll hint at some extra-marital affair. They usually do."

Stride grimaces. "I said there'd be more deaths, Jack, and I was right. Three men have lost their lives; one man is missing. Meanwhile, the man behind it all is still walking our streets, and we haven't a clue who he is, where he is and how to lay hands on him. We need a breakthrough, and we need it soon."

****

The reputation of the *Silver Quill* is growing incrementally with each article published. Lucy Landseer's latest piece on the 'Mystic Madonna of the Marvellous Metropolis' has caused quite a stir in literary circles. There have been letters to the editor. Some letters debunk the whole thing, suggesting that the *Silver Quill* really needs to get a grip, and not fall prey to every whim and fancy of crazy occultists.

Others, though, have come out in support of the writer, citing evidences of supernatural phenomena that they have experienced. A few admit to actually seeing the

Madonna themselves, and have invited the writer to explore with them the significance of her various manifestations at a time when London is deserting the True God and sinking into Babylonic squalor and paganism.

Of course, this polarity of correspondence is just what an editor loves, and a magazine thrives on, so Lucy has been invited, nay beseeched, to write more about the spectral Virgin. Thus, the afternoon finds her, notebook in hand, waiting on the up-line platform of Baker Street Station for some of the letter writers to join her. She intends to interview them about their experiences, and then confect their stories together in a sensational article that will, metaphorically, knock her editor's socks off.

Lucy hopes that the money she earns will give her some space to concentrate upon her novel, upon which she has been working furiously ever since she arrived in the great city. She expects to get it finished soon. Because at the end of the day, articles, short stories and little pieces are all very well, but a real writer needs to have a novel under their belt. Especially a writer who only has paternal funding for a year.

So far, Lucy has been forced to write her novel in the evenings, by candlelight, which tires her eyes. But she has made great headway, and she is sure that the book, (working title: *A Bohemian Love Affair*) is going to bring her great fame, and possibly some fortune.

Admittedly, she has never been to Bohemia, nor had a love affair, but she has discovered that it doesn't really matter. What she does not know, she makes up, describing places never visited with great vivacity. All her heroines are ravishingly beautiful, with geranium-hued dresses and water lilies in their long flowing tresses.

They order their clothes from Worth in Paris and inhabit a world of rose-tinted sunsets and delicate little suppers in discreet rooms decorated with silk hangings.

Her hero, Bertie Cecil Arbuthnot of the 1st Life Guards, is strong and handsome with wavy chestnut hair, and magnificent moustachios. He has a set of bachelor apartments in Knightsbridge, and his dressing table is full of gold-stoppered bottles and tortoiseshell backed brushes and little billet-doux on hot-pressed paper from ardent female admirers.

Every day, when he is not on parade with his men, he rides his bay charger in the park with an air of latent recklessness, and in the evening, and at weekends, he enjoys a good cigar, a novel, a glass of brandy and a hunt in the countryside. Not all at the same time, of course.

Lucy likes to imagine future female readers getting out their smelling-salts as they eagerly turn the thrilling pages, or hiding the book under the sofa cushions when prying mamas enter their bed chambers. She is certainly having immense fun writing it. She is also pretty sure that it is going to be the sort of book that Mr Mudie won't stock in his Select Lending Library.

After her interviewees have gone their various ways, and with eight pages of notes to unscramble, plus the promise that she will indeed include everything she has been told, Lucy Landseer decides to take a walk. Twilight is descending upon the city she has come to regard as home. She overtakes a couple of lamplighters on their rounds, presses though a crowd of moving people and is overtaken in turn by carriages and omnibuses.

Lucy feels a sudden overwhelming sense of joy. The infinite variety of the great city, the plethora of passing faces, the sense of continuous novelty, drawing out new sensations from within, this is living! This is where she belongs! Almost without any conscious decision on her part, her footsteps take her to the genteel locale of Baker Street, and the house she'd marked as that dwelling where resided the mysterious girl and her female companion.

She is in luck. Arriving outside the house, she discovers that the lights have been lit, but the curtains in the front room of the house are still undrawn. Lucy stations herself by the railings, pretending to search for something in her bag, while fixing her gaze upon the cheerful fire and the furnishings of the room.

Currently, there are two occupants: the girl, who sits at a round table, books open in front of her. She is copying something into an exercise book. Meanwhile, the older woman circles the room, now warming her hands before the blaze, now reading what the girl has written, and pointing out this or that mistake, always with a smile and a nod of encouragement.

Lucy makes a mental note: so, the woman is not the mother as she had first thought, but the governess. Seen divested of her outer apparel, her dress is too plain and simple for the well-furnished drawing-room. Her indoor cap is unadorned, and the shawl wrapped round her shoulders is also plain, and of a dark woollen material.

Her surmise is confirmed when another woman enters. She is younger, much prettier and wearing a green velvet gown and cashmere shawl. She is greeted rapturously by the girl, who immediately rises from her seat and skips towards her.

As the child is gathered fondly into her mama's embrace, Lucy suddenly catches sight of the expression on the governess' face. In the split second that it takes to draw breath, the woman has gone from fond indulgence to dislike. She grips the top of the vacated chair with whitened knuckles, glaring at the mother who, oblivious to the governess, is smoothing the girl's hair with her long white fingers.

Then, just as suddenly, the vignette is over. The mother ushers the girl out of the room, saying something to the governess as they leave. The governess takes her place at the table and begins to mark the written work. Next instant, a servant enters and draws the curtains, shutting off the room from its curious onlooker.

Lucy is left to make her way back to her lodgings. But what riches have been shown to her! The little scene she just witnessed being played out could have come straight from East Lynne. It is a pity that the author, Mrs Henry Wood, got there first, because she, Lucy Landseer, budding novelist, could have used what she has just viewed very profitably in her own work.

She walks on, working out alternative versions of the former wife/governess/new wife/former wife returning as governess paradigm, and decides that she will definitely return to the house. There is more to the woman and child than the girl's ability to see apparitions that may or may not be there. And who knows what interesting events she might also witness from the darkened safety of the street? There was, she observed, a large ivory-handled paper knife on the table.

****

The mantle of night disperses, and dawn breaks over the city, bringing with it fog and a stinging cold air. Muffled spectral figures glide out of side streets and alleyways into the main thoroughfares. They are the vanguard of the army of labour. As they trudge on their way, some whistling defiance to the weather, they are passed by the swift carts of the butchers, fishmongers and greengrocers en route to Covent Garden.

The sky lightens to a pale grey. The suburbs become alive with shop-boys, poor clerks, and needlewomen. The night cabs are crawling home. The day cabs are being horsed in steamy backstreet stables and mews. Milk men and women are the first street vocalists of the day, as blinds creep up in the windows of suburban villas. Newsboys shamble along, laden with the morning papers.

The postman's knock rings through the street and servants appear with brooms and buckets to cleanse steps and areas from the grime of the night. Hasty tea and coffee is being brewed and drunk, shaving pots filled, boots brushed, wives kissed, children chided, and men are sent on their way to labour for their bread.

The sometimes-silent city is filling at a prodigious rate. Here, for instance is the boy Muggly, who has arrived out of nowhere, unbreakfasted as usual. He is up a step-ladder, taking down the shutters of Mr Trinkler's shop, having been recently re-installed in his old employment, due to lack of interest in taking it on from anyone else.

Muggly is just contemplating the possibility of purchasing a stale roll to eat later, when a heavy hand is unexpectedly placed upon his shoulder, then the back of his jacket, and he is lifted bodily off the step-ladder. He turns, and feels the breath leave his body as the tall black pillar of the man whose message he forgot to deliver holds him at arm's length. His face is a mask of fury.

"So, ignorant cur: you thought to ignore my orders, did you?" His voice has a hollow ring to it, as if it comes from another unearthly world and has somehow skipped across that bourne from which no traveller returns.

Muggly yammers something about meaning to, but forgetting to, and was going to, and then, but, and …

"You are no better than a street dog! You are certainly as ugly and as stupid! Do you know how I deal with street dogs like you?" the man asks, as he brings the silver-topped ebony walking stick from behind his back and raises it in the air.

Muggly crouches down, covering his face with his arms. The man rains blow after blow upon him. Only when the dark figure has beaten himself to exhaustion does he cease, by which time, Muggly is curled up in a ball, blood running freely from his head.

"Let that be a lesson to you, cur," the man says, kicking the boy hard as a parting gesture.

He walks away. For a moment, there is silence. Then, the sound of soft sobbing, rising to cries of pain, as Muggly cowers on the filthy pavement, too shocked by the brutality and suddenness of the attack, to rise to his feet.

There is a patter of small footsteps. A strangled gasp. A small hand is laid upon Muggly's head; a finger strokes his cheek.

"Oh my Gawd, Muggly! Look at yer! What on earth happened?"

Pin (for it is she) dips the end of her pinafore in her pail and attempts to gently wash the blood from his head.

"You needs to sit up, Muggly. Come on, sit up!" she commands, putting a surprisingly strong arm round his shoulders.

Still sobbing and snuffling, the boy Muggly raises himself with difficulty to a sitting position.

"Is yer arm hurting, poor Muggly?" Pin says, gesturing to the boy's left arm, which hangs uselessly by his side. When he nods, Pin lifts off the pinafore, tears at the straps with her sharp pointed teeth and fashions a clumsy sling. Gently, she bends the boy's forearm towards his chest, and slides the sling under it, tying the two ends at his shoulder.

Muggly weeps with pain and hopelessness. Pin rips the rest of the pinafore and ties it round his head, giving him a slightly rakish and piratical appearance.

"It was *him*, wasn't it, Muggly? He done this to you. Don't say ~ I know it! I saw him in the street a while back heading this way. That's why I decided to come round to the shop to check on you."

Muggly nods, tears streaking pale runnels in the grime of his cheeks. Pin's eyes darken to black points of fury.

"Well, he ain't going to get away with it, Muggly. Evil swine that he is! Don't you fret, Muggly. He'll pay for this, or my name ain't Penelope Rose Klem. Now, you just sit here and don't move, and I'll be back in a jiffy after I cleaned a few steps."

And with that, Pin picks up her pail, and sets off briskly towards her next cleaning job. By the time she returns, the boy Muggly will have managed to stagger into the shop and collect his pitiful belongings from under the counter, after which he will limp slowly back to the dark little side street and the ramshackle house where he shares a room with two Irish families, who will do their best for him, out of the poverty of their resources. Pin will search in vain for him for several days, returning frequently to Trinkler's emporium to see if he has surfaced. But Muggly will not be found.

****

After a hard morning's work, a gentleman likes nothing better than to call in at his club and pass a few hours of rest and quiet with a glass of brandy, the daily papers and the company of like-minded souls. There are thirty-seven main clubs in the metropolis and they occupy the most magnificent buildings, as befits their status as exclusive haunts of the superior male sex.

On the corner of Pall Mall is the Athenaeum, one of London's most select clubs, where gather the intellectual cream of London society. Membership is fixed at 1,200 and each member must have attained distinguished eminence in the sciences, literature or the arts.

Here, bishops and scholars hobnob. Each man has his favoured armchair, where his newspaper is brought by one of the well-trained club servants, who are acquainted with every member's peculiarities and preferences, and can minister to them hour by hour.

Look more closely. As the occupant of one armchair reaches for his drink, the occupant of the opposite armchair, an old Indian army surgeon who has seen much service in the tropics, and has the yellow complexion, choleric disposition and destroyed liver to prove it, observes drily,

"Quite some bruising to that hand, what! Been in a fight of some sort have you, old chap? Should get it looked at."

Upon which the other favours him with a hard, reptilian stare and replies in a voice that is, if possible, even colder than the ice chinking in his glass,

“It is nothing that need concern you. A matter got out of hand. Chastisement had to be administered. That is all.”

The rebuffed medic harrumphs, and buries his nose in the newspaper, remembering that this particular individual, although a member by birth of one of the foremost families in the country, and reputed to possess a legal mind of ferocious brilliance, lacks an effusive manner and is not known for his ‘clubability’.

The silence that follows is only broken by the rustle of newspaper pages and the hiss and crackle of the great log fire. The surgeon, having enjoyed a good meal, closes his eyes. His companion reads on, pausing only to extract a small octavo notebook from an inside pocket, in which he notes down the current prices of various shares on the stock-market, and a couple of other matters that catch his eye.

Eventually, leaving his companion to snore through the afternoon, he orders up his coat, muffler and top hat and makes his way into the street, swinging his silver topped ebony walking stick as he goes.

****

Let us pause and consider the state of the City, currently a vortex of rumour and anxiety. An uneasy shifting mood swirls around the streets like fog. Everyone is jittery and on edge. The failure of the private bank Heywood & Co. coming so soon upon the heels of the failure of the Limerick and Tipperary Bank, has sent ripples of panic through both cashiers and customers.

Previously, bank clerks were much envied by those who know little about them. It was thought that, being in possession of permanent employment, their fortunes must be made. Now, the same individuals are whispered about by other clerks in more mundane employment, as if they are potentially part and parcel of the problem.

After all, it is bruited abroad, do they not handle daily vast sums of money? Are they not left in charge of vast sums of their customers' cash? Thus, those bank clerks who sought to distinguish themselves from their fellows by a certain fastidiousness of dress, appearing daily in clean linen, well-cut clothes, polished boots, scrupulously shiny hats, displaying a gold watch-chain and bright pea-green or rose-pink gloves, find their spotless character being blackened behind their backs.

How easy it must be for such a one to accept some *douceur* from a customer for favours rendered? It is even whispered that the chief cashiers of both banks may, indeed, have played a prominent role in the collapse of said banks by embezzling monies on their own account, and wilfully falsifying the books.

The febrile atmosphere is being gleefully stoked by the newspapers, who are predicting doom, gloom and the imminent collapse of the entire banking system. ***'Where will the Axe Fall Next?'*** is the rhetorical headline in *The Inquirer* which reveals it has an exclusive prediction from an 'anonymous source' in the City.

This financial futurologist claims to know the names of at least three major banks that are not just metaphorically scraping the bottom of the barrel, but are through and onto the muck it is standing on.

All of which is adding to the sense of frustration being felt in certain parts of Scotland Yard and causing Detective Inspector Stride to ingest far more coffee than is needful or advisable.

"He's out there somewhere Jack," he tells Cully darkly, for probably the fifth time in three days. "He's out there and he's counting his money and laughing at us all. I can hear him laughing."

Jack Cully, who has walked down this particular path on numerous occasions, nods thoughtfully and refrains from stoking the fire by pointing it out.

"He thinks he's cleverer than us," Stride continues, grinding the point of a pencil into his desk. "That's why he leaves the playing cards. He's taunting us. He's playing a little game. He's saying: this is my signature, but you can't read it or understand it."

"About those playing cards …"

Stride glances up, his expression warily hopeful.

"I'd like to borrow them, if I may. I told you my father-in-law is a bit of a card expert. He might be able to give us some pointers."

Stride smiles wryly.

"Can't do much with two cards, Jack. But, if you think it'd help," he pushes the cards across the desk. "Frankly, I'm happy to explore anything right now, because between you and me, I'm stumped. And I'm getting sick and tired of Dick Dandy and his penny-a-liner hacks trying to undermine what we do and suggesting that they could do it better."

Cully pockets the playing cards.

"Have we heard anything more from Miss Trigg about her brother's disappearance?" he asks.

Stride shakes his head.

"It's gone quiet on that front also. Lachlan has very kindly been keeping the young lady appraised of our progress, such as it is. Or is not."

Cully stifles a smile. His Scottish colleague's admiration for Miss Josephine King, Helena Trigg's employer, has been duly noted.

Stride pulls a face. "It's been a couple of weeks since the last clerk was murdered. I don't like it when nothing happens. It's always a sign that something is about to."

****

Something is indeed about to happen, but it is not going to happen to Stride or to Jack Cully. Helena Trigg is about to receive a letter. Here it is now, being delivered to her lodgings, where Mr Mutesius picks it up off the shabby linoleum, studies the envelope for a while, shakes it, sniffs it, then carries it into the downstairs sitting-room, where it is placed upon the mantelpiece to await her return.

For the rest of the day, the two Mutesiuses eye the letter suspiciously. It does not move, nor exude anything untoward, but they are not taking any chances. It is their joint unspoken opinion that there is Something Amiss with the upstairs tenants ~ the prolonged absence of one of them being a large part of it.

At the outset, Mr Mutesius had tried to extract the reason for the absence, but Helena had closed down his clumsy conversational attempts at delving into her brother's circumstances. Nevertheless. They have both heard footsteps pacing to and fro overhead in what they know to be the young female lodger's bedroom. They have also heard muffled sobbing ~ this, at least, is what Mrs Mutesius has reported hearing while brushing down the stairs.

Mr Mutesius did suggest that his wife, as a fellow female, might use her feminine wiles to draw out from the young lady what ails her, but the suggestion made Mrs Mutesius quiver all over at the prospect, and then have an attack of the conniptions, rendering her fit for nothing for the rest of the day.

In the end, they have both decided that, as long as Miss Trigg pays her rent on time (she does), they will inquire no more. After all, it is not as if she has committed any crime, unlike Mr Broderick, the former tenant, who not only smuggled young women and strong drink into his rooms, but then made off without giving notice, and with Mrs Mutesius' third best sheets in a holdall.

As soon as he hears her footstep in the hallway, Mr Mutesius slides open the sitting-room door and extends a beckoning forefinger. Helena, who has had a long day, made even longer by the lack of luncheon, feels her spirits sink. Now what?

She approaches the Mutesius' door, trying to arrange her features into as polite an expression as her bone-weary state will allow. Mr Mutesius produces the letter with a flourish, and hands it over, in the disapproving manner of somebody handing over a naughty child.

"There is a letter come for you, Miss Trigg," he wheezes throatily.

"A letter," comes the whispered echo from just behind his back, where Mrs Mutesius stands, wringing her hands in a slightly aghast manner.

Helena receives the letter, which is slightly damp to the touch, bobs her head in acknowledgement, and stuffs it into her basket. She can almost feel disappointment and disquiet oozing, in equal measure, under the Mutesius' door as she mounts the stairs to her own room.

Having lit her fire, and made a meagre meal of bread and butter, followed by a small wizened winter apple, Helena settles down to eat, and peruse the unexpected communication.

She reads:

*In response to the inquiry re: Information on the current whereabouts of Mr Lambert Trigg, former chief cashier at the London & County Bank, if **S** will be present under the clock at Charing Cross Station on Friday at 5.30 pm, they shall learn something to their advantage.*

The letter is unsigned and has been forwarded to her by the editor of the newspaper. Helena feels her heart leap in her chest. Tomorrow is Friday. At last, she is to receive news of her dear brother! But immediately, she is assailed by doubts: could this be a genuine communication? And what if the information her anonymous correspondent will impart will be the news she dreads hearing most in the world?

Helena stares at the letter, willing it to whisper what the writer knows, while her thoughts whirl uncontrollably in her brain. Finally, she lays the letter down on the table, and begins preparation for bed, and the sleep that she knows is not going to come.

Long into the night, Helena Trigg lies awake, staring into the blackness, her imagination throwing up images of Lambert, her heart longing to see him while her mind boils down to the hardness of facts. How her life has changed. How events have pivoted away from her so fast.

The sense of impending doom, the feeling of loss is always far greater in the dark hours before dawn. The idea that she might never touch his arm, stroke his forehead, or delight in his company again, is enough to bring tears to her eyes.

Finally, with night thinning and knowing that sleep has finally eluded her, she rises, lights the candle and paces to and fro, to and fro across the small room, watching the sky lighten and waiting for the thin, cold dawn of the day that will bring her triumph or tragedy.

****

But first, the thin cold dawn brings muffled up figures to the grey streets, as the mighty army of workers emerge from slumber and set out from all directions to be swallowed up by the immense city. Dawn also brings a small wiry girl wearing a workman's cap and a shawl that is made up of assorted holes surrounded by black wool. She lugs a large tin bucket in which reposes a fearsome scrubbing brush.

Making her way past the group of idlers already gathered round the beer shop, she approaches the spectral cobbler in his little open shed. Despite the early hour, he is already pounding away at the heel of a boot. Pin pauses for a moment to appraise the selection of black-leaded and cracked shoes for both sexes lined up for sale on the board in front of him.

Seeing nothing that is remotely in her size, she presses on until she reaches the silent shuttered shop of Mr Trinkler, Upholsterer and Preserver of Small Animals & Birds, where she sets down her bucket, unlocks the door with a key produced from a pocket and collects the step-ladder and the wooden pole.

Undaunted by the magnitude of the task ahead of her, Pin mounts the step ladder, stretches her full height, and unhooks the wooden shutters open. She then gently lowers them, using the pole to steady herself. Once they are safely on the ground, she hooks a slat and drags the shutters into the shop.

By this time, Mr Trinkler has entered the shop from the rear. He stares in a hostile way at Pin, who smiles back brightly.

"Done yer shutters, Mr T," she says. "An' now I'll just give them shelves a quick wipe-over shall I? An' then you can pay me what you'd pay Muggly, as we agreed, coz I ain't one to take advantage of a person wot has tempr'ly lost their best worker."

Before Trinkler has time to dispute the matter, Pin has brushed past him and gone into the little workroom, where she fills her bucket from the tap. She re-emerges, carrying a cloth and begins to wipe every surface assiduously, while Trinkler gets out the sales book and unlocks the cash-box.

"I see them kittens have gone," Pin remarks, to nobody in particular.

Trinkler ignores her completely. Pin's assumption of the boy Muggly's duties has happened without his agreement, as far as he remembers, but beggars can't be choosers, as the proverb goes, and his little tableaux are beginning to find favour with the newly monied, who see them as not just stuffed animals but as a desirable and decorative art-form, so a dirty unkempt shop is not going to attract them inside.

"I liked them kittens," Pin continues. "Though I likes them little mices going to school too."

The bell on the shop door tinkles, and the door swings open. Pin scurries to the rear of the establishment and is suddenly very busy dusting, her back to the tall top-hatted man who has just entered, swinging his ebony walking stick.

Trinkler puts down the ledger he is thumbing through and rests his hands on the wooden counter. He swallows nervously. The man leans in, until his hawk-like nose is within striking distance of the shop-keeper's face.

"I bid you good day, Mr Trinkler. And how does this morning find you?"

Trinkler attempts a jocular smile.

"Very well, honourable sir. And yourself?"

"Never better. Though there needs just one thing to make my day perfect … do you have that thing, man? "

Trinkler nods. "I shall fetch it, honourable sir," he says, ducking into the rear of the shop.

Pin freezes. She doesn't move a muscle. She is so still, she could be taken for one of the stuffed exhibits. But her sharp eyes do not miss a thing, and her sharp ears are attuned to every sound, and she sees Trinkler emerge with a small black book, which he hands over to the hawk-faced individual.

"Excellent. And there was no problem with the safe?"

"None at all, sir. Sweet as a nut it was and cracked open just like one. I have cracked many a harder one than that. They will never notice anything is missing."

"I can well believe it. And you did not touch the money?"

"Not a penny, sir. Just the cheque-book, as you ordered."

The man reaches into a waistcoat pocket and places a half-sovereign on the counter.

"For your trouble, Mr Trinkler. Ah, it was a lucky day for you when I took on your case at the Central Criminal Court, and got you off, was it not?"

"It was, sir. And I am forever in your debt for it."

"Indeed, you are," the man laughs. "And now, your next repayment is due. Listen carefully. This is what I want you to do."

He leans in towards Trinkler and lowers his voice. Pin strains her ears but can only make out the odd word. Eventually, the man straightens up, pockets the cheque-book and strides quickly out of the shop.

Pin resumes wiping the glass cases, her mind racing. *So that's your little game*, she thinks. She finishes the last case, collects her money from a reluctant Trinkler, and lugs her bucket and brush out into the street.

Later, after scrubbing floors, and whitening steps, she will buy food and take it round to the boy Muggly's newly-discovered lodgings. Today, Pin has learned some important information about the man with the cruel face and the stick. What she hasn't worked out is how to use the information to bring him down. Not yet. But she will.

****

Lucy Landseer is also trying to work something out, and it is equally as puzzling. In her role as investigative writer, she has befriended one of the Metropolitan railway employees ~ well, maybe not befriended, more elicited a certain willingness to pass the time of day, based on her regular appearance on the Baker Street platform.

Lucy is discovering that a pretty girl in a nice hat can achieve practically anything she sets her mind to. Currently, her mind is set upon solving the mystery of the Madonna, which she is also sure could be linked in some way to the governess and her charge.

It has been posited by one of her night school student friends that this suspicion does seem a little far-fetched, and possibly not worth the carriage, but Lucy is reluctant to abandon it quite yet. After all, stranger things have happened in the world of fiction. And many things in life are even stranger than fiction.

So here she is now, in her fetching hat, walking onto the platform, where she is greeted by the young guard who stands with his flag and whistle ready to board passengers and send off the next train. Lucy opens her blue eyes wide and twinkles a modest smile as she approaches.

"Here you are again, miss," the guard says.

Lucy nods her agreement.

"Is the weather still inclement up there?" the guard asks.

Lucy affirms that it is.

"I see there are a great many people standing at the end of the platform," she observes. "Why is that?"

The guard glances along the platform.

"Strange. They weren't there a moment ago," he says, frowning.

A train chugs in, emitting smoke and steam, and comes to a screeching halt. The guard shouts, "*Bak'r Streeet*," and steps forward.

Lucy strides off purposefully towards the crowd. As she draws nearer, she becomes aware of singing. It is a bit confusing, as there appear to be two songs being sung simultaneously. One song is being sung with great enthusiasm by a small group of very stern-faced individuals in dark clothes.

From what Lucy can make out, it appears to be about fighting a good fight and smiting infidels. The group are being conducted by a man with a heavy black beard, dark clothes, clerical collar and the deep-set eyes of a fanatical believer.

The other song is in Latin and is clearly a hymn to the Virgin Mother (Lucy isn't a daughter of the Manse for nothing: her childhood occasionally included an inter-faith tea and sing-song). The singers are choirboys in red robes and frilled collars.

"What is going on?" Lucy whispers to a woman bystander.

"Ah, you should have been here earlier," the woman says. "A train came in, and a young lady ~ well, she was more a young girl, I gather, got off, and told everybody that when she boarded the train at Paddington, she was suffering from terrible pains all over her body, but that now, she was no longer in pain, and she was sure the Madonna had cured her."

"Really?" breathes Lucy, wide-eyed with sudden interest. "Did you see the girl? What was she like?"

The woman shakes her head. "I believe she has gone. I myself only arrived a short while ago. When Father Desmond didn't attend our charity sewing-bee for Young Single Women Who Should Know Better, I went into search of him, and was told by the Verger that he'd taken some of the choir boys and gone to Baker Street Station, where a miracle had taken place."

"I see," Lucy nods. "And the others?" she asks, gesturing towards the impromptu choir, who are now trying to drown out the opposition by raising their voices to screech level.

"Oh, some very strange religious sect, I think. The man in the ticket office told me that they come here quite regularly to make a thorough nuisance of themselves. I believe the police have been sent for."

Lucy scans the crowd to see if she can spot the girl and her governess (for she is convinced they are behind the so-called 'miracle cure'). Meanwhile the station master approaches accompanied by a man in a well-brushed overcoat. Lucy recognises him at once. It is the same man she encountered upon a previous visit to Baker Street Station.

This time however, his face bears a stern, set expression, so she guesses that he is not here to meet his wife and daughter, as he was before. He elbows his way through the throng and taps the leader of the 'thorough nuisances' upon his gaunt black-clad shoulder.

"Detective Sergeant Jack Cully, of the Metropolitan Police. We meet once again, Brother Amos. And once again, I must caution you that the behaviour of you and your followers constitutes a breach of the peace. Please take yourself and your congregation elsewhere," he says in a patient-but-with-gritted-teeth voice.

Brother Amos turns a pair of dark, fanatically glittering eyes upon the police detective.

"Satan has been at work, officer!" he exclaims. "Do you not smell the sulphurous stench of him?" He gestures with a bony forefinger to the mouth of the tunnel. "There is his lair, and from there he spews forth his infernal poison and infects us all!"

Two choristers edge closer towards the tunnel, their eyes alight with sudden keen interest. The Verger hooks them back to safety as a train, its headlamps blazing, emerges from the tunnel and steams into the station.

What then follows, happens so fast that Lucy is hard put to remember it all sequentially, when writing her article later in the day. The detective and the station master lay hold of Brother Amos and half march, half drag him towards the exit. The followers pursue them, raising their voices in a discordant shout of indignation.

Another train arrives. Dis-boarding passengers mill aimlessly around on the platform, unsure what is going on, or whether they are in some sort of danger. A stray dog emerges from out of nowhere and starts attacking Brother Amos' long black robe with vigour. The choir stop singing and are hurried away by the Verger.

And in the midst of all the mayhem, Lucy suddenly espies a young girl stepping down from the train, accompanied by the familiar figure of her governess. They pause on the step, exchanging puzzled glances. Then the governess puts her gloved finger to her lips in a meaningful manner. The girl nods, takes her arm, and together they slip away, unnoticed, in the general melee.

****

Helena Trigg, in contrast, is hoping that her presence will be noticed. Especially by a certain unknown letter writer who claims to know something about her brother Lambert. Here she is now, making her way down the Strand in the direction of Charing Cross Station.

She enters the station, glancing round curiously. It is so busy, with porters shouting, cab drivers touting for customers, trains hissing steam, people meeting and greeting. Any one of these could be the person she is about to encounter. She feels a frisson of anticipation.

Helena walks past the W.H. Smith bookstall and makes her way to the black clock with its distinctive red and gold decorations. It is five twenty-five exactly. She stations herself underneath the clock, as instructed, and waits.

Five minutes tick by. Then another five. Helena checks the letter just in case she got the meeting time wrong. She has not. Another three minutes pass. She scans the faces of the passengers heading for the nearest platform. Nobody seems to notice her. Nobody approaches her.

Five more minutes tick excruciatingly slowly by. She stares at the spars of the roof, the pigeons flying to and fro, the triple globe lights on their iron stands. She remains unenlightened. Another two minutes crawl by.

Now Helena finds herself on the horns of a dilemma. Should she stay, in case her informant has been detained by some unknown circumstances which will be revealed when they finally appear? Or should she presume they are not coming, and walk away?

Five more minutes pass. Suddenly, she sees two station officials striding purposefully towards her. Helena's face brightens, her eyes sparkle. She had not thought there might be two people, but why not? The men come to a halt directly in front of her. She smiles at them expectantly. But their expressions are unfriendly. The older man reaches out and takes her arm roughly.

"Right, young lady. We've been watching you. We know what your game is, and you've been hanging around here quite long enough. You're not going to get any customers, and there are rules about people like you. Be on your way, or we shall have to summon a constable, and have you taken to a police station."

Helena gapes at him.

"How dare you! What are you suggesting?"

The younger man leers at her. “You know very well what we’re ‘suggesting’.”

Helena glares at him. “I am awaiting the arrival of somebody.”

“I bet you are. But you ain’t going to wait for him here. Get along with you, you saucy young hussy!”

Shocked to the core, Helena shakes herself free. She picks up her skirts and hurries back towards the station entrance as fast as she can, her face aflame with anger and humiliation, with the men’s derisive laughter ringing in her ears. She is sure everybody is looking at her and thinking exactly what the two station officials are thinking. Oh, the shame!

When she reaches the street, she pauses to draw breath. Only then do the hot tears come, scalding her cheeks. She had arrived with such high hopes. Now, they lie shattered at her feet. She has waited and waited in vain. And she has been insulted and called a prostitute.

Helena fumbles in her bag for a handkerchief to mop her streaming eyes. It takes her some time to regain her composure, but finally, she is ready to face the world once more. She takes a deep breath, squares her shoulders, and sets her face resolutely in the direction of home, determined to put the whole disastrous evening behind her.

As Helena walks away, a man emerges from the shadows of the station entrance. He is dressed in inconspicuous street clothes, the sort that do not mark him out as being of any note. He glances round quickly, then sets off in the same direction as Helena. He walks a few yards behind her, always keeping her in sight, but never getting so close that she becomes aware that she is being followed.

The man stays with her all the way to the door of her lodgings, crossing the road as she enters the house. He stands on the opposite pavement, watching silently, until he sees the small flickering light of a candle bloom in the first-floor window. He takes a note of the address. Then he disappears into the night.

Next morning, as a sleep-deprived Helena Trigg is wearily getting herself ready for another day's work, the man will share his findings with the person who gives him his orders. The one who wrote to arrange the meeting that was never going to take place. He will say that the quarry has been located. He will hand over the address and receive his payment. He will not ask any questions. He never dares.

****

Detective Inspector Stride is acknowledged, at least amongst his colleagues at Scotland Yard, as a man who can keep a calm head in trying circumstances. There are, however, three circumstances that can successfully destroy this impression: new boots, an insufficiency of strong coffee, and the press.

Nobody has ever before witnessed the effect of all three coming together. Until now. After limping painfully into work and discovering that his favourite coffee stall had decided to move premises somewhere else, Stride is now standing behind his desk, staring in disbelief at the front-page headlines of *The Inquirer*.

A small group of officers have gathered outside Stride's door, on the basis that their fairly wide vocabulary of invective is about to be widened even further. They step back as Jack Cully approaches the office bearing a mug of steaming tar-coloured liquid.

"You might like to wait a couple of minutes before going in, detective sergeant," one of the men says with a grin.

Cully is about to ask why, when a veritable tidal wave of secular and profane vocabulary comes flooding out.

"Ah," Cully nods. "He's seen it."

"Never heard that expression before," remarks one of the men thoughtfully. He repeats it slowly, in a memorizing sort of way. "Interesting. Can think of several occasions when I might use it."

There is the sound of various objects being hurled at the wall.

"He seems to have moved on," the officer says, in a slightly regretful voice.

"Never mind, we got the best bits."

"Yeah, we did. Thanks Mr Cully; shame not to hear DI Stride in full flow, I always say. A lesson to us all. Are you going in now?"

Cully smiles. "Might as well. I think it's reasonably safe," he says, pushing open the door. "Coffee?" he announces innocently, placing the mug carefully on the desk.

Stride points a quivering forefinger at the newspaper. "**Metropolitan Madonna Mayhem**!" he quotes. "**Detective Police Scuffle while Train Passengers Look on In Horror**!"

"Don't you always say you should never believe what you read in the newspapers?" Cully asks.

"Oh, I don't believe it ~ not for one single minute. I know Mr Dandy and his sense of the melodramatic. Perhaps you'd like to enlighten me as to what really happened, though? Before I receive a visit from the station superintendent, or a letter from the Home Office."

Cully picks up one of the many reports piled on Stride's desk.

"It's all in here. I took the liberty of writing it down, just in case. I have to say I didn't notice Mr Dandy present, nor any of his fellows."

"Oh, they don't have to turn up any more," Stride observes bitterly. "Such is the willingness of the general public to see their names in the newspaper, that you can bet somebody will always go hot-foot straight round to Fleet Street with the tale. In this case, it appears to be ..." he squints at the newspaper, "Mr G. F. Primmer (32) boiler maker of Pimlico Buildings. According to the aforementioned gentleman, you *'seized violent hold of an innocent member of the cloth, while uttering words not fit for the female ear to hear'*. Oh, and your ferocious dog attacked him also." Stride glances up, "You have a dog? I didn't know."

Cully waves away the dog.

"This Metropolitan Madonna business is becoming a thorough headache," he says. "I have lost count of the number of complaints we've received from passengers and station staff. There are now two constables from the Marylebone police office in constant attendance when they'd be far better deployed dealing with street crime.

"I have had to threaten Brother Amos with dire consequences if he is spotted on the Baker Street Station platform with his band of followers again. I suspect they will merely transfer themselves to another station. God knows where it's all going to end."

Stride rolls his eyes. "The main thing is that nobody gets hurt. So far, that hasn't happened. We have a duty to keep the public safe, Jack. That's all. If the Deity is favouring us with some sort of heavenly apparition (which I doubt), then He will have to accept the consequences. Any news from your father-in-law about the playing cards?"

Cully shakes his head. "I have posted them to him. I'm sure he will write back as soon as he can."

"It can't be soon enough," Stride says. "We're no nearer discovering who our murdering card-player is. He's already got the blood of two innocent young men on his hands. Possibly three. And I have a feeling in my water that he's not going to stop at that."

****

Meanwhile, over at the offices of J. King & Co. Helena Trigg's pale and wan demeanour has been noted by Trafalgar Moggs, who has decided to winkle out of her what the matter might be. He observes her covertly from his own his high wooden stool, observing the silent tears fall, to be brushed away by a quivering hand.

However, his concern is tempered by four years of marriage to the redoubtable Portia, and the birth of four small Moggses (three girls and a boy), which has given him rare and valuable insights into the female mind, insights that only a man similarly wifed and childed would know.

Thus, he does not attempt to approach the subject broadside on, as it were, but awaits a suitable opportunity to broach the matter. The opportunity presents itself in due time and he decides to seize it. Moggs sticks his quill pen behind his left ear, clambers off the stool and reaches for his bag, which is hung on one of the wall pegs. He pulls out a packet and pretends to examine it.

"Ah. I see my dear wife Portia has been baking once again," he remarks. "And once again she has overestimated my appetite. Miss Trigg, may I invite you to share some of this delicious fresh seed cake?"

Without waiting for Helena's reply, he breaks off a generous chunk of the egg-yellow delicacy and offers it to her with a smile. Helena is thus forced to look up from her work and meet his gaze. Moggs feigns instant alarm.

"But I see that my gift is unwelcome. I apologise, Miss Trigg. Let me not disturb you again."

Helena raises a weary hand. "No, Mr Moggs, you are very kind and of course I would love to taste the cake. It is not your gesture that has caused my distress. Indeed not. I think I have been the victim of a cruel trick, and it has upset me greatly."

Moggs sets the cake down on the edge of Helena's desk, where it hopefully won't get crumbs on the ledger, and stands waiting. Silently. He has learned that silence is the trick that opens the door and makes people confess. However long it takes. The silence stretches for a while. Moggs does not move. Eventually,

"I placed an advertisement in a newspaper asking for help in tracing Lambert. I received an answer suggesting that I should meet the writer under the clock at Charing Cross Station, but when I went there, nobody turned up."

Moggs nods quickly. "Do you still have the letter, Miss Trigg?"

"It is in my bag."

"And does Inspector Greig know of it?"

She shakes her head.

"Then I think you should send him the letter," Moggs says. "Describe the circumstances to him, just as you told me, and see what he says. If any further letters arrive, I advise you to take him into your confidence, and invite him to be a party to any future meeting."

Helena's eyes open wide.

"I know what you are thinking, Mr Moggs. But I assure you, I was never in any danger. The place was very public, and of course, I would never allow myself to go anywhere with a stranger. I am not so foolish. I know how to conduct myself."

Fleeting memories of the two station officials, and the impression that she clearly conveyed, suddenly surface in her brain. She bites her underlip.

"Nevertheless, that is my advice," Moggs says steadily. "I know it is hard for you, but in my experience, the detective police are best left to do their job."

"Except that they aren't doing it, are they?" Helena says with a sudden flash of anger. "The inspector has told me nothing. Days have gone by. He hasn't written. He hasn't talked to me. It is clear to me that he is no longer trying to find Lambert.

"I cannot just sit and wait for him to remember my request, Mr Moggs. My beloved brother has gone missing, a vile accusation blackening his good name. I know if the reverse were true, and I had gone missing, he would scour every corner of London ~ nay, of the whole world if necessary, to find me!"

Moggs holds up his hands.

"You must do what you think best, Miss Trigg. I merely advise you as a colleague and, I hope, as a friend."

Helena looks at him, her eyes filling with tears. She clasps her hands.

"Mr Moggs, you *are* a friend. A good friend. And I have no one else to turn to but you. Yes, I shall do as you suggest. Perhaps the arrival of my letter might remind Inspector Greig that he made me a promise."

"It can do no harm, and may, as you say, persuade him to re-examine your request. Write it now, and then you can post it when you go for your lunch. Meanwhile I shall deliver these invoices before Miss King returns from her meeting."

And having achieved his purpose, Moggs reaches for his hat and coat, picks up a pile of envelopes and leaves the outer office. Ten minutes later, Helena is scribbling busily, her expression far happier, and the piece of cake on her desk has vanished.

****

Freshly baked cake is a luxury rarely tasted by those who ply their trade much lower down the social hierarchy. Here comes one of the lowerarchy now. Pin is lugging her bucket to her latest cleaning job. Eschewing the latest Paris fashions, she is clad in her down-at-heel, out-at-toe boots, a threadbare black frock, with her sister's shawl wrapped round her small wiry body.

Pin has been making a study of the man she calls Evil Man, in order to familiarise herself with his movements. She has worked out that if the taxidermist has done some bit of business for him, Evil Man will arrive early, just as the shop is opening. Thus, for the past few days, she has turned up early as well, and busied herself with inconspicuous mopping and dusting.

Mr Trinkler is now so used to Pin's presence, that he treats her as part of the fixtures and fittings, even showing her where to find the hidden key to unlock the workroom at the rear of the shop. And apart from handing over her wages at the end of her cleaning duties, he barely seems to register she is there. Which is exactly what Pin wants.

Today, she is really hoping Evil Man will turn up because Pin has hatched a plan. Meanwhile, she has some shutters to lift down, and an interior to mop. She unlocks the shop and enters, greeting the various little stuffed animals in their glass dioramas. It is a source of great sadness to Pin that Mr Trinkler never talks to them. She is sure the animals feel it too.

Having said hello to everyone and patted the un-protesting stuffed dog on his head, she sets to work. A short while later, Mr Trinkler appears, grunts at her, and makes his way to the workroom where he is putting the finishing touches to a fox at bay, a commission for a sporting customer.

Pin continues mopping, letting her mind drift to its favourite topic: food. When she and the boy Muggly were growing up, they spent a lot of time together in the street, with their noses pressed to various grocers' windows. It was the nearest they ever got to a full belly.

Jam tarts, thinks Pin. Warm crusty bread spread with yellow butter. A big steak pie with a golden-brown crust and steam coming out of the pie-funnel. Her mouth starts watering. It has been a long time since she has eaten, and it will be many hours before she eats again. Her stomach rumbles.

The shop door opens. Pin glances round, then scurries to the back, secreting herself behind one of the big cases of birds. Evil Man enters, bringing with him the damp miasma of the street, and something else, harder to define, but whatever it is, it makes the hairs on the back of Pin's neck rise. As if she were a fox at bay.

He raps on the counter with his stick. The noise brings Mr Trinkler hurrying out from the back, wiping his hands on his overalls. When he sees that it is not a customer awaiting his attention, his obsequious expression changes subtly to fawning with a side-order of terror.

"Good day, honoured sir," he says, bobbing up and down like some large inadequate wading bird. "I have done as you requested, and I now have the address of the individual on me … somewhere."

Trinkler fumbles frantically through various pockets, his gestures becoming almost comic in their wild efforts. Eventually he produces a small piece of paper, and thrusts it across the counter, as if consigning it to the fire.

The lawyer picks it up, carefully reads what is written, commits it to memory, then casually crushes the paper with the fingers of one hand, letting the resultant paper ball drop to the floor. His smile is almost reptilian in its coldness.

"Yes. Excellent. You have done well. There will be more on this matter, Trinkler, much more, so make sure you are always ready for me. You can expect payment once it is finished. Not before. And now I must leave your delightful little shop, for I am due in Crown Court at nine. A case of mistaken identity, the defence say. But no matter. He will be found guilty and hung."

He hooks open the door with his stick and goes out into the street, leaving Trinkler leaning on the counter, breathing hard and wiping his brow. At which point, Pin emerges from her hiding place, carrying her floor cloth, which she allows to slip from her fingers as she passes the crumpled piece of paper.

"Ow, a right butter-fingers today, i'n't I?" she admonishes herself, stooping down.

A few minutes later, Pin, her bucket and her meagre wages, accompanied by the piece of paper, make their way to the next cleaning job. All day long, as she slops and dusts and is fallen over and called names, she thinks about the piece of paper in her pocket and wonders what it might say. Pin has never learned to read. But that is not a problem: her sister has.

****

We return to our den of thieves. Same thieves, but in a different den this time. For this is Gray's Inn, the stronghold of Melancholy, the Sahara Desert of the law, with its ugly tiled-topped tenements, and door posts inscribed like gravestones, where even the gardens, trees and gravel paths wear a legal livery of black.

Here are the chambers of Pin's nemesis. Here he resides in a first-floor set of rooms, dwelling in a shady half-light, as snug as an oyster, as the saying goes. One floor below is the front office, whose black door stands in dark ambush, half open and half shut all day. It is usually occupied by two lawyers' clerks, the occasional game basket from the country, dispatched by a grateful supplicant, papers, dust and despairing clients.

The front office is dusty and draughty. In Winter, the lamplighter goes about his rounds like an executioner, his wick striking little sparks that barely lessen the darkness. In Summer, when it rains, it rains smuts, so that both clerks must move their desks to the far side of the room, for to write by an open window means a thin veil of smuts covering the paper before the page is written.

The job of the lawyers' clerk is to issue writs, file declarations, and fair copy documents. From these individuals come the numerous ingenious methods that torture and torment Her Gracious Majesty's poor subjects. The lawyers' clerk enters his office at nine and leaves at eight, and his greatest delight is to 'get costs'.

The lawyers' clerk wears white neckcloths, plaited shirt-frills and black waistcoats, and has false sleeves so as not to spoil the skins of parchment, and he knows the legal price of everything, from common assault to breach of promise of marriage. Nothing is hidden from his baleful eye. He knows, for instance, that Sir Phizby Rakehell paid 500 guineas for an hour's advocacy with his master, and Lady Fanny Flirtface, three hundred for the same.

Step into the back office. Here is a smoky fire, a desk, a cliental chair (currently occupied), a bottle of record ink, some sheets of parchment and a quill possibly plucked from the wing of a hawk, a vulture or some other bird of prey. Shelves contain copies of Tidd's Practice, the Law List, books about trials, evidence and criminals, and bound copies of Parliamentary Acts. Unlike the front office, the furniture here is solid, though plain.

Seated in the cliental chair, with his elegantly-trousered and booted legs lolling over the side, is mine host Daniel Adonis, the dandy, from our former acquaintance. Lounging in the window recess, is the man of the turf, who has just hauled a gold repeater from the recesses of his pepper-and-salt waistcoat. Both have been informed by the front office that 'the Governor is out' and invited to step inside and wait his return.

"He's late," the sporting gent says. "And look at the place ~ it's like a bloody morgue. How can anybody live like this?"

The other puts a finger to his lips.

"He is a gambler; the thrill of winning is all he cares about."

"He has won enough to afford a better situation, surely?"

Adonis shrugs his elegantly clad shoulders. "This is how he prefers to live. Do not fret."

Even as he speaks, voices are heard in the front office, one peremptory in its tone. Then the lawyer enters, shrugging off his black gown and placing a bundle of tape-tied papers on a side-table.

"You are late," remarks the man of the turf.

He is treated to a long, level stare.

"Better late than *'late'*: as in the *late* Colonel Gerrard, eh?" the lawyer remarks evenly.

The words hit their target. The Colonel flushes.

"I see you apprehend my meaning. When one spends every working-day surrounded by the criminal fraternity in all its various forms, one develops a different perspective upon life. Or death. Patience is a virtue, my friend. Forget it for a single moment and the hangman's noose awaits."

"Come now, let us not fall out," the youngest member of the trio says, swinging his legs round and pushing himself to a stand. "You read my letter? Bosey wants his money, and we do not have enough between the two of us to cover the debt. We require a cheque from you for the sum of £12,000."

The lawyer's eyes narrow.

"So much? When does he want the money?"

"Yesterday. I have managed to hold him off for another twenty-four hours. If I do not pay, he threatens to put the word round that I am the sort of man who does not meet their gambling debts. He will do it too, you know what he is like. I couldn't possibly permit that to happen. It would mean ruination. I'd have to go abroad, and Cecy would divorce me. Her people have made it quite clear that I am already on borrowed time as far as the marriage is concerned."

Something dark and unpleasant flickers at the back of the lawyer's hooded eyes.

"Then of course I shall have the money ready tomorrow, my friend. Send your man round promptly at mid-day to pick it up."

He picks up the pile of papers on the side-table, seemingly unconcerned by the request.

"Now, if you will both please excuse me: I have to get these documents copied and out by close of day."

The two men bid the lawyer good-day and depart. He waits until the sound of their footsteps have diminished into silence, after which he returns to his desk and sits awhile staring at nothing. The expression upon his face could have been chiselled from marble.

A few minutes pass in silent contemplation. Then the lawyer opens a small drawer under the desk and takes out a chequebook. Dipping his quill into the ink, he writes out a cheque for cash from a well-known firm of solicitors to a person who does not exist. He signs the cheque with the signature of the senior partner, a signature he has practiced over and over, until it is perfect.

After blotting the cheque, he adds a covering letter, then summons one of the clerks, and instructs him to take the cheque to Barclay & Company in Lombard Street and cash it, making sure the money is paid out in £50 notes. He knows the numbers will be recorded, but by the time the bank realises they have been duped, the money will have left the country, having passed through various anonymous hands.

The lawyer now turns his attention to Simon Bosanquet, a deeply distasteful raffish young man, recently arrived from New York. 'Bosey' as he likes to be styled, has inherited a vast fortune on the death of his father, and is running through it at the tables.

At the same time, he is running through London society like a dose of salts. Whatever the time of day, he exudes a vague late-night whiff of cigars, brandy and the perfume of other men's wives. The lawyer feels the contempt rise in his throat, bitter as bile.

He thinks about what the young upstart has threatened to do. While he is thinking, he draws something on the blotter in front of him. The picture of a playing card. An ace of spades. He draws a skull in one corner and colours it in. Maybe he will not go so far … this time … but it is clear the young man must be taught a lesson.

Two nights ago, the lawyer's corvine profile was bent over some gaming tables at a very elite private gambling party, held in one of the smartest streets in London, where he won a tidy sum. Tonight, he will try the lamplit dens of Seven Dials, and the Holy Land rookeries. There are always men there who will, for the right money, do whatever one wants. No questions asked.

****

Dawn finds Lucy Landseer standing barefoot at her bedroom window. Her view, one that brings back so many memories of childhood, is of a small cemetery. Now, touched with the early morning light, it is luminous and mysterious, bounded by iron railings and a Cypress-shaded path.

She gazes out at the marble angels, their shrouded wing-tips still covered in a thin mantle of snow, at the serried rows of stone headstones, the crosses, and in the distance, the spire of the church, swathed in morning mist, rising up like an enchanted castle in some long-forgotten fairy tale.

Lucy feels a shiver of delight run through her, so intense it is almost like a pain. To be here, in this city! To wake up each day in this small, but now familiar room, with its desk containing her manuscript, and her own things gathered around her. To know that a whole day lies ahead of her, waiting to be unrolled. A day in which everything is possible, and anything is achievable.

She washes and dresses by candle-light, then descends to the ground-floor, entering the sparsely furnished dining room, where the hostel residents' breakfasts are being served by the diminutive maid-of-all-work-and-no-praise.

Lucy consumes the thick lumpy porridge and cold flabby toast with the youthful relish of somebody who spent their formative years in a country rectory. The concept of a sophisticated palate is alien to her.

She exchanges polite greetings with her fellow residents, who are gulping down their breakfasts, prior to leaving for their various employments. Some are copying-clerks; one is a head clerk in a City mercantile house. Several are nurses. Two are telegraphists at the Electric Telegraph Company. Lucy is planning to interview each of them in turn for a series of articles on 'The Modern Girl at Work'.

Having drunk her tea, and ignored the curious residue gathered at the bottom of the cup, she returns to her room to re-read the article she wrote last night. It is called *'The Power of Persuasion'* ~ though she suspects the editor will probably come up with something snappier.

The gist of the article suggests that, if enough people *think* something is true, it becomes, for them, the actual truth. Even if it may not be the truth at all. Apart from her personal observations about the Madonna of the Metropolitan Line, Lucy has managed to source some cogent examples of historical mass delusion, even venturing into the daring realms of unrequited passion. It is a strongly written argument piece, and after correcting a few words, she feels rather pleased with it.

Lucy Landseer, 'Modern Girl about Town,' sets out to deliver her work to her editor. This particular walk is one of her favourites. The streets offer so many interesting sights and sounds. An ever-changing panorama of carriages with glittering panels and glancing wheels pass her by. She takes note of the sleek-pacing horses and stiff liveried footmen. She likes to peep into the dim, cushioned, carriage interiors, catching fleeting glimpses of beautiful women in furs and velvets and costly shawls.

Everything is food for the imagination. London is her study: the buildings, the street-sellers' cries, the continuous procession of men and women, the shifting, rushing, bewildering, bewitching multitude. There, on the corner is the dark-eyed Italian boy with his red-coated monkey and his piano-organ. Lucy places a coin in the little animal's cup and gives them both a smile as she sails by.

Here are plate-glass windows full of bonnets on pegs, tempting cakes and bon-bons ranged round glistening barley-sugar cages. Here are prints and pen-knives and parasols, all given a fleeting glance of interest as Lucy hurries along.

Reaching a street corner, she pauses by the newsagent stand to skim the latest newspaper headlines. Amidst the reports of disasters natural and unnatural, scandals real or imaginary, one headline catches her eye immediately: **Cull Cully, Scotland Yard's Most Defective Detective!**

Lucy frowns. The name rings a bell. Then she remembers the incident at Baker Street Station. Detective Sergeant Jack Cully. Her mind throws up an image of him struggling to remove the strange religious leader and contain his vociferous followers.

But wait ~ was he not also the kindly man helping his wife and little daughter down from a train? The man who spoke to her, referring to the appearances of the Metropolitan Madonna as a 'mass hallucination' ~ the very words she had used in her article without realising where she'd heard them first!

Lucy glances once again at the unpleasant headline, and her eyes narrow. She reaches into her purse and hands over some pennies to the man in the kiosk, receiving a neatly folded copy of the paper in return. She dimples her thanks and continues her journey.

According to its sub-title, *The Inquirer* claims to speak for 'The Man in the Street'. Well, she may not be a man, but she spends much time 'in the street' and it assuredly doesn't speak for her. And she is going to let the editor know this, in no uncertain terms!

Sometime later, Lucy Landseer enters a discreet little tea room close to the British Museum. The tea room is full of women sipping drinks and sharing shopping experiences. It is the sort of place where a single woman can sit on her own, unmolested and unremarked.

She is shown to a table, and orders some coffee, a ham sandwich and a plate of fancy cakes. A nice little treat for finishing her article. While she waits for her luncheon to arrive, she unfolds the newspaper, gets out a pencil, and starts to peruse the piece on the detective.

It has been written by a journalist named Mr Richard Dandy, in prose so purple it could be cut out and made into a day-dress. Lucy is appalled. That millions of Londoners should, even now, be damaging their ocular nerves by reading *'the callous Cully continues to cause catastrophe'* doesn't bear thinking about! Yet she must think about it. She underlines the phrase, adding an exclamation mark in the margin.

By the end of her luncheon, the front page of *The Inquirer* resembles a map of the railway system of the British Isles as imagined by a splenetic spider. Lucy pays the waitress and gathers up her things. She will pass the afternoon studying at the British Museum. And her evening will be spent composing a stinging critique to the newspaper.

As she crosses Great Russell Street, carefully lifting her skirt to avoid a freshly deposited pile of manure, Lucy is struck by another idea. Perhaps there is something else she could also do to aid the much-maligned detective? Yes, there is! Her expression brightening by the minute, Lucy Landseer enters the British Museum by way of the massive finely-carved oak doorway, and climbs the grand staircase that leads to the Gallery of Antiquities.

****

By strange symbiosis, a letter is also preoccupying Inspector Lachlan Greig. In fact, such is his concern about it that he has brought it to show Detective Sergeant Cully, who reads it at his desk, a frown gathering upon his brow as he does so.

"Ah," he says thoughtfully, looking up.

"Aye. You see the difficulty," Greig says. "Miss Trigg puts an advertisement in a newspaper asking for information about her brother. Somebody writes suggesting they have information about him and arranges a meeting."

Cully steeples his fingers. "You have established that the handwriting is not that of the brother?"

Greig nods. "I also took the liberty of showing it to Mr Crace, the bank clerk who was Trigg's friend. He did not recognise the hand. So, it is not from the brother, nor from one of his colleagues at the bank. Then who sent it?"

"It is a mystery, that's for sure," Cully says. "And Miss Trigg writes that whoever sent the letter failed to show up. What could be the reason for that?"

"I'd have said life got in the way, but she has received no letter of apology, nor any request to set up a second meeting, so we can discount that as a reason," Greig says. "Therefore, I think whoever wrote the letter never intended to meet her, or rather, they wanted to see who 'S at Box 22' was. Think about it: a busy station, people hurrying by. Nothing easier than to fix a meeting place, then wait somewhere near by to see who turns up. The lassie did not know who she was meeting, so she would never know."

Cully gives him a quizzical look.

"Aye, I have a very suspicious mind and that is how it works," Greig agrees. "This person wanted to see whether they were being led into a trap. Or maybe they were setting one."

"Is it proof that Lambert Trigg is still alive, though?"

"Perhaps. Though we are no nearer finding him. I worry that she may now have put herself in harm's way unknowingly. And I don't like the thought of that at all."

Cully pulls a face.

"I can understand her impatience. Her brother has been missing for some time. She has heard nothing from him or about him. Meanwhile, as she writes in her accompanying note, she has also heard nothing from us about what we're doing to find him. She does not understand that these things take time."

"Nevertheless, she must not act in future without consulting us first," Greig says. "I shall now reply to Miss Trigg and tell her that if she receives any other letters, she must notify us immediately."

Good luck with that, Cully thinks, being slightly more appraised of the workings of the female mind.

"And I shall warn her to keep her wits about her whenever she leaves the house," Greig says. "If we could spare a man to watch her, I would order it, but we are several constables down already due to the winter influenza."

"I am sure Miss Trigg will heed every word of your warning," Cully says, keeping his expression strictly neutral. "She struck me as a sensible young woman. She is bound to listen to your advice and obey it to the letter."

Greig gives him a long thoughtful look. Then he picks up the anonymous missive and accompanying note, and returns to his own desk, where several other communications also await his response. He reaches for his pen, recalling as he does so, the numerous occasions when Detective Inspector Stride has railed against the never-ending tide of paperwork.

He is beginning to share his opinion.

****

Penelope Rose Klem (known to her friends as Pin) also has certain views, rising out of all the thinking she does. For Pin is a great thinker. When you spend your days mopping floors and whitening steps and dusting shelves, it leaves your brain free to cogitate.

Here is Pin now, up to her arms in hot soapy water, which is a treat on such a dismal day as this, and makes a pleasant change from Trinkler's Emporium, where the water is cold and the employer/worker relationship even colder.

While she enjoys the rare sensation of warm arms, Pin thinks about the piece of paper she picked up. '*Young woman*', it said. And there was an address. Pin wonders why Evil Man wants to know about a young woman. And what exactly he wants to know about her? One thing she is sure of: it cannot be anything good.

Now she is thinking about the boy Muggly. She thinks about his cuts and bruises, which have healed, and his broken arm, which has not. She is glad she has found him something to do that doesn't involve lifting or carrying. She finishes off mopping the floor and takes the bucket to the doorway to fling the dirty water into the street.

Pin moves on. Luckily for her, not all her clients are skinflint shop keepers who wouldn't appreciate a well-scrubbed floor if they fell on it. Part of her work takes her to some of the slightly better areas of the city and nicer employers.

Recently, Pin has inherited several places in Jermyn Street from a neighbourhood girl who, reaching the age of thirteen, decided if she had to spend her life on her hands and knees, she might as well move into the gentlemen's entertainment business, where the hours were shorter, the clothes nicer and you didn't continually get chapped hands from caustic soap.

Some of the places Pin cleans puzzle her, though. The bootmaker's shop is fine. The linen-draper also. But then, there is a Turkish divan, where men come to smoke cigars and drink. The smell in the morning catches her throat and makes her eyes water, but she is making a few extra pennies by picking up discarded cigar ends and selling them on later.

Pin finishes mopping the bootmaker's floor and hauls her bucket out of the door into the street. The Turkish divan, two buildings down, is her next venue. It is still very early; the usual morning rush has barely begun and the air smells of damp and rot.

She slides down the side alleyway and is just about to let herself in by the servants' door when it is suddenly thrust open, emitting a waft of warmth and stale cigar smoke into the cold air. Pin cowers back as two men emerge, blinking in the pale light.

They have clearly spent the night in the divan. Their evening dress is crumpled, their white cravats untied. They reek of cigars and brandy. The men stand in the alleyway, yawning and wiping their mouths. One of the men suddenly leans forward and voids the contents of his stomach onto the ground.

Pin stands as motionless as she can, scarcely breathing. But neither of the men notice her. She has frequently observed that street people, those who clean or sweep or sell matches or hold horses for the gentry, seem to be invisible. She watches the two men stumble towards the main thoroughfare. As they reach the end of the alleyway, the younger one claps the older one on the shoulder and gives a great shout of laughter.

Pin looks after them thoughtfully. Then, stepping over the steaming pile of vomit, she goes into the building. Mr Murad is standing in the tiny back scullery. He smiles when he sees her. Mr Murad likes Pin. She turns up. The feeling is mutual. Pin likes stories and Mr Murad has lots of thrilling stories about his ancestors, who were Turkish pirates. That's the main reason she turns up.

Now, she takes her bucket over to the tap and fills it with water.

"Them blokes wot just left 'ave bin sick in the alleyway," Pin remarks. "You want me to clean up?"

Mr Murad utters various choice words in Turkish.

"You are gud girl, Penelope," he says. "Gud girl. Not like that Fanny. You keep away from men like them, eh?"

Pin's face is a study in complete innocence, and her smile would charm the birds off the trees.

"I will. Why, Mr Murad, wot they done?"

A few more phrases in the vernacular of Mr Murad's birthplace are uttered. "They are bad mens, Penelope. They gambles for money, all night long. Then they come here to sleep."

"Then I shall take great care, Mr Murad," Pin's smile was so bright you could warm your hands at it. "Wot woz their names agin? Just in case I ever meets them, casual like."

"The young one, he is Mr Daniel someone or other, I am not sure. But the older one ~ he is the one to watch, Penelope. He is lawyer. Name is Jacob Jarvis. He is big wig in the law, as you say in this country. Very nasty man. When my cousin was accused of stealing cloth from a department store, which he did not do, he was lawyer for other side. My cousin was found guilty and deported."

Mr Murad points in the direction of the now empty alleyway.

"I will never forget this man. Never forget, and never ever forgive."

Pin picks up her bucket and cleaning cloth. Her face is now wiped so clean of all emotion she could be one of her own floors.

"Well, that's a sad tale, Mr Murad, innit. I'll just go and mop out the big room now, shall I?"

Mr Murad pats her shoulder.

"You go clean, Penelope, gud girl. I make some nice coffee and have little breakfast ready for you."

Pin hauls her bucket up the uncarpeted back stairs. So now she knows Evil Man's name. She repeats it to herself several times as she works, to make sure she doesn't forget it. Never forget, and never ever forgive. Pin nods to herself. She likes that. A good motto.

****

A short while later, breakfast is being cautiously served to Mr Mutesius, Helena Trigg's landlord, by an aproned and morning-capped Mrs Mutesius. She places the chipped coffee pot and a rack of toast on the red-bobbled tablecloth, then turns to her husband, who is staring fixedly through the heavy net curtains that keep the outside world where it rightly belongs.

"Would you like me to pour your coffee, my dear?" she whispers.

But to her great alarm, instead of granting the lodestar of his life permission to supply him with his morning beverage of choice, Mr Mutesius ignores her and continues to look out of the window.

"He's there again," he says.

Mrs Mutesius does some silent background hovering, coffee pot poised. She is awaiting instructions.

"Same place as yesterday. Same time too. What's he bloody well *want*?"

"Coffee?" quavers Mrs Mutesius, feeling that a question posed should be a question answered.

Her beloved rounds on her with a snarl.

"Of course he don't want coffee, you silly old fool!"

Mrs Mutesius' lower lip trembles.

Her life-partner reaches for his walking stick and hobbles on his bent and ancient legs towards the door.

"Where are you going?"

"I'm going to settle his hash once and for all, whoever he is!"

And having uttered this terrifying pronouncement, Mr Mutesius opens the living-room door, stomps to the front door, pulls it open a crack, and waves the walking stick threateningly.

"I see you! You clear orf! Clear orf! D'you hear me?" he shouts.

There is a long silence, during which Mrs Mutesius covers her face with her apron, and mentally prepares herself for a life of widowhood. Then, the halting steps of the man in her life sound outside the door once more, to be followed by the man himself, bent, gasping and wheezing.

"He's gone. I told him, I did. I said: you clear orf!"

Mrs Mutesius lowers the apron and stares at her Hero in the House.

"Will he come back?" she ventures cautiously.

The hero glowers darkly at the window.

"He won't dare. Not after the fright what I just gave him." He pulls himself upright creakily. "Where's my coffee then?"

Mrs Mutesius fills the cup and pushes it across the table. As her husband pours the brew down his wizened throat, they both hear the light patter of footsteps coming down the stairs.

"Is it Miss Trigg?" Mrs Mutesius ventures, in a suitably hushed tone.

"Well t'ain't the Angel Gabriel, that's for sure," Mr Mutesius says, chuckling at his own joke and ending up with a fit of coughing as his reward. He mops his eyes with a grubby handkerchief. "Which reminds me, her rent is due. And if that brother of hers isn't coming back, which it looks like he in't, I might have to think about letting his room. Could easily get two beds in it, and two more in her room and she could move upstairs to the box room. 'Taint as if we need a housemaid any more now you does all the cleaning. I'll speak to her about it tonight."

Meanwhile, unaware that she is the subject of conversation, Helena slips out of the front door, and begins the long walk to J. King & Co. At least the snow has gone, though the rain that arrived overnight still hangs about the streets like an unwelcome visitor. But she has had a hot drink and eaten some bread to fortify her before setting out, and Lambert's umbrella is a welcome accompaniment.

Passing the Mutesius' door, the smell of coffee almost overwhelms her. She remembers making early morning coffee for herself and Lambert, then sitting opposite him at the little table by the window, sharing their breakfast while discussing the day to come.

Helena crosses the road, noting how the red and blue lights of the pharmacists' shop are mirrored on the wet pavements. She reminds herself that she has her health, that she is fortunate to be working for a good employer, and that her rent is due, but that she has money to pay it. She thinks about what she might have for her supper after finishing work.

A pie man with a pony and cart has started going down the street at exactly the hour she gets ready to stop work. She has heard his cry: 'Pies all hot! Meat and fruit, pies all hot!' and the clip-clip of the little pony's hooves. Perhaps she might treat herself?

It is important to keep her mind busy on these practical everyday things, so that she doesn't worry. Because she is worried that she might be being followed. Inspector Greig's letter warning her that she put herself at risk by her actions came as a shock. She hadn't considered that at all.

Helena has an animal's sixth sense, a sort of prickling along her spine. She has had it for the past few days. She keeps stopping and glancing over her shoulder, hoping to spot the tell-tale signs on someone's face, that swift overlaying of fixed intent with casual indifference.

If only it were that easy! All the people she encounters on her walk to work and on her walk back home portray either expression. Once or twice she has been on the point of approaching somebody and challenging them. Luckily, she has thought better of it. Inspector Greig's words are imprinted upon her retina*: I beg you, Miss Trigg, try not to do anything to impede my investigation. It could mean the outcome we both dread.*

After some thought, Helena has decided, somewhat reluctantly, to take the warning seriously. For Lambert is alive, somewhere. She has no doubt of this whatsoever. After all, they share the closest bond: they are twins, linked by so much more than just family circumstance. If Lambert were lying dead anywhere in the world, she'd know for sure.

At the end of her busy day, Helena's walk home is enlivened by a mince-meat pie, eaten hot straight from the pie man's can. She arrives back replete and, to the best of her knowledge, unfollowed.

She has just crossed the threshold of her lodgings, shaking the rain from her bonnet as she does so, when her landlord's door creaks open and his wizened features appear round the side. He coughs modestly in an introductory sort of way.

"Ah, Mr Mutesius, it is rent day, is it not? I have it all ready for you," Helena says with a smile, holding the money out to him.

Mr Mutesius sidles into the hallway, thus giving Helena a clear view of Mrs Mutesius who stands in the lee of the doorway, wearing an overlarge afternoon cap and a worried frown. He takes the money, but instead of thanking her and edging away again, he stands his ground.

"I was a-wondering, Miss Trigg," he begins.

"Wondering Miss Trigg" comes the whispered echo from the doorway.

"Yes, wondering whether the time has come for you to make … other arrangements for your accommodation."

He peers at Helena with his rheumy eyes. She starts back.

"But I … I don't understand. I have always paid my rent on time. Why should I look elsewhere? I am perfectly happy where I am."

"Ah. But, you see, maybe we, Mrs Mutesius and I, are not happy."

"Not happy," repeats the echo.

Helena stares at him in disbelief.

"Please explain?"

Mr Mutesius deliberately stares over her shoulder, his fingers fiddling with a coat button.

"The rooms you presently occupy were let on the basis that there were two of you. Now there is only one of you. I have a small back attic room on the top floor that might be suitable for your changed circumstances. I could get it cleared out, maybe even give it a coat of whitewash. What do you think, Miss Trigg?"

"Miss Trigg," the murmurer repeats softly.

Helena bridles. Her colour rises. Suddenly, the ground beneath her feet is shifting again. She feels it slipping away, out of her control. She breathes hard, then replies, making herself speak slowly, listening to the words as if they emerge from some place within.

"Mr Mutesius, you are my landlord. I cannot argue with that. But if it is a question of my 'changed circumstances', as you call them, may I assure you that my brother will be returning very soon, and I do NOT think he will take kindly to having his sister treated in this manner while he is not here to defend her. No, indeed, I think he will be *exceedingly angry* that you are trying to turn me out of our settled home, for no good reason. I pay the rent you ask, do I not? Have you any complaints about me as a tenant?"

"No complaints at all," comes the unexpected reply from the doorway. Mr Mutesius rounds upon his spouse.

"What are you burbling about, you silly old woman. I thought we'd agreed."

"Well, I don't agree," Mrs Mutesius whispers. "I don't want no more strangers here, a-tramping up and down the stairs and talking loudly and keeping late hours and making more mess and work for me. It is my house ~ daddy left it to me not you. Miss Trigg stays."

It is the longest speech Helena has ever heard her utter in all the time she has been living here. She stares at the old woman in complete astonishment, as does Mr Mutesius, whose mouth actually falls open in shock.

"Thank you, Mrs Mutesius," Helena says quickly, before her cantankerous landlord has a chance to recover his equilibrium. "I am so glad we have reached an agreement. I shall now go and prepare my supper. I bid you both a good evening."

She turns, picks up her skirts and runs lightly up the stairs to her sitting room. Once safely inside, she leans against the door, feeling normalcy resume. She glances round at the familiar shabby furniture, the blue rag rug by the fire, the little china shepherdess on the mantelpiece, the photograph of herself and Lambert that they had taken when they arrived in London.

Everything in the room contributes to her feeling of safety. Everything anchors her. Without this, there is nothing. Only a dark void with no toe-holds. She hangs up her bonnet and mantle, puts some pieces of coal on the fire and lights it. Then she makes herself a drink. The sound of heated voices filters up through the floorboards. She smiles grimly. She can guess the topic under discussion.

Helena Trigg takes her hot drink, wraps herself in a blanket, and sits by the small coal fire that splutters and smokes in the grate. She has to stay here, whatever the cost, because if Lambert returns, and she is not here to welcome him back, he will never know where to look for her.

Dear Lambert. The thought of living the rest of her life without seeing his beloved face ever again, is too painful to bear. Helena pinches her lips together firmly. She needs to stay strong, for she must carry on. She *will* believe that her brother is returning very soon, as she said. After all, what else is there to have faith in?

****

The March wind doth blow, though there is no longer any snow. The coltsfoot, the first flower of Spring is all aglow upon the railway banks and in the waste spaces around the city. No cuckoo sounds, but the skies are fair, the air warm and dry, and the early morning sunlight seems to tell the happy-hearted Londoner that summer is a-coming in. Eventually.

Thus, Detective Sergeant Jack Cully starts out from his small terraced house with the determination that he will have a capital 'breather' before reaching Scotland Yard. Alas, it does not take long before reality shatters the spirit of that pleasant dream.

Fifteen minutes into his walk, he begins to get unpleasant whiffs of gritty matter. His eyes start to smart.

There is an unpleasant sensation about his teeth. The mud that has previously filled all the streets and footways is now being pounded into dust, and thrown around in all directions, to the infinite discomfort of himself, and the rest of the passers-by.

It is said that if one wishes to study the various phases of human anger, one can do no better than stand upon Westminster Bridge, or in Parliament Street, Oxford Street or the Mall, on a windy day in early March, just after the first fine weather has dried up the long-standing mud, and the cloud-compelling dust is being blown around the streets by the west wind.

Wiping his eyes, Cully eventually enters Scotland Yard, wondering how his good mood seems to have trickled away, leaving him cross and irritable. The desk constable hails him with a grin and the information that his presence is requested by Detective Inspector Stride.

Cully knocks lightly on Stride's door and enters. The small fire is doing its best to warm the air, helped by the strips of newspaper being currently fed into it.

"Ah, Jack, there you are. Have you seen the latest?" Stride says, picking up and waving a copy of *The Inquirer* at him.

Cully mentally braces himself. "Now what has Mr Dandy written about me?"

But to Cully's surprise, Stride is grinning from ear to ear.

"Mr Dandy has written nothing. On the contrary, he has been taken to task. It appears you have an admirer. Read this."

He riffles through until he finds the 'Correspondence from Our Readers' section, then folds back the paper, handing it to his colleague. Cully scans the page.

"Top of the first column, left hand side. I am reliably informed that this is the prime position for letters from the public," Stride says, still grinning.

Cully lets his eyes travel down the page, taking in phrases like: *'low and cowardly attack upon a public official ... prose worthy of a juvenile scribbler ... the nadir of popular journalism, only fit for the ignobile vulgans'*.

He is speechless!

"I do not know who L Landseer is, but he has my undying gratitude," Stride says happily. "He has put into words everything I feel about Dandy Dick and his vile outpourings. If I ever meet the man, I shall shake him by the hand and buy him a drink."

"He has an interesting turn of phrase," Cully remarks.

"Oh, he's clearly an Oxford man," Stride says. "Maybe a member of the medical profession ~ the Latin rather gives it away. Reminds me of Robertson on a bad day. Not that he has any other kind of day," he adds.

"I'm surprised the editor published it."

Stride waves a dismissive hand. "Fuel to the fire, Jack. He's hoping somebody will write in in defence of Dandy Dick ~ which they will, probably the man himself or one of his pals. Nothing like a controversial letter-fight to sell copies. Remember all the correspondence about the correct way to roll an umbrella? Went on for months."

Cully skims through the letter again.

"With your permission, I shall show this to Emily tonight," he says. "She will be highly amused." He hovers by the desk. "I have finally heard back from Emily's father," he says.

Stride looks up quickly.

"The cards?"

Cully nods. He draws the cards out of his coat pocket and places them on the desk.

"He writes that the cards are completely unlike the ones he used to gamble with in his youth. They are of a much better quality for a start. He also writes that the aces are different too. He thinks that a man who could afford a pack of cards like this ~ well, several packs, has a well-paid job somewhere. And is probably a serious gambler."

Stride focusses on the designs.

"Shame we don't know where they were bought," he muses.

"We do know where they were made, though." Cully points to the wavy scroll under the drawing of the ace where the words *Goodall, London* appear.

"By God, so we do! I hadn't noticed that before."

"I looked them up. Their business is in College Street. If you like, I could pay them a visit, and see if they can shed any light on where the cards might have gone after leaving the factory. It'd make a change from dealing with all this Madonna madness."

Stride nods, heaving himself out of his chair.

"Let's both go together, Jack. This is the first bit of solid evidence we've had in weeks. If they can tell us anything that might lead to finding our man, it'll be well worth the journey."

****

While Stride and Cully are making their way to Camden, let us divert, albeit temporarily, to Chancery Lane, the legal quarter of the city. Here are black-coated men carrying bundles of red-tape tied papers, and doorposts striped with names.

Here are stationers' shops hung with legal almanacs and skins of parchment, law lists bound in bright red leather, and law books in sleek yellow calf. Pause outside a furniture shop and observe the leather-topped writing tables, iron safes and japanned tin boxes, which look as if they have been dipped in raspberry jam.

On the corner of a side-street are the law offices of Harry & Persew. And here comes George Harry himself, tripping along the pavement on his way back from Court. He wears a black clerical-looking gown and a powdered coachman-like wig. He is red-cheeked from the wind, and jovial from ale drunk in the dingy public house opposite the Insolvent Court, from whence he has just come.

He enters through the open street-door, where he discovers his partner, Edmund Persew waiting for him. He is wearing a worried expression, but no wig and gown.

"What news on the Rialto?" Harry remarks gaily, tossing a bundle of court papers down onto a desk.

In response, Persew gives him a long, level pursed stare. He places a parchment-coloured forefinger to his thin, pale lips and beckons him into the inner office.

"I have just come from a meeting with the bank," he says, coldly. "It appears that we no longer have any credit with them. I have been told by the manager that you, George, have been writing cheques for vast sums of money that I do not recall being told about."

George Harry's legal eyebrows shoot up until they almost meet his legal wig. "I do not know what on earth you are talking about. I have written no such cheques."

"I put it to you, with respect, that you have."

"I put it to *you*, then, that you produce evidence of the accusation. Where is your proof, eh?"

In response, Persew silently lays out a selection of cheques on the desk. Each one has the law firm's name clearly printed on the top.

"Here it is. Proof one: Dated 17th of February, a cheque to a Mr Catesby Blackwell of Highgate for £2,888. Proof two: a few days later, a cheque for £4,200 made out to the same client. Proof three: the latest cheque, dated March 1st, for £6,000, also made out to Mr Catesby Blackwell. What is your response?"

George Harry's complexion turns as yellow as the law books on the shelf behind him.

"But … what?" he splutters, his usual verbal fluency dramatically forsaking him.

"I invite you to examine the signatures on the cheques closely, George. They are all yours, written in your hand ~ a hand that I, your partner of twenty years, recognise clearly."

Harry picks up each cheque in turn and studies it intently for some time.

"It is like my signature, I admit it, but it cannot be my signature. For a start, I do not know this Catesby Blackwell at all ~ he is not a client of this law firm. Never has been. And the ink on the cheques is a lighter blue than the one I use to write my cheques ~ see?" He holds up his inkstand for inspection. "I put it to you, on the balance of probability, that someone has got hold of one of our chequebooks, has used it to obtain large sums of money in my name and from our account."

"And would you care to surmise who that 'someone' might be?"

Harry shakes his head. "I only correspond with fellow lawyers, who are, *ipso facto*, above such base practices."

There is a long empty space where nothing is said. Each lawyer contemplates the significance of this event, and its future implications.

"What can be done?" Persew asks, finally. "He may have presented cheques to other banks, which will come back in time for redemption. We now have nothing in our account, George. Nothing. It has been emptied. I cannot even pay the clerks' salaries this month. What will happen when word gets out that Harry and Persew cannot pay their own clerks? We will be ruined!"

George Harry's expression is solemn.

"There's nothing for it: we must summon the forces of law and order. I shall write to Scotland Yard at once and seek their aid. Meanwhile, we shall carry on as if nothing has happened. I am in Court later. I suggest you go through the client accounts and see if there are any outstanding bills. If you find one, send your clerk to push for payment. Hopefully we can hold off future creditors for a short time on the strength of our good name and reputation."

The two lawyers head for their desks, where the sound of quill hitting letter-paper is the only sound to be heard for the next hour, followed by the sound of matches being struck, and sealing-wax sizzling. Then Harry rises to his feet, an envelope in his hand.

"I shall instruct Parvis to run straight over to Scotland Yard with this, and to wait for a reply. I shall attempt to return from Court by the time they respond."

He picks up his wig, which has been deposited on a chair, and claps it onto his head. Then, making a formal bow to his partner, he hurries out of the room.

****

The Camden Works of Goodall & Sons, card producers, is situated behind a terrace of houses in College Street. The building has previously been a gun factory, and there are still reinforcements on the windows, and black gunpowder stains running down some of the exterior walls as evidence of the former occupants.

Stride and Cully make their way to the front entrance, where an elderly man in a check cap and brown workmen's overalls is loading wooden boxes onto the back of a pony-cart. Stride shows him his card.

"Is the boss in?"

The man gestures towards an open side door.

"He's a-sorting the orders."

They enter the factory, where row upon row of workers are unrolling thin sheets of card, laying them on rollers, feeding them into printers, cutting them, sticking layers together, flattening them, trimming them, applying the designs, and subjecting the finished cards to careful checks.

The heat is intense, the noise of machinery deafening, and there is a strong smell of chemicals and glue. Overseeing the various processes is a stooped, round-faced man with a receding hairline, a walrus moustache and a suit with a limp collar.

He wears spectacles over puffy-lidded eyes, which, along with the tufts of hair above his ears, gives him the appearance of a myopically genial owl. This is Josiah Goodall, son of Charles, and brother of Montague who is currently supervising some of the picture artists.

Stride introduces himself and Cully. He explains, without going into too much detail, why they have come.

Then he hands Josiah Goodall the two playing cards, folds his arms, and waits. The card manufacturer studies the cards from all angles, turning them over and over, peering at them sideways, and stroking the edges with a thumb and forefinger.

"So, what can you tell us about these cards," Stride asks, after several minutes of close and silent examination has taken place.

Goodall goes on studying the cards.

"Well, detective inspector, I can tell you that these belong to the new ace of spade designs. You see, the Old Frizzle duty ace won't do for today's players. Oh no. They want quality and novelty, and we aim to supply them."

He peers at them over the top of his rimless spectacles.

"We started making this design in 1862 ~ you see the little imp sitting on top of the drawing has a feather in his cap: that's how you can tell it's an original Goodall & Son card. This particular design tends to be favoured by serious card players. They like cards with plain backs to them. I can tell that these cards have been well used ~ the corners are slightly worn. What usually happens is that the old pack is superseded by a new one when the cards have reached this stage."

"And do you have a list of people you supply to?" Cully asks.

Goodall nods. "We do. It is a rather extensive list, for we supply private clubs, shops, department stores, stationers, societies and of course, we also export to the continent."

"Just the London ledgers will do," Stride says. "Perhaps the last two years only?"

Goodall goes to fetch the sales ledgers. He places them on a work bench and glances at them expectantly.

"My colleague will examine them." Stride says.

Cully puffs out a sigh, gets out his notebook and pencil, and begins leafing through the pages. Meanwhile Goodall turns to Stride, a gleam in his eyes.

"Have you see our latest double-ended court cards, detective inspector? No? Let me show them to you while your colleague is occupied."

He reaches down an ornate box and takes out a pack of cards, which he fans through with all the speed and dexterity of a street gambler, laying the picture suites on the counter as they appear in the fan.

"They are becoming quite the fashion. Rather fine do you not think? Last year alone, we sold over two million packs of cards. De La Rue cannot come near that, can he!"

"I'm sure he can't. They are very … jolly aren't they," Stride says, sensing that a positive response is called for, although truthfully, he hasn't a clue what the man is talking about.

"You're a card-player yourself?" Goodall asks, hopefully.

Stride shakes his head. Playing cards, along with mud, and peddlers who knocked on the door with unwanted household items, are all regarded in the same light by Mrs Stride, who has had a strict Presbyterian Scottish upbringing.

"Shame. Ah well, I expect your line of work keeps you too busy, eh? Now then, here's another fascinating fact, as I like to call them: do you know why every ace of spades has to carry the maker's name?"

Stride shakes his head again. He shoots Cully a meaningful glance.

"I'll tell you why: it's all to do with the Playing Card Duty ~ I bet you didn't know there was such a thing, did you? No, I can see from your face that you did not. Well, that's the reason. It showed that the printing house had paid its taxes ~ now, you noticed I said 'paid', didn't you? And you're asking yourself: why did he speak as if it was in the past."

Stride, who is actually asking himself something completely different, merely smiles weakly.

"This is the reason, detective inspector," Goodall leans forward slightly, as if about to confide an enormous secret, and despite himself, Stride finds himself leaning forward in sympathy.

"Three years ago, the government reduced the duty on playing cards from one shilling to threepence. Now you've learned something, haven't you!"

"Indeed, I have, Mr Goodall," Stride says earnestly. "But I think my colleague and I have trespassed upon your valuable time quite long enough. Ready to go, Jack?"

Jack Cully, who has only reached the mid-point of the first of the three customer sales books, raises his head, catches his colleague's expression, reads it, and closes the book.

"Yes, I think I have everything we need."

Josiah Goodall shows them to the door, a satisfied expression on his face.

"You are welcome any time, detectives. My goodness, to think that a pair of playing cards from Goodall & Sons should be involved in a murder inquiry! It's like something out of one of those penny dreadful novels the wife likes to read. I can't wait to tell brother Montague."

Stride holds up a hand, "If you wouldn't mind, we'd prefer if you didn't speak to him. I'm sure I don't have to explain to a man of your intelligence why."

Goodall frowns. Then his brow clears. "Why of course, detective inspector. I understand completely. Mum's the word, as they say."

He shakes their hands, then stands in the doorway, watching them leave. As soon as the two detectives are out of earshot, he hurries back into the factory, and heads straight to the small sales office. This is too good a story to keep to himself. Admittedly, he *had* promised the senior detective that he wouldn't speak to Montague. He had promised nothing about writing to him though.

Meanwhile Stride and Cully are making their way back to Scotland Yard.

"Just as well you came to the rescue back there, Jack." Stride says, pulling a face. "I was seriously contemplating hitting the man. He wouldn't shut up about cards! Is it me, or do I just attract these strange people?"

Wisely, Cully decides to divert the conversation. "I don't think this line of inquiry is going to lead us anywhere. The company seems to supply every department store and stationery shop in London."

"So, what do you suggest?"

Cully walks on in silence for a while. Then,

"What is it you always say: to get the right answer, you first have to ask the right question. We're asking where the murderer bought the playing cards. Maybe we should be asking why."

"Go on."

Cully continues, "We suspect he is highly intelligent, as well as manipulative and convincing. He can express himself well and is well turned out. He also seems to know how the City operates. That suggests someone in a well-paid profession ~ perhaps a private bank or a brokerage firm?

"It occurs to me that someone who will go to such lengths, must be a gambler, probably playing for high stakes, and losing. He is using the money to fund his habit. The bank clerks are not his primary target, they are merely in his way."

Stride stops and turns to face him.

"You are absolutely right, Jack! And that would also explain why he leaves an ace of spades playing card on each of his victims. Game over. What was it L. Landseer called you in his letter: perspicacious and something or other. Such men possess a reckless streak; it will undo him eventually.

"Let us make judicious inquiries around the other police offices and see if they have any contacts who might be able to help. Now, a spot of luncheon is on the cards ~ ha! What do you say to Sally's? We are always assured of a warm welcome at Sally's. Let's celebrate that letter of yours with a pint of Sally's best."

****

Little does Stride know, but the epistolary facilitator of the celebration is even now making her way to Euston Road and Gower Street Station, having spent a morning in the British Museum studying the ancient Assyrians and the far less ancient visitors.

Lucy Landseer is preparing material for another of her 'Modern Girl About Town' articles, which are proving to be so popular with the magazine's readers. She has lunched *en plein air* on a succulent ham sandwich and a mug of coffee, purchased from a street-stall. She has paid the small crossing sweeper to see her over the road. Now, with her notebook full of ideas and sketches, she is heading for her final destination, Baker Street Station.

Lucy's inspired idea is to write a kind of Madonna diary, charting everything that she sees, or that is told others have seen, as well as her own observations. When she has gathered together sufficient evidence of the public deception taking place, she will write various articles offering her version of events. One in the eye for *The Inquirer* and its verbally incontinent chief reporter!

Now she stands on the down-line platform, waiting for the train to come puffing out of the tunnel. She clutches her satchel firmly. It also contains the notes for her next essay. On Tuesday evening, the handsome lecturer from Cambridge University paid her a compliment about her previous one, and she is sure his gaze fell upon her several times during the evening's lecture.

She studies her fellow passengers. All human life is gathered here in this small space. The platform is crowded with women in bright apparel (she does like the word 'apparel'), eager children peering into the tunnel, women with babies in arms, men in city suits and men with cloth caps, bundles and empty dinner baskets.

Glancing across to the opposite platform, she observes that there is now no such thing as a dead wall. Every square inch is audacious with posters in all colours of the rainbow, each advertising some product or performance. It seems to have happened overnight. She can't recall seeing such a profusion of printed puffery before. Or maybe she was too preoccupied?

Lucy considers the variety of tempting offers for hair restorer, tonics, ovens, furniture, clothes, pills and potions offering miraculous results, plus the upcoming bill of fare at the Victoria Music Hall. Then the train chugs into the station, and hisses to a halt to a shout of *'Gow'r Streeee!'* from the guard. Doors open, people, baggage and the odd dog descend. She clambers aboard and settles herself in one of the second-class carriages.

The guard blows a shrill blast on his whistle. The train seems to gather itself together, then lurches forward, entering the tunnel. Lucy stares out of the window, which becomes a mirror as the train enters the tunnel. A pretty girl in a fetching bonnet smiles at her. Her own reflection in the glass opposite. Her companions doze or read the daily newspaper. Suddenly, there is a brief sensation of white light, just beyond the window. Something sparkles enticingly for the briefest second. Then it is gone.

Lucy's eyes widen. Is it the Madonna of the Metropolitan Line? Glancing round her fellow passengers, she meets the eyes of an elderly couple, sitting close together at the far end of the carriage. Their expression in rapt. They clutch each other's hands. Whatever she thought she saw, they clearly saw it too and know what it was.

Lucy Landseer pinches the back of her hand, hard, to check that she is awake and not hallucinating. The pinch hurts. So, she must be awake. When the train finally enters Baker Street Station, she alights hurriedly.

The first people she encounters, as she makes her dazed way towards the exit, is the old couple from her carriage. They are heading towards the shrine at the other end of the platform, along with many other passengers, all with ecstatic expressions upon their faces. The old couple stop and smile at her.

"She only appears to those who believe in her. Or to those she is going to bless," the old woman says, somewhat cryptically.

"I don't …" Lucy begins, but the old woman holds up a gloved hand.

"There are people who think she doesn't exist, my dear. They write terrible things in the newspapers about how we, who have seen her and worship her, are just foolish. You must have read some of the things. But we aren't foolish, are we? Because you saw her too, clear as day, didn't you? And you're obviously a clever young woman."

Lucy bites her bottom lip.

"Why don't you come and thank her for yourself," the old woman continues. "You could say a little prayer."

"No, I'm so sorry, I have a previous engagement," Lucy says, turning away.

The old woman shrugs, then trots docilely after her husband. Meanwhile Lucy slowly climbs the stairs that lead up to the street, trying to make sense of what she just saw, which goes against everything that she, a modern and rational young woman, (albeit one who was brought up in a country rectory), believes to be true.

Ghosts and apparitions do not exist. It is all superstitious rubbish. After all, hasn't she just written a well-reasoned article affirming it? With cogent examples. But after what she has just seen for herself, what on earth is she supposed to believe now?

****

Inspector Lachlan Greig knows definitively that there are no such things as ghosts. He is not even entirely convinced in the existence of a deity. He has, however, unwavering faith in the power of coincidence. He is about to have his belief confirmed.

An unexpected summons to the front desk presents him with an anxious stoop-shouldered young man in a dusty black coat and ink-stained fingers. He introduces himself as Egremont Parvis, clerk to Harry & Persew, solicitors.

He then hands Greig a red wax-sealed letter and informs him that he is to wait for a reply. Greig breaks the seal and reads the letter carefully. Twice. After which he nods thoughtfully to himself a couple of times, before telling the clerk to wait while he gets his hat and coat.

****

There is nothing like a good luncheon to fortify the spirits and put heart back into a man, and even if the fare at Sally's Chop House just about scrapes into that category by the edge of its fingertips, Stride and Cully emerge from the chop house's smoky interior with hope renewed and expectations raised. They are met, on their return, by Lachlan Greig, his eyes alight with interest.

"Gentlemen, come and view what I have," he invites them.

They follow the tall Scot to the small back room used by the Yard's constables to write up their reports. Greig unfolds the letter from Helena Trigg's unknown correspondent. He places it on the table. Then he places a couple of cheques alongside it and stands back.

"D'you see it? I swear they are by the same hand! Look at the g's and the p's. The way they loop down and then hook back on themselves."

Cully bends over the writing. "You are right, Lachlan. But where do the cheques come from?"

Greig relates the events of earlier on, including his visit to the offices of Harry & Persew where he examined the safe, which, he was told, had not been examined prior to the discovery because it bore no visible signs of a break-in.

"When the forged cheques turned up, they took a further look, and it now appears the lock was picked, and the safe opened, and then closed. But no money or papers were taken, only a single cheque book."

"How did the forger manage to copy the lawyer's signature?"

"I asked the very same question myself, and I was told that he must somehow have got sight of the firm's legal correspondence."

"I thought we were dealing with a man of intelligence; I was quite right," Stride says.

"A man who can murder, forge a cheque, assume a false name, break into a lawyer's office, and pick the lock of a safe?" Cully muses. "That's a very unusual person indeed. Surely, we are dealing with a gang, don't you think? Someone gives the orders, others carry them out."

Stride tries to pick up the threads of his thoughts but fails to weave them into anything coherent.

"Whoever the man at the top may be, he does not stay with any one device for long. He moves from bank to bank, from one fake identity to another, from forgery to forgery. He never seems to make a mistake." He spreads his hands. "How do we even begin to track him down?"

"He has one weakness," Greig says. "He gambles. Such men are risk-takers; it's in the very nature of their habit. And with respect, you are wrong: he has already made a mistake."

He picks up the letter to Helena Trigg.

"Lambert Trigg is alive. Or at least, he has not succumbed to the machinations of this man. This letter proves it. He is desperate to find the clerk, and subject him to the same fate as the others.

"While Trigg lives, our man can never feel truly secure. The knowledge that there is somebody out there who can identify him, will be dogging his footsteps like a bad smell. And a man who daily risks exposure is a man who will trip over his own cleverness. We do not need to give him enough rope, for he already has it. We need only to watch and wait for him to tie the fatal hangman's knot."

****

It is the end of the working day, and the city streets are full of weary workers returning home after the day's labour. Omnibuses are packed to their knife-boards. Small steamers chug downriver, while those whose labour does not afford them the luxury of paying for transport, avail themselves once again of shanks' pony.

Home calls them. Home, sweet home. And nowhere is the *domum* more *dulce* than the small terraced house rented by the Cully family. And here is Jack Cully himself coming in through the back scullery, after cleaning his boots carefully on the doorscraper.

And there is Emily, Jack's dear wife, one hand massaging her aching back, the other stirring a pot of scrag end of mutton stew that has been simmering on the hob for the past few hours, filling the tiny kitchen with its warmth and fragrance. At her feet, young Violet Cully nurses her ragdoll and chatters away to it in a language only the two of them understand.

Jack greets his wife with a kiss, then picks up Violet, placing his cold cheek against her soft one. The little girl shrieks and wriggles with terrified delight.

"Good day at work?" Emily asks, placing three bowls on the red-checked tablecloth.

Jack Cully sets his daughter on the ground once more and produces a copy of the lunchtime edition of *The Inquirer* from his pocket.

"Same as before. Here's the newspaper, Em."

"No letters about you today?" Emily twinkles at him.

Jack Cully rolls his eyes.

"The less I read about myself, the better. We are here to track down criminals, not appear in the gossip pages of the newspapers."

Emily starts to serve the stew. Jack takes Violet to wash her hands. When they return to find their supper on the table, piping hot, the little girl tugs at her mother's skirt.

"Tell papa about the man," she whispers.

Emily lifts her daughter onto her chair and tucks a bib round her small neck.

"Now, Violet, we agreed that it was nothing, didn't we?"

"But TELL him," Violet insists.

Emily sighs.

"It's something about nothing, Jack. Violet says she can see 'a man' in the road tunnel. She has seen him, she says, for some days. Now she refuses to walk home that way."

"There is a man," Violet says, setting her small jaw. "He is all white and he has a big nose and I don't like him." She digs her spoon into her bowl.

Jack and Emily exchange bemused glances over her head.

"It is a nuisance, because we have to walk quite out of our way to come home," Emily says quietly. "I'm hoping she'll forget about it."

"I won't," comes the small obstinate voice.

Jack smiles at his little daughter.

"Tell you what, Violet, why don't you and I go and see the man after supper. I'll tell him to go away and stop frightening you, shall I?"

"Oh Jack, please don't humour her," Emily pleads.

But Jack Cully is a man of his word, and so, leaving Emily to do the dishes, father and daughter set out, carrying a small candle in a jar to light their way. Hand in hand, they walk until they reach the tunnel, where they stop. Cully lights the candle. Then, holding Violet's hand firmly, he walks her into the tunnel.

"There he is!" Violet gasps, pointing to the wall.

Jack Cully lifts the candle. On the brick wall, just above his head, there is a greenish-white shape patterning the limestone brickwork. It glows softly in the candle-light with a pale luminosity. He stares hard at it, trying to see what his little girl sees.

"There's his nose," Violet points. "And his feet. I don't like him, papa. Let's go."

Cully sets down the candle. Then he lifts her in his strong arms and walks her towards the wall. As Violet whimpers and shrinks back, hiding her face in his coat, he takes one of her hands and places it on the bricks just by the outline of the man.

"Violet, he isn't a real man. It's just a shape on the bricks. It looks like a man to you, but it isn't. I think all the frost and snow we had recently caused it to happen. But he isn't real, I promise you."

He sets her gently down. And then Detective Sergeant Jack Cully suddenly makes an important connection. In ancient Greece, this would be called a eureka moment, and might involve a bath and a naked philosopher. But this is London in 1865, and the night air is rather nippy on the skin, so he merely stands stock still for several minutes, thinking very hard. Then he murmurs,

"So that's what it is. Yes, of course. Why didn't anybody realise?"

"Papa?" Violet asks.

Jack Cully lifts her up and sets her on his shoulders.

"You are a little genius, Violet Cully. Thank you!"

And to Violet's great delight, he dances her all the way home.

****

Meanwhile, London dines. In the great Park Lane town houses with their white pillars, sumptuous dinner parties take place. Menus are written in French. The numerous courses, under their silver-domes are placed on the sideboard, *à la Russe.* Here are white-gloved company directors, dukes and duchesses and elegant young people in the latest evening fashions.

In the many clubs, where gentlemen retreat from the stresses of the day and the cares of the marital home, huge saddles of mutton, sides of beef, champagne and rich heavy puddings are paraded and consumed. Meanwhile, abandoned wives dine at home on cold cuts and the latest novel by Scott (in whose culinary passages there is a great deal of good descriptive nourishment).

London eats. The fried fish shop is crowded. Vinegar bottles are being shaken and salt taken with finger and thumb from the big salt boxes on the counter. Elsewhere, jellied-eels are ladled into white china basins and 'hot floury 'taters' are eagerly consumed by a continuous stream of customers. In taverns and public houses, crowds of tired city workers eat chops and potato and a glass of brandy and water. Others stand under the flaring naptha lights to enjoy whelks, cockles and mussels, 'a penny a plate'.

London starves. For those too poor to afford any dinner, the streets offer the torture of watching others fill their bellies. Restless and emaciated, the shivering poor roam the gas-lit streets seeking anything they can find. Small children pick through discarded vegetables and rotting fruit. Older ones hang around the street stalls in the hope of a charitable handout.

Look more closely. Here, outside a pie shop, are two familiar figures. A shambling boy, very out at the elbows and short in the trouser department and a small wiry girl wrapped in an old shawl. Together, they are contemplating the circumference of a pie.

"I like beef-steak best," Pin says, her small nose pressed to the window glass.

"That's nice Pin. Eel pie's good. And kidney too," Muggly nods.

"With a thick crust of pastry, like that pie there," Pin says, devouring the object of her desire with her eyes, which is the nearest she will ever get to tasting it.

Even as she feasts her gaze upon it, the pie is lifted out of the window and disappears into the depths of the shop. A short while later, a woman with a large covered basket emerges, glances up and down the street, then sets off in the direction of the nearest public house, where the object of her affections is regaling himself with a small aperitif before dinner.

"The lovely pie's gone, Pin," Muggly says mournfully.

"So it has."

"What're we going to do now?"

Pin screws up her small face.

"Let's go and find my sister."

They turn their faces from the warmth of the pie shop and start walking. The gaslight offers little isolated pools of light in the darkness. Nobody is about.

"Lot of stars up there," Pin says, tilting her face upwards.

Muggly contemplates the vast scoop of sky, vertiginously high and clear.

"What are stars, Pin?"

"Stars are holes what lets in the light, Muggly," Pin says.

"Are they?" Muggly regards the firmament with new, enlightened eyes.

"It's the light what makes them shine like that."

Muggly nods in a satisfied manner. Pin takes him by the hand. They walk on together in companionable silence.

****

Night wears on. The last train has passed through Baker Street Station, and reached the end of the line, where it has been greased up and oiled in preparation for the coming day. The platform has been cleared of passengers, the globes of light hanging from the ceilings are dimmed. The ticket hall is dark and the booth shuttered up. The staff are all departed for hearth and home.

The only sounds now are the scuffling of the rats as they pass and repass along the pitch-black tunnels and the drip-drip of water seeping through from puddles and leaking pipework in the street above.

To begin with.

Gradually, another sound can be heard, at first faintly in the distance, then coming closer. The rhythmic sound of boots marching somewhere deep in the tunnel. The sound approaches, getting louder. It is accompanied by a pinpoint of yellow light that flickers from side to side, as if someone is swinging a dark lantern as they walk.

Given that this is not the usual behaviour of rats, it can be assumed that whatever approaches is human in origin, an impression fortified by some tuneless whistling and the odd curse.

Eventually, two men enter the station, their lantern throwing grotesque shadows. They move in single file onto the platform. The leader sets down the lantern and glances around him. The other sets down a pail and a brush.

"There?" he asks, pointing to a spot on the wall.

His companion swings a leather bag off his shoulder.

"If you say so," he agrees, opening the bag and extracting a rolled-up poster, which he carries over to the wall. The lantern-bearer applies the paste and the job is completed in under three minutes.

"'Nother one on the other side, p'raps?" the paste supremo suggests.

They cross the rails and stick a second poster to the wall, after which they gather the tools of their trade and set off in the direction of Paddington Station.

"Still think it's a funny thing to put on a poster," the paste person remarks as they head for the tunnel.

"None of our business, is it? We just do what we're told, and what we're paid to do. And we're paid to do this. Come on, couple more stations, and then we're finished."

There is the sound of two pairs of boots trudging rhythmically into the dark maw of the tunnel accompanied by a ragged chorus of song, becoming fainter and fainter, until only the sound of silence punctuated by the odd rat remains.

****

Helena Trigg closes the front door to her lodgings, pauses on the step, glances swiftly up and down the street, then pulls her muffler up as far as possible, hiding her face from view, except for a small pink-tipped nose.

She sets off for work, occasionally stopping and turning around suddenly, a gesture that results in tutting from those walking directly behind her. Once again, she sees nothing suspicious, though she reminds herself that just because she doesn't see anybody, it doesn't mean they aren't there.

On the advice of Inspector Greig, Helena catches the omnibus, waiting at the stop with a queue of other people. None of them pay her any attention. Most are engrossed in the early morning newspapers. She slides her hand into her bag, feeling about until she locates the outline of the fish knife.

Helena is not sure she ought to have a fish knife in her bag, but it is preferable to the bread knife, which was her first thought. Being found in possession of a bread knife could be misconstrued. Whereas a fish knife can be explained away as an item of cutlery one might be going to buy more of, once one has matched the pattern.

The main thing is, if push comes to shove, she has a weapon, and she is not afraid to use it. Well, she hopes she is not afraid. She squares her shoulders and clamps a confident expression on her face.

Helena reaches the building housing J. King & Co. and climbs the stairs. Entering the outer office, she hangs her coat and bonnet on a peg, and looks around. This place is her sanity. This is where she comes every day to deal with the figures. There is a calmness about additions and subtractions, a logic that does not occur in the erratic course of life.

She walks to the desk next to the window. Her desk. She knows every whorl in the surface, every contour. Her pens rest in the ridge, her white china inkwell sits in the round hole next to it. Helena has always relied upon the consistency of mathematics. Balances, debits, credits, these she understands. There is safety in numbers. They are old familiar friends.

Now she rests her hands upon the desk and peeps out of the soot-encrusted window. Down in the street, she sees top hats and bonnets pass by in an endless stream. So many people, all strangers. She marvels how everybody rushes in London. Everybody has a somewhere to be. She hears a sound behind her and whirls round, her heart in her mouth.

"Good morning, Miss Trigg. I hope you are quite well. I think it will be a fine day once the fog has cleared," Trafalgar Moggs greets her, as he enters the office, swinging his (shabby) umbrella.

Helena Trigg returns the greeting. She fetches the sales ledgers from the shelf and prepares her pens for her morning's work. Meanwhile Moggs removes his muffler and gloves, blowing into each finger.

"There were snowdrops in the park this morning, Miss Trigg. I saw them as I came to work. It is a hopeful sign, is it not? Spring is on its way. Let us hope it finally brings you good news."

Helena stares out of the window at the small triangle of grey sky. Snowdrops. Small and white and exquisite. When they were children, her heart always lifted at the first sign of the little flowers, pushing bravely out of the cold earth and reaching their pure petals up to the sunshine. I will not give up, she vows. I will never give up, until you are back, my brother, and your name has been cleared, and the one who did this to you is behind prison bars.

****

Jack Cully is also not a man to give up, which is why he is even now approaching Baker Street Station at the steady pace known throughout police forces everywhere as 'proceeding'. Also proceeding is a day constable and Inspector Lachlan Greig, on the basis that whenever one is going to propose an activity that might elicit a refusal, it is always good to arrive with persuasive reinforcements.

They reach the station to find it unexpectedly busy, in that there is a crowd waiting expectantly outside. The detectives exchange puzzled glances ~ it is not even remotely the beginning of the working day and most of the crowd do not look like working people.

Nor do they seem like regular users of the underground railway. They resemble rather the sort of random individuals who materialize from nowhere whenever something of an interesting or ghoulish nature has happened.

Greig and Cully push their way to the front, show their badges to the man in the ticket office and then make their way down to the platform, which is full of people waiting for the next train to arrive. Many of them are standing in front of a wall poster and gesticulating at it in an excitable fashion.

The detectives approach, are recognised and greeted by the station master. They join him in front of the poster.

"Ah," Cully says, nodding thoughtfully.

"There's the self-same poster on the other side of the platform," the station manager tells them gloomily. "Two more at Paddington, one at Gower Street and Edgware Road, two at Farringdon Road. It's a positive plague of posters."

"How did this happen?"

The manager shrugs. "People put posters on the walls. We try to stop them when we catch them. We just don't often catch them," he admits lamely.

Greig leans in and studies the poster closely.

"Whoever did this must have access to the stations outwith the train times. I can think of no other way this could have been carried out."

"You could be right."

"Has anyone from the railway company gone into the tunnel to see whether there is actually anything there?" Cully asks.

The station master frowns.

"I don't understand: what sort of anything?"

Cully explains his theory, in the light of Violet's 'man'.

"Everybody claims to see the apparition, or whatever it is that they see, close to the crossover of the two lines in the Baker Street tunnel. But suppose what they see is not an apparition? Suppose it is just something in the brickwork after all? A trick of nature. I think we should go into the tunnel and see for ourselves."

"But the trains …"

"If we stay close to the tunnel wall, surely we should be safe?"

The station master's face radiates doubt and reluctance in equal amounts. Cully makes a sweeping gesture with his left arm, taking in the shrine with its candles, small statues, prayers, offerings, crutches and people on their knees, the passengers milling round the poster, and sundry members of the True Bethel Bible Believing Brethren who have managed to insert themselves into the general melee despite being, in theory, banned from setting foot on the station concourse.

"Is this how you wish to conduct the day to day running of this station? This noise and chaos? Devout believers turning up all the time? Religious fanatics invading at will? Seriously, would it not be worth the risk to find out the truth, and put an end to it once and for all? If you discover it is all a hoax, at least life will return to normal. Do nothing, and the worshippers will only increase. Do you want the station to become a place of pilgrimage or a place of business?"

"If you put it like that, I suppose …"

Greig consults his watch.

"There is a train due in two minutes. I suggest we take our cue from its departure and enter the tunnel as it leaves. That will give us a good five minutes to be in place before the next train arrives."

"I'll get a lantern," the station master says.

Greig strides on his long legs to the end of the platform. Cully and the constable follow him. As the lights of the train appear in the tunnel, like a set of blazing eyes, he squats down, calculating the distance between the edge of the platform and the ground below. Then, as the last carriage of the train pulls into the station, Greig jumps.

****

Leaving our gallant Inspector mid-air, as it were, let us return to Scotland Yard, where less than gallant expletives are emanating from the office of Detective Inspector Stride. The cause of Stride's current woe lies before him, as it does each morning, thanks to one of the newer constables who is tasked with purchasing the early morning editions of the London papers, placing them upon Stride's desk, and then getting out of the office as fast as possible.

"I told him," Stride mutters furiously. "I distinctly recall telling him! And now he's gone and done this!"

The 'him' in question is Montague Goodall, whose benign spectacled features are staring out at him from the front pages of *The Inquirer*, *The Times* and *The Daily Telegraph*. Along with a photograph of various ace of spades playing cards.

Each newspaper offers a slightly different slant on the basic story, which is that Scotland Yard approached, and are now relying upon, the skill and expertise of Goodall & Sons (of Great College Street) to help them solve a series of gruesome murders, and thanks to the help of the aforementioned Goodall & Sons, have been able to open up other promising lines of inquiry.

The help has come in the form of an explanation of the mysterious ace of spades card, the **DEATH Card**!!!! ~ the number of exclamations vary, on each of the murdered men. At this point, Stride strikes his forehead with his fist, while uttering the words *'No, no, no!'* in a despairing voice.

Gripping the sides of his desk with whitening knuckles, he reads on. After the revelation that Stride had ordered not to be revealed, is revealed, the various newspaper articles morph from unwelcome fact into pure unfounded fiction.

New details, previously unknown to the forces of law and order may have come to light! Apparently. Key witnesses have divulged vital information that could soon identify the killer! The arrest of his accomplices will then be enacted, leaving the honest man in the street of the Greatest City on Earth to go about his business without fear of being assaulted by murderers bearing playing cards! This is according to *The Inquirer*.

It is all couched in suitably vague, though at the same time very dramatic, glittery language ~ exactly the sort of thing that will excite the mob and guarantee the outer office filling up in no time with citizens eager to share their interpretation of events, in return for whatever reward might be on offer.

Each article ends in the same vein: with a big puff for the card manufacturer, featuring various novel designs and listing other products, such as games, stationery, fountain pens and toilet paper, all produced by Goodall & Sons, and available from numerous retail outlets at very reasonable prices.

Stride strongly suspects this is the sole reason the Goodall brothers decided not to heed his advice and to contact the press in the first place. The rest is down to penny-a-liner hacks eager to increase their paper's circulation by purveying fake news and false information, all of which is now seriously going to impede the progress of his inquiries.

By the time he has finished reading the various misrepresentations of his investigation, Stride has mentally migrated to some country south of apoplectic. Brushing the offending journals from his desk as if they were annoying insects, he goes to the door.

"CULLY!! Jack Cully!! Get in here quickly!" he shouts.

But Jack Cully left the building a long time ago.

****

Without the background noise of passengers, and the rumble of trains, the tunnel is a wide arcade of echoes. The four men walk in single file, Indian fashion, into the semi-darkness. Smoke swirls around them, acrid and pungent.

They have just reached the crossing point, when the next train approaches. The head-lamps of the engine flicker. Sparks shoot up between the tunnel and the train. The light goes from black to yellow and black once more. Blue imps dance around the cables.

"There!" Cully shouts, pointing to an archway. "There it is!"

They follow his pointing finger. There is a long pause.

"Didn't see anything," the station master admits, raising his lantern high.

"It was just for an instant, as the light fell on that bit of the wall. Something sparkled and glowed, high up," Cully says.

"I'll take your word for it, detective," the station master says.

"So that's the Madonna of the Metropolitan Line," Greig murmurs. "A bit of phosphorus and a lot of imagination."

"And the posters?"

"Somebody seizing a golden opportunity."

"Maybe the same somebody who created it in the first place?" Greig says.

"I hadn't thought of that," Cully says. "But you could be right. However, this whole business has to be nipped in the bud quickly and quietly, before it gets completely out of hand. We need to set the record straight."

They walk back along the tunnel until they regain the safety of the Baker Street platform, where things have quietened down somewhat.

"I could put a blackboard up in the ticket office?" the station master suggests. "Attention: There is no Madonna, it's just a trick of the light ~ that sort of thing?"

"I'd strongly advise against it," Greig counters. "You will only encourage people to venture into the tunnel to see for themselves ~ and that could lead to accidents of a fatal nature."

"Ah. Hadn't thought of that. So, what do you suggest? Because we need to get the truth out there as quickly as possible, don't we?" the station master asks.

Cully chews a thumbnail thoughtfully.

"Perhaps you could get your men to clean the tunnel wall? And take all the advertising posters down while they are about it. That would be a start, wouldn't it?"

****

Let us pause for a moment, and consider the pernicious revolution enacted upon London society by the advent of the advertisement. Not a wall, not a wooden hoarding, not a fence nor a plate-glass window nor an omnibus can now be allowed to remain in its pristine condition, but it must contain some huge wall poster advertising anything from circuses, to cures or cocoa.

No longer can a man (or woman) walk down a public street without their ocular senses being assaulted by large brightly coloured displays of various goods or entertainments, none of which they want. Their eyes are bedazzled and their mind befuddled by promises that are so extreme that they cannot possibly be fulfilled.

Who among us has not been jostled off the pavement by some unfortunate individual who has hired himself out as a walking advertisement? The sandwich man has become as common upon our public thoroughfare as the small urchins who follow and plague him. How often has the cry of *'where's the mustard, then?'* been heard, shouted in some scornful piping treble.

For eighteen pence a day, these men must perforce walk the streets of the city, rain or shine, from ten to five in winter and ten to six in summer. They are not permitted to take the boards off but must be constantly on the move. New products demand more and more of them to appear, until the innocent foot-passenger finds himself positively blockaded by human advertising machines.

It has been said (especially by Detective Inspector Stride, who says it quite often) that advertising is the brazen mask of the age, behind which all conditions of people proffer their products or plead their wants to the entire nation.

Nowhere more so than in the pages of the newspapers, where the insertion of large type and illustrations thrust themselves upon the unwary reader in an aggressive and unwelcome manner. Teas and tortoises, pills and powders, every newspaper or magazine now carries page after page of advertisements.

For the sum of 8 shillings, or whatever the advertising fee charged, the man (or woman) in the street may offer their houses, their horses, their housemaids or themselves to any stranger who picks up the newspaper. Everything and everyone in the city is reduced to a commodity with a price.

Helena Trigg's brush with the murky world of the personal advertisement has not encouraged her to advocate on their behalf. Not for her the lure of the perfect complexion (she has one) or a 'comfortable home' in return for governess services (she has a job) nor does she need to appeal 'to the benevolent' for help to alleviate her poverty (she is generously remunerated by her employer).

In most people's eyes, therefore, one would think Helena Trigg possesses the necessary requirements that go to make a happy life. And yet here she is, staring into the fire, her hands curled round a cup of tea. The gas jets on either side of the mantelpiece hiss gently in their white globes. Images curl inside her like smoke, creating pictures of a time long-ago and faraway.

Memory leads her back. Here are the two of them, Lambert and herself, dressed in black, folding clothes into two tin trunks in an empty house. The furniture has been sold. Their train tickets to London have been purchased. There is nothing left now. Nothing to hold them to this place, their magical childhood home. Just silence and sunlight dappling the wooden floorboards, and a thin spiral of dust-motes rising.

London. How is it possible to live in a city that is so immense in scale and so crowded with people, and yet feel so alone? It is a question that has increasingly troubled her, as the days string themselves along casually like so many beads.

Walking home this evening, a little wind driving the fallen leaves along the pavement, she had felt fear grip her heart with its cold hand. The rustling leaves whispered that one day, like them, she too would be swept away, and no one would ask where she had gone.

The revelation hit her hard, like a door unlocking itself on a cold night. For a second, she stopped in her tracks, undone by the strength of it, and had to stand motionless, paralysed, until the force of her will swung the door shut once more.

Since her brother left her, the days have been pulled out of shape and won't return to how they used to be. The wind funnels down the street and blows dust into her face. The air tastes as if it has been breathed before, hundreds of times by hundreds of people. The world has become frightening, impossible in its thinness.

Helena holds a cushion, hugging it to her chest. The cushion has a faded blue cover, embroidered with pansies. It belonged to her mother. Her hands had sewed it. Reminding her of the childhood home, of when the sun always shone, and she was loved.

Time telescopes. Memory seduces. Helena follows the enticing trail, knowing with part of her mind, that wherever she is trying to return to has already gone. Nevertheless, she watches the firelight flicker and fade, and wonders how far back she can go.

****

This is a den of thieves dissolving. It is happening inconspicuously, in the opulent setting of the smoking-room of an exclusive gentleman's club in Pall Mall. It is also taking place without of one of the group, who is currently prosecuting a case at the law courts of Westminster Hall. *In absentia*, the remaining two members are discussing the dissolution of the partnership.

"He has definitely gone too far this time," says the sporting member.

"So it would seem," the dilettante member drawls, blowing a series of perfect smoke rings at the ceiling overhead. "I was not happy about that Bosey business, I admit, but at the end of the day, he was an American and needs must, and all that sort of thing, eh."

The sporting member takes up one of the better-quality newspapers (we are in the purlieus of the affluent, where copies of *The Inquirer* never see the light of gilded chandelier).

"He promised us nothing would ever get into the papers. Promised us. You were there."

"I recall the occasion well. He boasted about his ingenuity and sophisticated methods. He said he would always outwit Scotland Yard, what with his Inner Temple chambers and his practice in criminal law. They would never catch him, he said, which makes these revelations all the more disconcerting!"

"This article clearly links two murders with that playing-card nonsense he told us about. It even suggests the murderer might be one of London's gambling elite. Short of naming him outright, it is running him pretty close. I don't understand how this has happened, do you?"

The other sighs.

"Sadly, I understand it all too well. He has fallen prey to the oldest of lures: the thrill of winning and losing: I have known him for some time, and I believe that he regards the risk of detection as part of the sport. It quickens his blood. But it has made him reckless ~ the playing card business, as you rightly say, was utter folly. But it leaves us with a dilemma: if we are not astute and act speedily, we might also be drawn into the net that is closing about him and be brought down as well."

"You think he would give our names to the police?"

The dilettante gives him a look that says*: Oh, come on: he'd have his own mother transported if she tried to stand in his way.*

"It's not only that, it's his 'grateful clients' that I fear. He has a network of accomplices all over town. I firmly believe we both wouldn't be able to walk the streets safely if he goes down. I have destroyed all letters, IOUs and communications between us and I intend to leave England tonight, while Cecy is with her people in the country. I shall travel East and stay abroad until this matter is resolved. Jarvis may give my name to the police, but they will never find me."

The sporting member pulls at his moustaches.

"Good idea. There's no proper racing until the Derby and the Oaks. I have a contact in New York ~ he's been asking me to go out and visit him for a while. Think now's the time to take him up on the offer, eh?"

"Now is the best and only time, my friend," his companion says, tossing down the last of his brandy. "I am off to put my affairs in order and then pack my traps. Tonight, I catch the Dover packet for the Continent."

He stands, carefully smoothing his fine cloth trousers. Then he requests a member of staff to fetch his overcoat, umbrella and hat. While he waits for them to arrive, he leans down and says, *sotto voce*,

"Let us determine that we never met, that this conversation never happened, and that we never knew each other."

"I agree wholeheartedly."

The dilettante tips his hat to the colonel, and walks swiftly out of the club, ignoring other members. Out in the street, he glances quickly around, then slips down a side-street, where his closed carriage awaits. He climbs in, settling himself into one of the butter-soft leather seats.

"Home, Francis," he commands, "and don't spare the horses."

****

Meanwhile, Mr Mutesius and his much put-upon partner in life are enjoying an early dinner. Or rather, Mr Mutesius is enjoying his, having helped himself to all the tastier bits of bacon, leaving the rind and the fat to his wife.

"Nuffink like a tasty hot dinner to set you up for the evenin', I allus says," he remarks with his mouth full.

Mrs Mutesius, who is enjoying nothing like a tasty hot dinner, cuts the fat into tiny pieces and nods. It is some days since her one attempt at matrimonial defiance resulted in the lady lodger remaining on the first floor. She is not sure she will attempt rebellion again. Old bones bruise more easily and take longer to heal.

Mrs Mutesius stirs her watery tea and listens to the slushy noise of her husband eating. She tries to remember why she married him in the first place. He was her parents' lodger, a small man with smaller prospects, who went every day to some nondescript office near the docks, where he sat at a desk until it was time to come back to the house.

But then her parents died, one after the other in quick succession, leaving her the house. Could she have done better for herself? There was a rather charming floor-walker who rented the top left attic, she recalled. But apart from the house, she had little to offer in the way of matrimonial attraction, being rather squat of figure and plain of countenance.

So she settled for what she could get, and now here she is, and here he is, till death do them part. She stares at the back of her hands, with their age spots and raised blue veins, like knotted ropes. So preoccupied are they both with the business of eating, and regretting, that the knock at the front door comes like a thunderbolt.

Mr Mutesius starts, drops his fork on his plate with a clatter, then swears loudly.

"Oo the hell is that, now? I'm havin' me dinner."

Mrs Mutesius half-rises.

"Shall I answer the door?"

Her better half considers the matter. The knock comes again. He goes to the window and twitches aside the net curtain.

"Ain't the post carrier. Looks like some smart city gent. P'raps he wants to rent a room? If he does, that girl can pack her bag, and I don't care what you promised her."

He crosses the room and goes out into the hallway. Mrs Mutesius follows him. The old man wrenches open the door, which, ever since the frost got into it, has tended to stick.

"Yers, can I help you, sir?" he says, by way of greeting.

The man on the step, of whom Mrs Mutesius can only see a sliver which seems to contain a lot of black, together with a very sharp nose and chin, raises his shiny top hat.

"Please excuse me for calling round at this hour, my good man," he says, his voice smooth like oiled silk. "I am looking for a certain Mr Trigg, whom I believe lodges here."

"Not at the moment, he don't."

There is a brief heartbeat of a pause. Mrs Mutesius strains her ears.

"So, he no longer lives at this address. Ah. I understand."

"Beggin' your pardon sir, but no you don't. I said he ain't here *at the moment*. But he's expected back very soon. His sister, what lodges here, told me this the other day."

Another pause. Slightly longer this time. Then,

"I see. Thank you for this information. I shall call again, if I may. Oh, and would you do me the great courtesy of not mentioning this to the sister. It is a private matter between men, if you understand. Not something for the ladies to bother their heads about."

A crafty expression crosses Mr Mutesius wrinkled features.

"Ah. One of *them* sort of private things, eh? Hur, hur," he chortles. "So that's why he buggered off so sudden like. I might of guessed."

"Precisely. But you are sure he is expected back?"

Mr Mutesius turns his head, "Oi, Clarrie, didn't the girl say she was expecting her brother to return very soon ~ was not them her *exact* words?"

"Yes," Mrs Mutesius whispers.

"Thank you, dear lady," the man calls out. "And now, I have another favour to ask of you: upon this card is an address where I can be contacted. The owner of the emporium knows where to find me. When the gentleman in question returns, please contact the shop immediately. It is of the utmost importance. And 'mum' is the word. I cannot stress that too highly."

Mr Mutesius studies the small pasteboard square he has been handed. His lips move in time with his brain, which is laboriously working out what it says (actually, they move slightly behind his brain, but the effect is very similar).

"And this *Mr Trinkler, Upholsterer and Preserver of Small Animals & Birds*, he'll pay me for the information wot I give him, will he? Coz it's a long walk to his shop and I'm not as young as I used to be."

The man on the doorstep smiles urbanely. "Oh, I am quite sure you will receive, in due course, exactly what you deserve," he says.

"Well, that's orl right then."

"Good. So glad we have had this conversation. I thank you for your time, Mr … and I bid you and your lady farewell."

"Yers. Farewell it is then."

Mr Mutesius shuts the front door.

"Well, now then, what did you make of that?" he says.

Mrs Mutesius shrugs. She has learned the hard way that having an opinion on any topic is not a good idea, even if one is requested of her. She trails meekly and silently after her lord and master, who sits back down at the table.

"Well, I ain't going to eat this now: it's gone stone cold," he grumbles, pushing his plate to one side. "You'd better go and fry up some more bacon. Make some more tea while you're about it too. And hurry up, I haven't got all evenin' to waste."

****

Lucy Landseer is not one to waste an evening either. For several days, she has been confined to her room with a nasty cold, but she has not been idle. No, indeed, perish the thought. Three articles from the *Silver Quill* have been composed, even though the writer has been indisposed and are waiting upon the bureau, and she has also spent some of her indisposition wrapped in a shawl, writing her novel.

It is progressing nicely.

Her hero (who wasn't based upon the handsome Cambridge lecturer before she met the handsome Cambridge lecturer, but now totally is), has just perceived the error of his philandering, idle ways, and is about to fall at the feet of the poor, but highly intelligent heroine he previously ignored, as he now sees her in her true colours.

There is a lot to be said for being 'laid aside on a bed of sickness' as the Anglican prayer book has it. Except for the actual imagery, of course, which has always made her feel distinctly nauseous. She dips her nib into her ink pot and writes on. Time passes. The sky empties out into a broad black vacancy and the lamps are lit in the street below.

Lucy Landseer finishes writing the touching and emotional scene that she hopes will bring a tear of joy to the future reader's eye and lays down her pen with a sigh of relief. She glances at her little wristwatch. Where did that hour go to? Her stomach reminds her that it is time for supper.

She gets up, pushing the chair away, and stretches her cramped back, while she contemplates her options. On the one hand, she does not fancy the hostel's invalid fare.

Woman cannot live on weak beef tea alone. She craves something more substantial and filling.

On the other hand, is she well enough to brave the evening streets? She decides, upon reflection, that she is, and so a short while later, warmly wrapped, bonneted and gloved, she emerges from the Young Women's Christian Association and heads off into the sparkly night in the direction of more tempting fare than is on offer back at her lodgings.

Pausing only to post the articles to her various editors, Lucy walks briskly towards the small restaurant to which she and her fellow students often repair after their evening lectures. Here, coffee can be drunk, and a delicate supper eaten in discreet confines, without the unwelcome attention of gentlemen with the wrong idea.

It is a clear night, for the haziness and smoke from factories and a million and more houses is being blown away by a steady breeze. After so many days inside, the evening air is almost intoxicating, and Lucy is in fine spirits by the time she reaches her destination.

It is too early for her fellow students to be in place, but she seats herself at their usual table, and orders a plate of hot beef, potato, some vegetables and a fruit tart to follow. While she awaits the arrival of her supper, she picks up one of the evening papers, left conveniently upon a side-table for customers to peruse (another reason she patronises this establishment).

The front page has a long peroration upon the state of the city streets, and the number of potholes, caused by the recent frosty weather. She skims it and a few more articles, in a similar-vein. Then, turning to the centre page, her eyes widen as she sees a half-page advertisement.

Lucy Landseer stares very hard at the advertisement, her brow gently furrowed. She glances quickly round at her fellow diners. They are all engaged in either their meal, or their dining companion. As quietly and furtively as she can manage, she tears out the page, folds it up small and slips it into her bag. Her cheeks redden. She has just committed a theft!

Sending up a quick prayer to the God of her father, whom she is sure understands completely why she just did what she did, Lucy Landseer tucks into her hot supper with relish.

Later, in the silence of her room, she will smooth out the stolen page, and study it intently. Other people might judge an advertisement by its face value alone, but Lucy Landseer is both a reader and an author of sensation fiction; therefore, she has a vivid imagination which enables her to look behind the surface, beyond the surface, even to ignore the surface altogether, and come up with a completely different narrative.

Later still, lying in her bed, with arms folded behind her head, she is still focused upon what she has seen. *So that's what it was all about*, she thinks, and feels that exultant writerly thrill that comes when a rather difficult bit of plot suddenly releases its secret.

****

It is a far cry from the virginal bedroom of a youthful flậneuse to a gentlemen's club in Leicester Square. Here, within an elegant stone structure (the building was originally erected from a design by Mr Decimus Burton), we find The Chichester, where gambling, betting, card-playing and games of chance are readily available, for the place is entirely devoted to play.

Admittance to this particular gambling house is restricted to those who are known to the management, and to individuals who 'look all right'. However, the *modus operandi* is pretty much the same here as for all other such places. One pulls a bright-knobbed bell. The door is unchained and opened by a big speechless man in a dark suit whose job it is to admit or bar and later, escort to the same door any who infringe the rules and thrust them out into the street.

He closes the door quickly behind the newcomer, who follows him down a passageway until they reach a handsome gas-lamp and another door covered in red baize, which gives way to a series of brilliantly-lit rooms with ornate friezes and gold embossed papers on the walls.

Here are tables covered in green cloth, set up for whist, French hazard or roulette. *Chemin-de-fer* and *rouge et noir* are also popular here, bets being laid between onlookers as to whether the banker or punter will win.

Two or three men always sit at the tables, exhibiting a lot of flashy jewellery. These are the Bonnets ~ in the pay of the management. They are there to entice visitors to play. The Bonnets are all men of good education, who, having lost the fortunes they started out life with, are now employed by the proprietor, for a weekly stipend, to lure others to the gaming tables to lose theirs.

On one side of the first room is a bouffet, covered with wines and liquors. Next to it, a walk-in humidor, storing cigars in mahogany drawers. Everything is laid out with the sole purpose of parting the patrons from their money. Upstairs are supper rooms, where chefs from the continent serve up the finest food, however late at night the members might demand it, for much business is also done informally here.

Tonight, the club is crowded. Several fortunes have already been won and lost in the course of the evening's play. The croupiers wear their customary imperturbable countenances. The Bonnets appear intent on the game, as if the results were life and death to them, and there is a group of lively young bucks who have caught the eye of the management, but not in a good way.

All at once and unexpectedly, given the late hour, the street doorbell sounds. The door is immediately part-opened, and the appellant scrutinized. Then the chain is lifted, and he enters. To get here, the late-comer has walked down one dark street after another, through one dark square to the next, like chess pieces on a board.

He sheds his black cloak and hat, hands over his ebony walking cane, and enters the brightly lit room, where his presence is instantly acknowledged by the croupier, who bids one of the Bonnets to move up and make room for him at the table. However, the newcomer shakes his head and stalks off.

He reaches the second room, and stands in the doorway, arms folded, his eyes scouring the tables with their busy occupants. Unsatisfied, he retraces his steps, mounts the staircase and enters the dining room. A white-aproned waiter hurries over.

"Good evening, sir. Table for one tonight, sir?"

Sir shakes his head.

"Tell me, have Adonis or the Colonel been in tonight?" he asks.

"Haven't seen either of them in here tonight, sir."

There is a pause.

"When did you last see them?"

The waiter's brow furrows as he tries to recollect.

"Last week, sir. You were all playing cards downstairs, as you usually do on a Thursday night, and then you came upstairs for a bite to eat. As usual."

"Yes, that is indeed what we 'usually' do," the lawyer murmurs to himself as he turns away. "But tonight, it appears, we do not. And as no carriage arrived to collect me, I have had to walk here. Both their houses are shut up, from which I deduce that my two boon companions have flown the city. But whither, and why? That is what I must find out."

He makes his way back downstairs. For a brief moment he stands in the doorway, listening to the croupiers' voices rise and fall, watching the eager faces of the players. He is tempted to join them, feeling the adrenaline rising up inside him like the sap of youth. Then, abruptly, he turns his face away and demands his outdoor clothes.

The lawyer walks. Such is his parsimony that he does not keep a carriage, relying upon the carriages of others to convey him wherever he wishes to go. Such is his fastidious nature, that the thought of sitting in a common hackney cab or a public omnibus, where anybody may have sat before him, is total anathema.

It is 2.00 am, the hour between sweet dreams and black despair. As the sound of his footsteps echo through the silent streets, his thoughts are dark and bitter. Before tonight, he would have sat down at one of the tables and joined the players, his heart high, his expectations eager. But that was in another time, and another place.

As soon as he reaches his own dismal quarters, the lawyer lights a candle and picks up a copy of *The Times*.

But instead of turning to the legal pages to read, once again, the triumphant reports of his own recent successes in Court, he re-reads the front page, concentrating upon an article with a drawing of a playing card.

Enlightenment. An epiphanic moment. He has been on the wrong track entirely. He thought he had eliminated all the obstructive ones: the young man at the gaming table who recognised him from a time before his London legal triumphs. The bank clerk, and that other clerk, whose imminent return has been the source of his current anxiety.

In the end, he has been stabbed in the back by his own side. *'Et tu, Brute?'*

So, this is what it has come to? After all he has done for them. The scrapes he has liberated them from. The scandals he has closed down. The foes he has dealt with on their behalf. The money he has disbursed. The people he has silenced. And his reward: to be betrayed to the press. To have all his devices and desires revealed.

The lawyer breathes sharply, opening his thin snake-like lips, as if he feels a sudden pain deep inside his chest. Then he rises and goes to his desk. He opens an under-drawer and takes out a walnut wood games box with gilded bronze fittings and cantered edges. Its top is decorated with four large cabochon onyx stones.

He lifts the lid, revealing four packs of playing cards lying in blue silk compartments. From two of the packs, he selects the ace of spades cards and sets them aside. So, they think they can outwit him by their absence? They think by this, they have evaded his grasp?

They have not. They will not.

In his mind's eye, the lawyer conjures up the image of a courtroom, with his two former friends arraigned in the dock before him. He reads out the charges against them: betrayal, treachery, disloyalty, ingratitude, cowardice, desertion.

'Gentleman of the jury, how do you find the accused?'

'Guilty, M'Lud. Guilty on all counts.'

He places the black cap upon his own head and passes the inevitable sentence. Justice will be done, however long it takes. The cards cannot lie. The lawyer changes into his nightgown, snuffs out the candle-stub, and climbs into bed, but even there, in the deep darkness, his thoughts roll on, slow as breakers, on the edge of sleep.

****

Morning arrives, bringing with it fog. A downright thorough London fog. A silent, stealthy beast of prey kind of fog. A closing in and shutting out the world sort of fog. Overnight, the whole city has been embedded in a dilution of yellow pease-pudding, just thick enough to get through without being totally choked or completely suffocated.

The smell and taste of the fog fills people's mouths, as if all the smoke that had ascended for years from thousands of chimneys and factories had fallen back down at once, after having rotted somewhere above the clouds. Every time they breathe in, they partake of it. People breakfast, dine and sup on it. They fall over it and curse it and lose themselves in it.

Yet despite the fog, the morning tide still flows in an endless stream along the city streets, for London hungers for its crowds, and soon the shops, warehouses, factories, counting houses, banks, eateries and places of business swallow them up, to spew them forth again at evening.

Look more closely. Here is Pin, with a large scrubbing brush and red raw hands, cleaning fog from a doorstep. And here, coming round the corner, is the Boy Muggly, bearing two stale bread rolls.

"Look what I got, Pin," he crows delightedly, handing one to her.

Pin squats back on her heels, wiping her hands on her apron. She tears off a piece of the bread and pops it into her mouth, half-closing her eyes.

"My, that is good, Muggly. It's almost like it was fresh. But it still tastes of bread, if you know what I mean."

Muggly hasn't a clue what she means, but he grins.

"I been helping the baker fill his shelves, an' he let me take these two rolls. They fell on the floor, but I wiped them on my sleeve."

Pin finishes her roll and licks her lips.

"We all got to eat a peck of dirt before we die. I heard my sister say that many a time. Thanks, Muggly, that'll keep me going till tonight."

Pin picks up the scrubbing brush and attacks the step with renewed vigour. Muggly stands awkwardly by, watching her work.

"'Ave you seen …" he says, letting the words tail off.

Pin's expression hardens.

"No, I ain't."

Muggly scratches under one armpit.

"I seen him though, Pin. He was at the door of that house talkin' to the old 'un."

"When was that, Muggly?"

Muggly screws up his face, in an effort to place the incident precisely.

"It was two days ago. I think. In the evening. I was watchin' for the young lady to come back, like you said I should. I got a new place to stand now, after the old 'un shouted at me. I saw him knock at the door. He and the old 'un had a great long talk. Thick as thieves, they was. Then he left. They didn't see me though. I made sure of that. Nobody sees me."

Pin sits back on her heels, her expression darkening.

"He is up to something, Muggly. That's for sure. You'd better take care you watch very carefully. I dunno what it's all about, but if we can do him down, we will. For what he did to you, Muggly. Revenge is a dish best served cold. I heard someone say that once, and it's true."

Muggly repeats what Pin has just said. Slowly.

"What does it mean, Pin?"

"It means he's going to get what's coming to him." Pin nods her head emphatically. "And when that happens, he won't be able to hurt you anymore, and we won't be scared of him."

"Are you scared of him, Pin? I fort you wasn't scared of nobody."

Pin stares fiercely into her bucket of hottish water.

"I ain't scared of many people, Muggly, but I'm scared of Evil Man, coz he's cruel and nasty. He reminds me of a man who used to live in our court. I seen him pick up a little black cat what crossed his path and bash it against a wall."

Pin's eyes fill with tears.

"I took that little cat onto my lap, and I stroked and stroked its fur, but it was no good. It died. I'll never forget it, Muggly. Evil Man is like that. I'm scared of him, but he's not going to hurt you nor me, nor anybody else, if we can stop him."

Muggly looks doubtful.

"But how can we stop him, Pin? Just you an' me on our own, like?"

Pin stares up into his round, good-natured moon of a face.

"We'll find a way, Muggly. Trust me. Now, you get back to watchin' and I'll get back to scrubbing, and we'll wait and see what happens. Coz something is going to happen, that's for sure. An' we need to be there when it does."

****

Inspector Lachlan Greig also shares Pin's opinion that something is going to happen. He sits at his desk in the small back parlour of his rented rooms, hunched over a piece of writing paper. A gas lamp by the desk hisses and murmurs. Odours of cooking filter under the door. Outside his window, the backstreet is silent and deserted. A quarter moon hangs over the rooftops. He chews the end of his pen.

Dear Miss King, (he writes)

I am writing to you as the employer of the accounts clerk Miss Helena Trigg to alert you to the possibility that she may now be in some danger. You have no doubt read a story in the press about new information received by the Metropolitan Police which is going to lead to the arrest of the man accused of defrauding various city banks and causing the deaths of various employees.

Regrettably, I have to inform you that, to the best of our knowledge, no such information has reached us. However, the impression given that it has, may well drive the actual perpetrator into engaging in some rash act of recklessness.

As we are all aware, he has already attempted to locate the whereabouts of Miss Trigg's brother. He may well draw the erroneous conclusion from the articles in the various newspapers that it is Mr Trigg himself who has now come forward and identified him to the police.

I am afraid that if this is so, he could try to contact her again, possibly to harm her, in the belief that she knows where her brother is concealed. Let me assure you and Miss Trigg that I have no proof of this, it is merely just my professional opinion, coupled with a deep suspicion of the criminal nature of such people, and the way their minds work.

I am aware that Miss Trigg is unwilling to change her lodgings ~ though in my private opinion, that would be the best solution to the current situation. It might be good, therefore, to find some brief employment for her that removes her from London for a while.

I shall leave it in your capable hands. I have decided to write rather than call, as I do not wish to alarm Miss Trigg unduly. Perhaps the employment could be offered without any hint as to the real reason why? I leave that up to your good judgement, though.

As indicated, I have no proof that any harm may befall her, but I wish to forestall it if I can possibly do so. Please write, at your earliest convenience, and inform me what actions you have seen fit to take.

I remain, yours most sincerely,

Lachlan Greig (Inspector)

Greig re-reads his letter a couple of times. Then he blots the sheet of writing paper, and places it in an envelope, addressing it to Miss Josephine King, J. King & Co., Commercial Road. He pictures her opening it tomorrow morning and reading what he has written. He pictures her face as she does so.

Lachlan Greig has not found the transition from Scotland to London an easy one to make. The city seemed, at first, a dark and heathen place, with its smog-washed buildings and hurrying impassive crowds of people who never made eye contact as they pushed past.

The hectic sprawl of the place, with new streets ever emerging from behind great hoardings, the constant reminder that he was a 'foreigner' who spoke in a strange and therefore mimicable accent, the dust, the masses of pigeons and feral children, all made the place seem like something from a nightmare.

It has taken a long while for the handsome inspector to find his feet. The kindness of Jack Cully and his sweet-natured wife Emily, who both welcomed him into their house, has helped him slowly to acclimatize. As has the small flame lit in his heart ever since he first met Josephine King.

Greig has been hit by Cupid's arrow before, and the experience was not a pleasant one. Now he is naturally cautious about repeating it, fearing scorn and rejection once again. It has taken his heart a long time to heal from the last encounter.

But as he thinks about that painful time, he finds he can no longer bring it to mind with the same clarity. It is as if the door to the past has closed upon it for ever. Greig places the letter in his greatcoat pocket, ready to post first thing in the morning. Then he reaches up into the desk lamp and turns it out.

****

By contrast with the foggy, shabby bricken wilderness that is London, in Paris, the sun is shining. In Paris, the Seine is sparkling, and the wide leafy boulevards are full of elegantly dressed Parisiennes going about their morning tasks ~ which are mainly to walk elegantly along the wide boulevards, soliciting the admiration of other Parisians.

In a café in Montmartre, a young man is idling over a late morning coffee and the British newspapers, which are also late, but only by a couple of days. The young man has a notebook and pencil, and every now and then, he stops to write something down.

Perhaps he is studying the language? His appearance certainly reminds one of a student: his hair is slightly longer than normal. He wears an easy black necktie, and his loose buttoned frock coat is frayed at the cuffs, and out at the elbows. He is also smoking a small pungent black cigarette, much favoured by the local artistic community.

The impression is reinforced by the arrival of another young man with an equally second-hand air about his clothing. He sits down, snaps his fingers and orders '*un café, s'il vous plaît'* from the waiter, who balances a tray aloft on the palm of his hand with a dexterity rarely seen in any London coffee house.

"So, mon ami, how goes the world with you this bright morning?" the newly-arrived asks. "Has la belle Sarah finally granted you an audience dans son boudoir?"

The young man smiles thinly. "I leave all that sort of caper to you, Henri. I am sure you are far more adept at love-making than I."

Henri gives a Gallic shrug, and makes the sort of dismissive sounds that suggests he is exactly as described, and quite happy to be so. For a few minutes, the two friends sip their coffee, and contentedly contemplate the passers-by. Then,

"What are you reading?" Henri asks, gesturing towards the newspaper. "What news from Angleterre?"

The other folds back a page, and points with his pencil to one of the columns. Henri produces an ornate pair of pince-nez from a waistcoat pocket, balances them on the end of his nose, and squints at the print.

"Ah. Je comprends. Et alors …"

"Exactement."

The young man swallows the dregs of his coffee in one swift gulp. He pushes back his chair, then holds out his hand.

"I must go. Thank you for everything you have done for me since I arrived in Paris, Henri. I am forever in your and your family's debt."

Henri also stands, then impulsively embraces him, kissing him on both cheeks.

"Travel safely, mon ami. And take great care. Do not put yourself in any danger. Remember, you always have a home here in Paris with us."

"I know it, and I am eternally grateful."

"So, now we must part. Bon voyage. Send me word when you reach l'Angleterre."

"I shall."

The young man gathers up his few belongings and sets off down the hill at a brisk pace. Arms folded, Henri watches him go. His expression is both sad and uneasy at the same time.

"Bon courage, Lambert," he murmurs, as his companion swings around the corner of a side-street and disappears from view. "Vraiment, j'espère, que tout va bien pour toi."

****

Detective Inspector Stride also wishes things would go well. Alas, they are currently going far from well. Mrs Stride, a stickler for cleanliness, (which she always asserts to be superior to Godliness, in that you can't see the deity, but you can see the dust) has begun preparations for her Annual Spring Clean.

Mops, cakes of soap and buckets are being positioned just where he is most likely to fall over them. Meals have suddenly become skimpier. A neighbourhood girl has been hired, a chimney sweep ordered, and Stride has been asked his opinion about various colours of paint.

To top off the whole miserable business, when he went to his wardrobe last night, he discovered several shirts and an old brown suit that, admittedly, was falling apart at the seams but possessed great sentimental value, had all mysteriously vanished.

Thus, Stride has arrived at work feeling out of sorts. The motley crowd waiting in the outer office has not helped alleviate his mood. His warning to Jack Cully that the many spurious articles in the daily papers would spawn their own peculiar brand of murder devotees has proved correct. Here they all are, *en masse,* ready and eager to pass on to the detective police their collective wisdom. Such as it is.

To reach the shores of sanity as quickly as possible, Stride splits the crowd with Cully. Nevertheless, what follows is a couple of hours listening with barely-feigned politeness to weird and wonderful theories, expounded by strange and peculiar people, including a very earnest woman, dressed in a long robe adorned with sigils, whose breath smelled foully of rotten meat. She offered to do tarot card readings. By lunchtime, Stride's jaw has set in a painful rictus, and he has developed a great desire to throw things at the opposite wall.

The two detectives are just getting ready to leave for Sally's Chop House, where Stride secretly intends to lurk for as long as possible, when there is a knock at his door. The desk constable sticks his head round. He is newly recruited to Scotland Yard and his bemused expression clearly indicates that this morning has been one of those experiences not covered in the Police Handbook.

"No," Stride says automatically. "Absolutely not. We're leaving. We're going to lunch."

"I was told to give Detective Sergeant Cully this card," the desk constable says, cautiously placing a small pasteboard calling card on the edge of Stride's desk before backing rapidly towards the door.

They glance down at the name on the card. *L. Landseer*. The letter-writer who bested the ubiquitous Dandy Dick, Fleet Street's foulest. They exchange a meaningful glance.

"Tell him we'll be out in a minute," Stride says.

The police constable gives them a funny look. Then he shrugs and returns to his desk duties.

"Right. Lunch temporarily postponed, I think," Stride says, replacing his outdoor coat and hat on the peg. "Let's see what our Mr Landseer has to communicate."

Jack Cully, whose stores of patience have been sadly depleted over the course of the morning, is tempted to point out that Landseer's presence is probably related to the case he is investigating, but the glint in Stride's eye forbears any counter-suggestion.

"Bring him back here," Stride says, shuffling the reports on his desk into some sort of 'I-am-a-busy-man' semblance before going to fetch a third chair from one of the interview rooms.

Jack Cully makes his way to the front office. To his surprise, he finds it empty, apart from a rather attractive young woman sitting waiting composedly. She is looking all round, her eyes robin-bright and curious. Puzzled, he stands in the doorway.

The young woman rises.

"Detective Cully? I am Miss Lucy Landseer. You have received my card? I should greatly appreciate it if you could spare me some of your valuable time. I wish to talk to you about the Metropolitan Madonna. I believe I may have solved the mystery of her numerous appearances. And I also think I know who she really is."

****

Many hours later, as Jack Cully and his wife Emily sit contentedly either side of the fire after supper, he describes the momentous meeting between his colleague and the erudite letter-writer.

"I've never seen Stride look quite so thunderstruck in all the years we've worked together, Em," Cully grins. "When I went back into his office, with Miss Landseer in tow, and introduced her to him, well, you'd have thought the ceiling was about to cave in. I was afraid he was going to have an apoplectic fit."

Emily glances up from the baby's dress she is smocking.

"He does seem to have a problem with working women," she observes crisply. "I recall his comments upon Miss Josephine King, when she took over her uncle's business, and more recently, what he said about that poor Miss Helena Trigg. He really is old-fashioned, Jack. Only rich ladies can afford to stay at home tinkling out tunes on their pianos and waiting to be married. The rest of us must work to earn our bread. If I hadn't found work as a dressmaker, when my best friend Violet and I first came up to London, I'd have starved."

Jack Cully regards his wife with amused affection. From what he remembers of their courtship days, Emily was frequently on the point of starvation: indeed, it was the combination of overwork and under-feeding that caused her complete collapse at the time.

"So, what happened once he got over the shock?" Emily asks, biting off her thread.

Cully stares ruminatively into the fire, bringing to mind the scene in Stride's office. Once Stride had got over the surprise of L Landseer's actual identity, he was almost sent bowling back down by the announcement, made in a calm, matter-of-fact tone as she sat down and removed her gloves, that the young woman earned her living by her pen.

"A *writer*?" he'd queried, in the same horrified tone of voice that he might have uttered the words 'a cockroach'.

Miss Landseer had regarded him evenly. "Is that not a good thing?" she'd inquired coolly. "The public like to read. Somebody has to provide them with reading matter. That is what I do. After all, the bible was written by various people, was it not? And people like to read that, do they not? Indeed, I believe it is the most read book in the English language."

Stride had looked stricken at the comparison, muttering something about having very little time or inclination to read. At which point, Miss Landseer had glanced significantly down at his cluttered desk, her eyebrows arching slightly upwards over her expressive blue eyes, and a slight smile had played about the corners of her mouth.

There had then been a short pause. After which the astonishing young woman had opened her bag and produced a full-page advertisement, cut from one of the London papers. She'd unfolded it and placed it on top of a pile of unread documents.

Cully recognised it at once: it was the same advertisement as the poster he'd seen on the wall of Baker Street Station. That poster had featured a slender young woman in flowing white robes, her long fair hair steaming over her shoulders. Light radiated from her head, and her right hand rested lightly against a scroll bearing the words:

Virgin Face Cream ~ Beautifies the Complexion

The scroll went on to affirm that ***Virgin Face Cream*** was *'the only natural and perfect skin purifier, preservative and beautifier. It removes pimples, wrinkles and other disfigurements and makes the skin strong but velvety.'*

There was plenty more in a similar vein, finishing with a promise that the purchaser of ***Virgin Face Cream*** would instantly acquire a smooth and beautiful skin, and that a box of the ***Cream*** together with a cake of ***Virgin Soap*** might be purchased from any reputable pharmacy or department store.

And here it was again, smaller, but word for word. Exactly the same.

"You will not remember me, Detective Cully, but I met you on the station platform at Baker Street once ~ you were with your wife and little daughter," Miss Landseer had continued, when they had all studied the advertisement in silence for a while. "You will not recall it, but I do. You told me that, in your opinion, there was no such thing as miraculous apparitions."

"And there isn't," Cully says. "I have proved it quite recently on another occasion, and I intend to demonstrate it publicly. The Madonna of the Metropolitan Line does not exist. I have gone into the underground tunnel and looked for myself. There was nothing there but some phosphorus on the surface of the brickwork. It must catch the light when the trains pass, and someone has mistaken it for a religious vision."

"I think you are right," Miss Landseer had said, nodding sagely. "But it is not a mistake. It has always been an advertising stunt, carefully thought out, and taking full advantage of people's gullibility."

At which point, Stride had leant forward in his chair, steepling his fingers under his chin in what Cully mentally called his sceptic pose.

"All well and good, Miss Landseer, you seem very sure of yourself, if I may say so. Perhaps you can furnish us with some proof of your theory."

Without missing a beat, she'd come straight back at him.

"It's not a theory. I have taken a close interest in this matter and investigated it carefully. I am here to present you with my findings, which will explain exactly how the trick has been carried out."

The young woman had then produced a large notebook from her bag. She flipped it open.

"I recognised the figure in the advertisement immediately I saw it: she is the governess of a young girl. They both use the Metropolitan Line daily, sometimes twice daily. They travel at different times, and use different carriages, sometimes second class, sometimes third class. They alight at different stations. On every occasion, the child 'claims' that she saw something in the tunnel."

Now Cully leans in, his eyes focused upon her face.

"You have made notes? May I take a look?"

Smiling, she showed him the first page.

"As soon as I began to wonder why they took the train so frequently, I decided to investigate them. Here are my findings. They may not be complete, of course: obviously I have other things to do with my time than travel on the underground railway all day, every day.

"And here is the address where they live. I am sure that if you question the governess, you will soon get to the truth and be able to lay to rest the 'Madonna of the Metropolitan Line' stories once and for all."

And with that, the astonishing young woman had consulted her pocket watch, then got to her feet, adjusting her bonnet.

"Thank you for sparing me the time, detectives. I shall, of course, leave you my notebook. Now I must go. I have some articles to deliver to my publisher. And an essay to write for my tutor. I bid you both good-day."

"You're a very clever young woman, aren't you," Stride had said, somewhat reluctantly.

Miss Landseer had turned in the doorway and dropped him a saucy curtsy.

"Why thank you, detective inspector. What a lovely compliment," she'd said. Then added, with a look of complete innocence, "my father told me I must always respect the wisdom of the aged."

And with a flurry of skirts, she was gone, leaving the bewitching scent of rose-water in her wake.

Emily Cully's face is alight with amusement.

"And was she right, Jack?"

Jack Cully takes a pull at his pipe.

"She was as right as right could be, Em. In the afternoon, Stride and I paid a visit to the house. A family called the Mastersons live there. He works in the shipping business. They have one daughter, Imogen. Pretty little girl. Her governess, Miss Cassandra Dickens, was also there, and after a little gentle persuasion, she admitted that the whole business was a trick.

"Her father put her up to it. He has a company making soaps and complexion creams, and skin foods and he thought up the Madonna idea to drum up publicity for his new range of products. Of course, he never thought it would take off as it did and become the talk of the town, such that people would put up a shrine and actually start praying to it."

"Men rarely think these things through, I find," Emily says drily.

"Too true Em. Of course, once the first people 'saw' the vision, it just snowballed. Create the right conditions and people will do the rest; they make their own reality. If an innocent child says she saw the Madonna, then the Madonna was there. It is not lying exactly, just not telling the truth.

"However, now the governess has promised that there will be no more 'sightings', and the station has cleaned the tunnel wall and removed all the shrines and candles, I hope things will gradually die down, and the whole matter be forgotten."

Emily Cully grins mischievously, "I shall have to try some of this Virgin soap!"

"I wouldn't go wasting your money, Em. You don't need that rubbish. In my eyes, you're the most beautiful woman in London," Cully says. "Besides, you know I'm not a religious man, but all the same, I don't approve of using Bible names like that. It's wrong. Virgin soap, Virgin cream ~ whatever next? Virgin trains?"

"I'm sure you're right, Jack," Emily says, rolling up the little dress and placing it in her workbasket. "Miss Landseer sounds like an interesting young woman though. I'm sorry I never met her."

"Oh, she certainly was most interesting," Jack Cully nods. "And very helpful. But I expect we shall not hear from her again."

It is rare for Jack Cully to be mistaken about anything, but on this matter, he is going to be proven wrong. Lucy Landseer will go on to finish and publish her debut novel, to some critical acclaim, although it isn't what she'll be most remembered for. That accolade will belong to her thrilling series of crime fiction stories, featuring Belle Batchelor, a daring private detective and her faithful canine side-kick, Harris.

The novels will, of course, be written under an ambiguously gendered *nom-de-plume*. Only a couple of her devoted readers will know her actual identity: the Cambridge professor with whom she lives (unmarried), and a certain member of the Metropolitan Police, anonymously credited with supplying the author with various crucial insights, from time to time.

****

But that is for the future. Back in the present, Helena Trigg, female clerk, finishes adding up the last column of figures in her ledger. She has started working late, as the money she was sent has all but run out, and she must find a way to pay the double rent for the rooms she and Lambert occupy. And eat, though eating is somewhat lower down her list of priorities.

She picks up her quill pens, and her inkwell and puts them, with her ledger, on a shelf behind the desk. She then covers her desk with a cloth and tucks her high wooden stool neatly under it.

Helena places her two hands on either side of her spine and stretches her back. Her shoulders ache and her fingers feel as if they have been bent out of shape. She slowly and painfully straightens them, pulling each finger until the joints crack.

She is about to don her bonnet and outdoor coat, her mind already way ahead of her and thinking thoughts about supper and how cheaply she can do it, when the door to the inner office opens, and Miss King, her employer, comes out.

"Ah, Miss Trigg, you are still here," she says briskly. "Can you spare me five minutes of your time?"

Helena follows her into the office.

"Please sit, Miss Trigg," Josephine says.

Helena Trigg, her heart full of ominous misgivings, lowers herself onto a hard chair, and clasps her hands on her lap. What on earth has she done? Her mind desperately runs backwards over her work. Has she been inattentive? Has she made some gross error that has put the business on a wrong footing? Or has she been distracted? Unable to give her work the full attention it deserves?

A hundred and one possibilities rush through her mind ~ the foremost being that if she is about to be let go, she will have to vacate her lodgings at once, and where, oh where should she lay her head? And what about Lambert? If he should return and find her gone? She knows she cannot rely on her landlord and his mouse-scared wife to pass on any details.

Josephine notices her expression.

"Do not worry, Helena, you are not in any trouble. In fact, quite the opposite. I need your expertise to help me in my new venture."

Helena's shoulders un-tense.

"I expect you know about the new business I intend to start?"

Helena nods.

"I have made an offer for a firm in Birmingham ~ it is similar to King & Co., but the owner is elderly, and he does not want to continue running it. I need someone with your eye for figures to go up there, look through the books and see if anything is amiss. I should not like to find myself saddled with a failing business that might drag King & Co. down with it. Might you be able to do this?"

"When would I go?"

"If you agree, tomorrow by the first train. I shall arrange for a cab to pick you up from your lodgings and take you to the station. You will be met at the other end and put up at a good hotel."

Helena thinks hard.

"How long would I be away?"

"That is up to you," Josephine says. "If the books are all straight, maybe a couple of days. If there are problems, you must telegraph me straight away, as we would then have to consider our best course of action under the circumstances. I'd go myself, but I do not have your mathematical expertise."

"Then, of course I will go," Helena says.

"Thank you, Helena. I was sure I could rely on you," Josephine says, rising. "I shall now telegraph Mr Allen, the business owner, to alert him of your arrival. The cab will be at your door at seven o'clock tomorrow."

"I shall be ready," Helena says.

Later, on the walk back home, Helena Trigg thinks about the prospective venture. She hasn't been out of London since she and Lambert arrived. She has certainly never travelled on a railway train. It will be a new experience for her, as will visiting Birmingham. She feels a ripple of excitement. She decides she will write it all down, so that she can share it with Lambert, when he returns.

Helena buys a small baked potato from one of the food stalls, nursing it in her hand until she reaches a quiet corner, where she devours it greedily. She is so hungry, but she must eke out her food supplies. Paying the rent on time and in full is her top priority. And buying a new pair of boots.

Everything else must wait. At least she will be fed at the hotel, she tells herself. That is something else to look forward to. She lets herself into the house, climbs the stairs to her room, and starts her packing.

****

It is late at night. So late that it is almost the next morning when a figure in a black travelling cloak arrives at the front door of the Mutesius' lodging house. Fumbling in a pocket, the figure draws out a key and quietly lets himself in.

Making no sound whatsoever, the figure tiptoes upstairs, entering a room on the first floor. Briefly, the flickering flame of a candle is seen blooming at the window. Then it disappears, and all is dark and silent once more.

****

Unbelievably, as it is a rare event, Detective Inspector Stride is having a reasonable day. Thanks to the anonymous tip-off he and Jack Cully sent out, most of the newspapers are now leading with the revelation that the 'Metropolitan Madonna' was not some religious apparition, as previously thought, but the result of frost and a chemical reaction in the limestone bricks used to build the railway tunnel.

Some of the more up-market newspapers ~ the kind read by professional people who possess a complex vocabulary and matching intellectual rigour, have called in various professors of chemistry, and a geologist from the British Museum to explain the phenomenon in detail, with mathematical formulae to prove it.

"We did it, Jack!" Stride crows triumphantly, waving the morning edition of *The Inquirer*, whose front-page banner headline reads: ***Many 'Mortarfied' by Madonna Mistake!***

"I wonder how long it took them to come up with that?" Cully says. He resists the temptation of pointing out that it was Miss Landseer who provided them with the necessary information, and his own small daughter who set them on the road of discovery.

"One investigation resolved, satisfactorily. Meanwhile we are still no nearer to tracking down our card-carrying killer," Stride says. "Despite the steady stream of visitors to the front desk, not a single person has been able to supply us with anything helpful." He sighs and rubs his forehead with one hand. "I had hoped one person ~ just one person, might provide us with a lead. It seems I was mistaken. I've sent a constable out for some coffee. Then I intend to read through all the case notes once again. There must be something that we've missed."

****

Mr Mutesius wakes up late and instantly, with a foul taste in his mouth. From outside he hears the sound of passing traffic. There seems to be more of it than usual. He sits up, leans forward, and spits out a tooth. It is yellow and decayed and smells rotten. He stares at it in disgust. Second tooth in as many weeks. Soon he will be toothless and forced to eat slops like a baby.

He consults the old repeater watch he keeps on his bedside table. It is too late to be sleeping. He should have been up hours ago. He throws back the bedclothes and lowers his skinny blue-veined legs to the floor.

Where is his wife? How dare she get up without his permission? And why can he not smell coffee brewing or bacon frying? Muttering threats and imprecations, Mr Mutesius throws on his dressing gown and stumps off to see what is amiss.

Entering the front parlour, he finds Mrs Mutesius standing motionless, staring up at the ceiling. She looks terrified. He gives her a slap across the shoulder.

"Oi, what d'you think yer doing? Where's my breakfast?"

But to his surprise, instead of scurrying away to the basement kitchen to fetch the food, Mrs Mutesius remains exactly where she is. Silently, she points upwards.

"There it is again. Did you hear it?" she whispers, her eyes wide with fear.

Mr Mutesius inserts a finger into his mouth and feels round to find the hole left by the rotten tooth.

"I don't hear nothing. You've gone stupid again. Like the last time. Stupid old woman. I'll have you locked away in an asylum, you see if I don't."

There is a crash. Then the distinct sound of footsteps crossing the room overhead. Mr Mutesius' fist hovers mid-air but does not come to land upon his best beloved, who stands shaking in her slippers, her mouth opening and closing like a stranded guppy.

"Who is it?" she whispers, clutching his sleeve. "It ain't Miss Trigg, coz she's gone away for a few days. She told us. So, if it ain't her, then who's up there, a-walking about and dropping things?"

With surprising strength for a thin old woman, Mrs Mutesius propels her husband urgently to the bottom of the stairs. She hands him a broom.

"You go and see who it is. I'll stay here and keep guard."

Clutching the broom in one hand, Mr Mutesius slowly and reluctantly mounts the stairs. He is wheezing and coughing by the time he reaches the first-floor landing, and his head is spinning. Lack of breakfast, he thinks.

For a moment he hesitates between going on, or possibly going back and dealing with the intruder on a full stomach (by which time whoever it is might have scarpered, thus saving him the bother).

While he is still hovering between the Scylla and Charybdis of indecision, the door to the upstairs sitting room suddenly opens. Mr Mutesius takes a step backwards, trips over the broom and goes flying head over heels down the stairs, landing at the bottom in a crumpled heap.

Mrs Mutesius, who has been standing in the lee of the stairwell, gives a scream and rushes over to him. She gets down on her knees and shakes him.

"Stand up, Edwin! Open your eyes! Speak to me!"

A muffled groan is the only response.

Mrs Mutesius scrambles awkwardly to her feet and stares accusingly upwards.

"Oh, it's you!" she exclaims.

****

It is the beginning of evening, balanced between twilight and dusk. The lawyer sits in a hard chair in an unlighted room on the top floor of his dingy chambers, contemplating the evening ahead. The walls of the room are bare, the furniture sparse. The remains of an unappetising meal sit congealing in a pewter plate.

The poet who wrote that that *'no man is an island'* had never encountered Jacob Jarvis, the exception to the rule. Solitary by nature, and now solitary by circumstance, he sits by the empty grate, letting the cold work into his hands, his feet and his heart.

His existence is pleasure-free, apart from the time spent at the gaming tables. At the age of fifty-one, he senses that he has reached his peak, and from now on, his life will fall into the sere. But before that happens, he desires just one more triumph.

He has recently drawn £400,000 out of two banks: Coutts & Co, and Twinings, via several bills of exchange presented in the names of his former partners in crime, using false letters of introduction. The signatures on the bottom of each letter, vouching for him and granting him permission, have been forged (given their absence) by himself. It is his final act of revenge.

In three months' time, when the bills are returned to the issuing banks, both men will face bankruptcy, ruin and public disgrace. The lawyer intends have a ringside seat in the court where they will be tried, and he will use every ounce of his influence as a man of law to make sure both end up being transported for life. There is more than one game of cards; more than one way of playing the ace.

Meanwhile, his fraudulent actions have now secured him a not inconsiderable sum of money, which he intends to disburse at the gambling tables. The lawyer rises and makes his preparations. Once again, he feels the familiar quickening of the blood as he contemplates the thrill of the game. Win or lose, it matters not.

London is full of thousands upon thousands of souls, all wanting something that they cannot have. It is the human condition to want. Want loves want. It grows and breeds. This is what he wants. He claps on his top hat, pinches out the candle, and goes out into the night.

****

Some mortals have a splinter of ice in their hearts; others have hearts of gold. Here are two of the latter mortals: Pin and the boy Muggly, sitting side by side on the doorstep of Pin's building, sharing a slice of bread sprinkled with damp sugar.

Pin is telling Muggly about the new diorama at Mr Trinkler's Emporium. It is a Schoolroom of Mice, with desks and tiny slates. Pin has spent some time with her small nose pressed to the glass case, trying to make out the letters on the tiny slates, and wishing she'd learned to read.

"I reckon them mousies has a better chance of a good job than I have, Muggly," she says, licking sugar from her fingers.

"But they are stuffed, Pin, and you ain't," Muggly says, with a rare spark of enlightenment.

Pin cocks her head to one side.

"That is very true, Muggly. But I still can't read. My sister keeps promising to teach me my letters, but by the time she finishes work, she is fit for nuffink."

"I can't read, Pin."

Pin puts an arm round his shoulders.

"When she learns me, I'll teach you, Muggly. Promise. That'll be prime, won't it? You and me, reading stuff, just like them clever people. And then when we can read, we'll have all sorts of lovely food. Pies and puddings and tarts. You just imagine that, Muggly!"

Muggly ponders the mystery of reading. Yet another of the great mysteries that fill his head with wonder and puzzlement. How do birds stay up in the air? Why does one slice of bread still leave a gaping hole in his stomach?

And how did the young lady he has been watching so sedulously go away, and then come back as a man? There is so much he does not understand.

****

Meanwhile, here is the young lady herself, ensconced in a second-class carriage, on her way back to London. The train hurtles along at a reckless fifty miles an hour. It is utterly terrifying and completely exhilarating.

She shares her carriage with a couple of commercial travellers, who have spent the whole journey discussing sales and prospects, and a family relocating to London. They are surrounded by bundles and carpet bags, which they refuse to entrust to the guard's van. They are also accompanied by two small children and a teething baby.

Helena Trigg is still not sure why she was sent to Birmingham by her employer. The elderly owner of the business, who met her at the station and conducted her to her hotel, wasn't sure either. The books were all in order, written up in his meticulous copperplate, and it only took her a morning to look them over and find everything satisfactory.

As her return train ticket was booked for a few days' hence, Helena had time to look around Birmingham, 'the City of a Thousand Trades,' as she gathered it was called by the residents. At first, she was overwhelmed by the noise. The hammering of presses, the clatter of engines, the whirling of wheels, the runaway cattle in the Beast Market, it was an assault upon her senses! And it never stopped. Day and night, the red glow from a thousand furnaces lit up the sky, so that the stars were hidden from view.

She'd thought London was loud and dirty, but it was *nothing* in comparison to Birmingham. The air was heavy with sooty smoke, and the back to back begrimed houses in the city centre with their broken windows stopped up with filthy rags or yellowing paper seemed far worse than anything she has seen in London.

It was hard to reconcile the glittering watch-chains, necklaces, buttons, bracelets, buckles and snuff-boxes that she saw displayed in shops with the squalor and poverty, the children fighting over scraps of food, the sullen, whey-faced women in doorways, and the piles of stinking filth that clotted up her throat and made her feel sick.

And now she is returning. To her own fireside, her own bed, her known routine. How glad she will be when her foot crosses the threshold of her little sitting-room, and she sees the kettle waiting to be filled, and the old familiar things from home waiting to welcome her.

But until that happy moment, there is scenery to stare at, and the whoosh of trains going in the opposite direction. At every station, small shoeless children run up and down the platform, offering fruit, or flowers to the passengers, and newsboys bawl the latest headlines. Then the guard blows his whistle, and the engine hisses and jerks into life and they are off again.

Time ceases to exist in any linear form. There is only now … and then now … as the train rushes through countryside and past fields of cows and small villages, leaving them behind to rush on to the next ones. The baby cries fretfully. The commercial travellers unwrap sandwiches. The children squabble and bicker and clamour for sweets.

A sudden shower of rain patters on the roof, slaps with unexpected ferocity at the windows, and is gone. The landscapes all merge into one: rural, urban, industrial. She doesn't have a clue where they are, only that they are travelling south ~ a station is rushed through, but the train is going far too fast to read its painted boards.

Helena closes her eyes. She feels travel-soiled; her mouth is dry; the skin of her face is taut. She lets the clickety-clack rhythm of the train wheels soothe her unsettled spirit. She thinks about how her life has changed in small instances, almost without her knowing it.

Then the engine screeches, the two commercial travellers check their watches and begin to fold up their papers, and the family starts packing away the children's bits and pieces. They are approaching the terminus.

As soon as the train comes to a halt, Helena Trigg picks up her case, then hefts it along the platform to the barrier. It is far too heavy to carry all the way home, so she will have to find a cab. Through the arching roof, she catches a glimpse of the grimy familiar London sky. She is back.

She reaches the barrier, sets down her case, and fumbles for her ticket. She is just replacing her purse in her bag, when someone picks up her luggage. Startled, Helena looks up to see who it is, and feels the colour drain from her face. She staggers back a few steps, as the world spins dizzily around her. For a moment, she cannot breathe.

Then she is in her brother's arms, the tears coursing down her cheeks, and he is hugging her tight and murmuring her name. Oblivious to the curious stares of the passers-by, brother and sister hold each other tight. So tight, that it seems as if they would never let each other go again.

****

It is early next morning, and the streets glitter with rain. Every street, every narrow lane, every broad highway is crammed with people walking to their place of work. Similarly, the conveyances are packed full of human beings, jammed as compactly together as the stones on the paving underneath. It is as if London is made up of arteries, sustained by thousands of human globules who circulate through the city, sustaining its life and energy, and beyond it, the whole land.

Here are two such: they have just alighted from an omnibus and are making their way to an office. They mount the steps to the first floor, where one unlocks the door, letting the other enter. Preparations are made for the day's business: quills are sharpened, inkwells refilled, and ledgers lifted from their shelves and set upon the two wooden desks.

Eventually, a step is heard on the stair. The two exchange a look. The door to the landing opens and Josephine King steps inside, untying the strings of her bonnet as she enters. Seeing the two awaiting her arrival, she stops short, her eyes widening in surprise.

"Good morning, Miss King," Helena Trigg says. "May I present my brother Lambert to you. He arrived in London two nights ago from France, though I gather you have already corresponded with him."

Josephine King's glance travels quickly from brother to sister and back again. "I am delighted to make your acquaintance, Mr Trigg," she says evenly.

Helena Trigg continues, "Lambert has returned because he read in the British newspapers that the man who swindled the banks out of so much money, and killed a senior bank clerk, was about to be exposed and arrested. He decided to come back and offer his services to the police to help identify him."

"The stories in the press are untrue," Josephine says. "I have it from Inspector Greig himself. The newspapers are trying to make something out of nothing. Nobody has come forward, and the police are currently no further in their investigations. I am sorry to be the bearer of this bad news. But I cannot help thinking you would be better off returning to France at once, Mr Trigg. Your return has put both you and your sister in danger."

Helena stretches out an arm and clutches her brother by the sleeve.

"No, I couldn't bear to be parted from him again."

"I understand your concerns, Miss King," Lambert Trigg says calmly, "but as it is evident that I am no longer a suspect in their eyes, I must try to clear my name by helping the police as much as I can. And my poor sister has been entirely without anyone to protect her, something I blame myself for. I am staying in England. It is decided. I made a little money while I was in Paris, which will help us with food and rent. The responsibility for both has been a heavy burden upon my sister. I should never have abandoned her in the first place ~ I understand that now."

"You did what you believed to be right," Helena counters fiercely. "And you made financial arrangements for me."

"Which have now run out."

"But here you are, in the nick of time to save the day!" Helena says, her mouth curving upwards.

Josephine frowns.

"Much as I admire your sentiment, Mr Trigg, I am not sure what help you could be, until the suspect is traced and apprehended. I know Inspector Greig is worried that the man knows where your sister lives and may even now have somebody watching the house."

"I have seen nobody, and I have been keeping an eye out every day," Helena interjects.

Josephine bites back the urge to tell her that not being seen is the primary requirement of being a good watcher.

"May I suggest a possible course of action?"

Brother and sister nod in unison.

"Write to Inspector Greig, Mr Trigg. Inform him of your return, and the reasons you decided to come back. Let him decide how best to employ you. In the meantime, I'd recommend that you stay indoors as much as possible. It would only be for a couple of days, I am sure. What do you think to my suggestion?"

Lambert Trigg nods quickly. "I think it is a good one. I need to find another job, and it'd give me a few days to read the situations vacant and get up a letter of application."

"Are you intending to go back to the life of a bank clerk?" Josephine inquires.

"It is all I really know, but I may have to spread my wings. I fear my previous employer would not give me a good character, even though I can prove I had no part in the fraud perpetrated upon the bank."

"I see." Josephine eyes him thoughtfully for a few seconds. Then she says,

"I'm sure your sister has told you that I am thinking of taking over a similar business in Birmingham. I shall need someone to set it up for me, hire staff, engage with the local finance houses and act as my representative. The trains to and from Birmingham are frequent, and although it would mean living away from London in the week, you'd return at weekends. Think about it ~ don't give me an answer now. It would be a temporary post, but it'd tide you over if you can't find anything suitable."

"Oh, Miss King, how kind you are. Isn't she, brother?" Helena exclaims.

"She is very kind ~ and very unwise to trust her new business venture to someone with as little practical business experience as I have."

"And how much experience do you think I possessed, when my uncle died, and I took up the reins here?" Josephine counters. "I knew absolutely nothing. I was lucky in having Trafalgar Moggs to instruct me, and I am quite happy to lend him to you, if he is willing and should you decide to take up my offer."

Helena tugs at her brother's sleeve.

"Say yes, Lambert, please. It'd make me happy to see you settled at work again, and at least I'd know where you were!"

Lambert Trigg holds out his hand, "Then, yes, it is, Miss King. And thank you for putting your trust in me. And now I'll leave you both to get on with your day's work. Helena, I shall be back to collect you at the end of the day. Miss King, your servant."

Trigg gives Josephine a bow, tips his hat to them both, and goes out. Helena turns a joyous face to Josephine.

"I cannot tell you what this means, Miss King. I have Lambert back at last, and now he has a job!"

Josephine bites down her misgivings. It seems to her that in the pleasure of their reunion, both brother and sister are ignoring the obvious: that somewhere in London, a murderer lurks, and from what Lachlan Greig has told her, he is cunning, utterly ruthless and will stop at nothing to preserve his anonymity. She hopes Lambert Trigg has made the right decision. She hopes that she has too.

****

A couple of hours later, Inspector Lachlan Greig is brought a letter. It is marked Personal and Urgent. He slits open the envelope and reads the contents. Several times. After which he sits and thinks for a while, and then takes the letter to show to his colleague Jack Cully.

"This could be the break-through we have all wanted," he says. "If Mr Trigg is willing to come in to Scotland Yard, we can ask him what he remembers about our man. We might get him to work with the police artist to produce a drawing. Once that is done, we could send it round to the newspapers and see if it flushes him out of wherever he has gone to ground. What do you think?"

"I agree," Cully says.

"Then I shall write to Mr Trigg at once, and suggest he pays us a call at his earliest convenience. There is no time to waste."

Lachlan Greig is a man of his word. The letter is written, blotted and dispatched within the hour. He is also a man of honour, so while he spends the rest of the afternoon with Josephine's letter folded in his inside pocket, next to his heart, he does not reply to it. Yet.

The letter he wishes to write to her must wait until this case is over, and the murderer is behind bars. As his old sergeant in Edinburgh always said: *'Never mix business with pleasure, laddie. That way ruin lies.'*

To everything, there is a season, as the Good Book has it. Greig hopes the season will be Spring, already showing in leaf and bud.

****

The reappearance of Lambert Trigg might be a source of joy to his sister, but it is proving to be a source of great frustration to his landlord Mr Mutesius, whom we last left as a heap of rags and bones at the foot of his own stairs.

Three days have now passed, and the old man has barely moved from his bed, where he lies bruised, bandaged and fuming. Beef tea has been administered at regular intervals by his long-suffering wife.

A doctor has visited, examined the patient, declared that the patient has broken his left wrist, bruised several ribs and is suffering from mild concussion, but given the circumstances and the age of the patient, he is lucky to be alive, and that'll be two guineas please.

Mr Mutesius stews in his frowsty bed and thinks about the reward coming his way for reporting his tenant. Only it won't even approach the outskirts of his expectations unless he sticks to his part of the agreement. And at the moment, that is out of the question.

He might have written a short (ill-spelled) note, but alas, he is left-handed. He could get his wife to write at his dictation, but he feels it would be making her part of the agreement. She might even, oh the horror, claim part of the reward.

Meanwhile, he hears the tenant walking about overhead without a care in the world. He hears him going up and down the stairs and opening and closing the front door. He hears him whistling and singing snatches of some song in a foreign language. And his frustration grows apace as every hour passes.

Where's he off to now? Mr Mutesius thinks, as the light tread is once again heard outside his door. Grasping his stick, he levers himself upright and hobbles to the window. He leans against the sill, catching his breath. Then, thrusting aside the net curtain, he peers out at the day.

It is early afternoon, and a thin sun is trying its best to impart some warmth to the ground. Mutesius watches sourly as the tenant, wearing, he notes, a smart suit and a striped cravat, makes his way towards the main highroad leading towards the West End.

"Yerss, you come and go happily now, but you an't going to be doing it soon," he mutters darkly, surprising Mrs Mutesius, who has just entered the room with her customary cat-like tread.

"Oh. You are out of bed. Is that really a good idea? Did not the doctor prescribe a week of rest?" she says, setting down a cup of beef tea on his night stand.

Mr Mutesius turns from the window. "I can't stay in bed for ever, and I won't drink any more slops," he snarls. "You cook me a nice hot dinner, with plenty of meat and potatoes. I got important business to get on with, so I don't care what that quack said, right?"

As she scurries to do her lord and master's bidding, Mrs Mutesius wonders what he means by 'important business'. She has her suspicions, which is why she has covertly taken the business card he was given, out of his jacket pocket and hidden it somewhere he won't find it. Mrs Mutesius experiences great comfort in such small acts of defiance.

Meanwhile, her husband returns to his bed. Groaning loudly, he heaves himself back into it and pulls the covers up to his whiskery unshaven chin. Tomorrow, he promises himself, after he's got a couple of good meals inside him, he'll set out on his mission. And then the tenant will get exactly what he deserves. And so, with a little bit of luck, will he.

Unaware that his every move is being carefully monitored from below, Lambert Trigg makes his way to Scotland Yard to keep his appointment with Inspector Lachlan Greig. It is mid-afternoon when he enters the building and is shown immediately into a paper-strewn office. Two officers sit behind the desk: one, a middle-aged man with pouchy eyes in an unslept face is introduced as Detective Inspector Stride by his younger colleague, who then introduces himself to Trigg as the writer of the letter.

Stride eyes the young man with mild disfavour.

"About time you came to us, Mr Trigg. We could have done with your help weeks ago."

Lambert Trigg acknowledges the comment, but his head remains high and his glance is level.

"I would give my life to preserve my beloved sister, gentlemen," he says proudly. "If my leaving England meant that she was saved from harm, then I do not regret my decision for a single second, even if it has inconvenienced you. And it has given me a chance to think about what happened ~ I am sure that my bank wasn't the only one being defrauded by this man. I see from your faces it is so."

He reaches into his pocket and draws out a brown manila envelope which he places upon the desk. He turns to Greig.

"This is some of the paperwork that passed across my desk. It is in the handwriting of Mr Godwin Fitzwarren. You might like to compare it with anything else you possess. You asked me in your letter whether I could recall the features of the man who called himself this. I answer you now: yes, I can. Every line, every whisker. I have gone over it time after time, etching the memory of his face into my mind for just such an occasion as this.

"I am willing to work with your artist to recreate this memory, but I cannot do so right now. It is late, and I must meet my sister from work and walk her home. She tells me this evil man has discovered where we live. My first duty is to protect her. I will return tomorrow morning first thing, after I have seen her to her office, and then I shall be at your disposal all day."

He rises, shakes hands with the two detectives, and is shown out by Greig. When the Inspector returns, he finds Stride has taken out the paperwork handed to them by Lambert Trigg and is comparing it to the letter from Helena Trigg's unknown correspondent, and the cheques passed to the police from the solicitors Harry & Persew.

"Come and look at this!" Stride exclaims, rubbing his hands. "Three different items, but without doubt, the same hand has written them all. This is our man, Lachlan! We have him! By God, we have him at last!"

****

To the visiting tourist, the young gentleman with matrimony upon his mind, or the married man with a discreet rendezvous or a guilty conscience, there is nothing that more bespeaks the picturesque London scene than the London flower girls.

You will find them all over the West End, sitting with their backs to a convenient wall, their baskets of violets, primroses, lilies or moss-roses next to them. In the minds of many Londoners, the arrival of the flower girls with their fresh scented bouquets marks the arrival of Spring.

Look more closely: here is one you may recognise.

Penelope Klem, known to her friends and family as Pin, sits by a shop doorway on the corner of Drury Lane. She has filled her cleaning bucket with bunches of flowers and her piping cry of *'Vi-lets…luverly spring vi-lets'* vies with the clop of carriage horses, the shouts of fruit costers and the general din of the busy street.

Technically, this is not Pin's pitch, belonging as it does to two sisters from Shoreditch. But as they have not appeared to claim it for a few days, and as Pin has decided to diversify, she has moved in, along with an even smaller child, who is selling bruised oranges.

Pin is four bunches in profit, when an elderly and rather scruffy old man approaches her pitch. He leans heavily on a stick, and there is something unsavoury about his long greasy hair and battered billycock hat. Pin eyes his approach and makes the instant assumption that he is after something other than violets.

"Oi, you, girl," the man rasps, his breath coming in wheezing gasps. "I'm looking for a shop wot sells stuffed animals. You know where it is?"

Pin does indeed know, having recently migrated from cleaning duties in the very shop itself. She gives him directions, then holds out her bucket of flowers, smiling in a winning customer-friendly way, her head on one side.

The old man ignores this blatant sales-technique. He stomps off, his gait lurching and unsteady, without uttering a word of thanks. Scarcely has he gone, when Pin hears a strange noise: a kind of whistling, hissing sound. She glances in its direction and spies an edge of the boy Muggly peering at her from round a doorway. She stands up and waves at him. Muggly hurries over and grips her arm.

"That's him!" he whispers, pointing at the retreating figure of Mr Mutesius, who is heading towards the emporium of Mr Trinkler, Upholsterer and Preserver of Small Animals & Birds.

"What's him?"

"The man."

Pin bites down her irritation. Getting information out of Muggly is sometimes like getting a reluctant winkle out of its shell: you have to ease it out with the right equipment.

"What man?"

"That man. The one I told you of. Lives in the house wot I been watching for us."

"Ah."

Enlightened, Pin sets down her bucket of flowers.

"Right then, you mind them flow'rs, Muggly; I'll be back in a tick," she says briskly.

Leaving Muggly to replicate her winsome advances to the passing trade, Pin sets off at a run. It takes little effort for her to catch up with Mr Mutesius, who is progressing in a series of erratic crab-like movements, so she reaches the door of Trinkler's shop a nano-second after he has entered.

Easing the door quietly open, Pin leans her head against the lintel and tunes her sharp little ears to the interchange taking place within.

"I got some information," Mutesius croaks.

Trinkler eyes him suspiciously and is eyed suspiciously in return.

"You tell him Trigg's come back," the old man says. "That's all. Trigg's come back. He said I woz to tell you, and it woz urgent. And now I've told you, so you can tell him I wants my reward."

Having delivered this cryptic message, the old man turns, and lurches unsteadily towards the shop entrance, now a Pin-free zone, although a canny observer might spot her lurking in the opposite doorway, her eyes bright and alert. She returns to her flower bucket, which is being sedulously guarded from potential customers by the boy Muggly.

"Come on, Muggly, we have to warn her!" Pin says, tugging his ragged jacket. "You gotta show me where the house is."

Muggly blinks a few times as his brain shifts up a couple of gears. Then he nods and stands up.

"Oi, Sukey," Pin addresses the orange seller, "You're in charge of them flowers now. Don't take no less than thruppence a bunch, and I know how many bunches is in the bucket."

Having thus completed the requisite staff training, Pin takes Muggly by the hand, and they set off as fast as their legs can carry them, and the pavement traffic permits.

****

Mrs Mutesius hobbles down to the basement kitchen and fills the kettle from the tap in the scullery. She sets out the tea things, ready for Mr Mutesius' return, adding a plate of ginger biscuits to the tray. She knows there will be complaints, her husband's teeth are deserting his mouth like rats leaving a sinking ship, but she likes a ginger biscuit to dip in her tea.

She lights the gas, noting that the house is completely silent. All the tenants have left for work. The only sound is next door's dog barking at a pair of blackbirds. It comes to her that this is what it would be like every day, if her cantankerous, violent and bad-tempered husband were not here anymore. She tries not to focus on the idea. It goes against her parents' teaching about marriage.

She is not to know that Mr Mutesius is even now pouring the reward that he has not received down his throat in a series of pint pots. Nor that he will be found at closing time by the landlord slumped under a table, out cold. Nor that the same landlord will drag him out and dump him in a side alley, where the night air, the alcohol, and various undiagnosed outcomes from the fall downstairs will finally do for him what his wife can only dream about.

Mrs Mutesius finishes her preparations and climbs the stairs to the ground floor. She turns the handle of the basement door and steps into the gloom of the hallway. In the half-light, she is suddenly aware that there is somebody standing just inside the front door. It is clearly not Mr Mutesius, unless he has grown a foot in height and acquired a top hat in the process.

She takes a few steps towards the dark figure, her face staring and surprised. For some strange reason, there is a tall dark man in a top hat standing in the hallway. She cannot make out his features. She is puzzled by this and takes a few more hesitant steps forward. The man is carrying an ebony walking stick with a silver handle in his right hand. He raises the hand and walks towards her in a threatening manner.

With a speed that she has never exhibited before, nor knew she possessed, Mrs Mutesius scurries back along the hallway, slides herself through the door to the basement, then slams and locks it. She stands on the top step, listening to her heart pounding away in her elderly chest. The door handle is turned a couple of times, and she feels pressure being applied to the door itself, but it does not yield.

Gasping for breath, she descends the stairs and secretes herself in the larder. Whatever it is, whoever it is, she is not going to emerge until Mr Mutesius comes back. Let him deal with it. She shuts her eyes tightly, and begins gabbling all the prayers she can recall from her childhood.

Meanwhile Lambert Trigg has spent a fascinating, but ultimately exhausting, morning with the police artist. It is one thing to remember the features of a person, it is quite another to communicate accurately the same features to someone else who has never seen them.

Over and over, he has had to correct himself: no, the forehead was broader, the eyes closer together, the brows thinner, the cheeks more sunken, the expression more reptilian. It has taken several hours, but finally, the artist has produced a likeness that Lambert Trigg thinks most resembles the man he regularly faced across his desk, and whose actions caused him to lose his employment and flee the country.

Pleased with what he has accomplished, he sets off home to prepare the evening meal ready for Helena's return. The Scottish detective has told him that the likeness will be in all the main newspapers by first edition tomorrow. He is reassured by this, but he knows neither of them will feel really safe until the perpetrator is captured.

Lambert Trigg reaches the Mutesius' house and lets himself in. There is no sound from the ground floor flat; the door to the basement kitchen is closed. The assumption must be that his elderly landlord and wife have gone out. He runs lightly up the stairs to the first floor. And stops dead on the landing.

When he quit the house that morning, Lambert Trigg was careful to close the outer door to their sitting room. As instructed by one of the detectives, he had carefully inserted a small piece of paper, low down, between the door and the frame, as a security measure. The door is still closed, just as it was when he and Helena left. However, the piece of paper now lies on the floor.

****

Pin and Muggly are London waifs and strays, and as such, their knowledge of back alleys, cut-throughs, and dead ends that aren't, are second to none. They make swift progress and the light is just beginning to fade from the sky when they reach the house Muggly has been watching.

There are no lights in any of the windows, which is either a relief, as it means they are not too late, or a warning that Evil Man is hiding inside waiting to pounce. Having carefully questioned Muggly to discover which route the young lady prefers to take on her return journey home, Pin decides they will set out and meet her halfway.

They have been walking for about twenty minutes, eyes peeled, when Muggly suddenly clutches Pin's stick-thin arm and points.

"There she is, Pin."

Pin sees a neatly dressed young woman in a plain straw bonnet. She carries a leather work satchel under her arm and wears a worried expression on her face. She seems to be scouring the streets, as if she is also looking for somebody.

Pin steps boldly out, right into the young lady's path and holds up her hand, as she has seen the traffic policeman do at Regent Circus when there is a lock. The young lady stops walking and stares down at her.

"You can't go home," Pin says, by way of formal introduction.

The young lady frowns.

"I am sorry, I don't understand. Who are you? And why can I not go home?"

Pin takes a deep breath.

"You tell him Trigg's come back," she says, doing a passable imitation of Mr Mutesius. "That's all. Trigg's come back. He said I woz to tell you, and it woz urgent."

Instantly, the colour drains from the young lady's cheeks.

"When did you hear this?"

Pin reveals her sources. The young lady's face goes candle-white, her eyes huge with shocked surprise.

"Oh, Lambert! Why did you return, only to lose your life at this evil murderer's hand? Why, my brother?"

Muggly edges into the frame.

"I fort you said there wasn't nobody in the house," he whispers hoarsely.

The young lady stares at him.

"The house is empty? Then we must hurry. If Lambert hasn't returned, we may be able to get back first and stop him! Come, we have not a moment to lose!"

Pin gives Muggly a frantic glance. She hangs onto the sleeve of the young lady's jacket. Muggly attaches himself to the other sleeve.

"Not so fast, miss. When I said there wasn't anybody there, I meant anybody we could see. But there might have been, if you take my meaning. I think we should be careful. We don't know who might be lurking around, do we?"

But Helena is deaf, dumb and blind to Pin's protests. She races along the pavement, elbowing passers-by aside, with the two youngsters frantically trying to keep up with her. Reaching the house, she barrels through the front door, slamming it behind her, and rushes straight up the stairs, leaving Pin and Muggly staring up at her, open mouthed.

Helena goes into the sitting room. It is empty. She takes the box of lucifer matches from the mantelpiece and lights the two lamps on either side. Then as she steps back, she is suddenly aware of movement behind her.

She spins round. And feels the breath leaving her body. A tall saturnine man dressed from head to toe in black, is standing in the doorway to Lambert's room, regarding her with keen interest. He makes no sound, nor movement, but manages to exude such an implicit aura of menace that Helena reaches for the poker.

"Please, do not bother with any of that nonsense, Miss Trigg," the man says, his voice smooth as oiled silk. "I am far stronger than you and I am sure, in any encounter of a hostile and pugilistic nature, that I would come off best. And it would be such a pity to hurt one so young and fair. I am sure your brother would agree, would he not?"

Helena grips her fingers round the poker and makes herself stand tall.

"Where is my brother? What have you done with him?"

The stranger gives an imperceptible shrug. "I thought I heard him on the stair a few hours ago. Maybe I was mistaken. Whatever it was that I heard, I know he will return sooner or later. And I shall be waiting for him. I have unfinished business to enact with that young man."

He points to one of the armchairs.

"Please sit down, Miss Trigg," he says, his voice cutting through the air like a whip. "You and I are going nowhere."

****

Meanwhile, the cab carrying Lambert Trigg, Inspector Greig, Jack Cully and two armed constables makes its way through the early evening rush hour. Greig is of the fixed belief that when going to arrest a man, it is always best to arrive mob-handed, which is why, as soon as Lambert Trigg arrived at the front desk, hot and breathless, and blurted out his story, the inspector sprang into action.

"Can we not go any faster?" Lambert asks, desperation in his voice. "Helena will be almost at the house by now."

"We are making good progress," Jack Cully says. "See, we are at the corner of your street now."

The cab pulls up outside the house, disgorging its occupants. Lambert Trigg rushes up the front path, closely followed by Greig, who lays a restraining hand upon the young man's shoulder.

"Easy, laddie," he says quietly. "Fools rush in, eh? Let my men deal with whoever is up there. They know their trade. You stand by."

He reads Trigg's agonised expression.

"No harm shall befall your sister. Or yourself. Of that you have my word as a Scot."

Greig turns to the constables, who have drawn their truncheons.

"Now, my good men, you know the rules. No blows to be struck unless in self-defence. Ready all? In we go."

Greig steps forward and kicks the front door wide. He runs up the stairs, closely followed by Cully and the two constables. They push past Pin and Muggly, who are cowering on the top step. Then Greig steps into the sitting room, Cully at his shoulder. The constables take over the doorway.

At their entrance, Helena Trigg leaps to her feet, her eyes desperately seeking the one face she longs to see. Her eyes bespeak her disappointment. Her companion also rises, donning his top hat. He faces Greig, smiling affably. His face shows no sign of anxiety whatsoever.

"Good evening sir. Your entrance is a little precipitate! I have been visiting my niece. A pleasant encounter, but now I must take my leave. My dear, I bid you farewell," he says, walking calmly towards the door, his stick clutched firmly in his fist.

"Not so fast," Greig says, moving swiftly to bock his exit. "I am Inspector Greig of the Metropolitan Police's detective division, and I have reason to believe that you have questions to answer at Scotland Yard. Questions about bank fraud, forging cheques and possibly murder."

The lawyer's mouth works. "I'm afraid you must be mistaken, officer. As I said, I am here to visit my niece. Is that not so my dear?"

"No, it is NOT so!" Lambert Trigg pushes his way between the constables. "She is no more your niece than I am your nephew. Inspector, I identify this man to you as Mr Godwin Fitzwarren. He passed forged cheques and bills of exchange across my counter, and nearly brought down an old and well reputed city bank."

"The game is up, sir," Cully says quietly. "We are now arresting you, and you will accompany us to Scotland Yard, where you will be questioned about this, and other matters. Constable ~ place this man in handcuffs and escort him to the cab."

The constables step forward, one reaching for the cuffs in his belt. The lawyer holds up a black gloved hand.

"Not so fast, gentlemen. Not so fast, if you please. Under what name are proposing to arrest me?"

"Under the name you used to defraud this man's bank: the name of Godwin Fitzwarren," Cully says.

The lawyer waves the suggestion aside. He laughs scornfully, "But Godwin Fitzwarren does not exist. He was a mere figment of my imagination. A phantom of the mind. A character in my little play. He has no birth certificate, no papers, no London address. Nothing. You could not bring him before any court in the land. You will have to do better than that, I am afraid. A phantom cannot be arrested. You must either detain me under my proper name, or the law says I may walk free."

There is a long silence. The constables wait for further orders. The two detectives exchange desperate glances.

Meanwhile the lawyer watches them, arms folded, hooded eyes bright with malice, his lipless slit of a mouth open in a triumphant grin.

And then a small defiant voice calls out from the landing. “His name is Lawyer Jacob Jarvis. An’ he broke Muggly’s arm with his stick.”

****

Later, after the police detectives have left, taking the handcuffed lawyer with them, Helena puts on the kettle, makes a huge pile of hot buttered toast, and listens with growing amazement as Pin relates the story of how the two ragged youngsters’ lives became entangled with hers and her brother’s.

Pin enlightens Helena as to the identity of her secret stalker, and Muggly stands by shyly, a delighted grin on his face, as Helena embraces the girl, and then Lambert shakes his hand until it almost falls off.

“How can I possibly repay you both for all that you have done?” Helena asks, as she shows them both out into the darkening street.

Pin thinks hard for a while. Then she tells her.

****

A fine Saturday afternoon. There are crocuses and daffodils blooming in the public parks and the private squares. Birds sing in the plane trees and the air smells of incipient Spring and hope.

Look more closely. A man has just got off an omnibus. He is tall, above the average height for a man of his age, has bright chestnut hair, a handsome face, and is wearing a good tailored suit and a well-brushed top hat. His gloves are immaculate. He is clearly meeting a young lady, because he pauses to buy a small bunch of primroses from the flower girl outside the pharmacist shop.

The man crosses the busy road, dodging the horses and smart equipages that dart to and fro (for this is Hampstead High Street and the traffic, like the shops and the inhabitants, is up-market in nature). The man makes his way down a side street, stopping outside a small tea-room. It has a freshly-painted sign saying: *The Lily Lounge. All baked goods freshly made on the premises* and it appears to be full of customers.

The man's face which, up until this moment, has borne an expression of cautious optimism, changes immediately he spies a young woman sitting on her own at a window table. She has removed her bonnet, and her unruly flame-red hair is escaping from its pins in small fiery curls.

The man smiles, his dark eyes lighting up at the sight of her. The young lady sees him, returns his smile, then lowers her gaze, her face suddenly suffused with a very becoming blush.

For a moment he pauses on the threshold, as if savouring an event that has been a very long time in coming. Then, carefully holding the small bunch of flowers in front of him as if they were a protective shield, Inspector Lachlan Greig pushes open the door to the tea-room.

****

Later still, as dusk falls and the lamplighters begin their rounds, Helena and Lambert Trigg sit on either side of their fireplace. Supper has been shared, and now they are enjoying the peace and companionship. Helena is trimming last year's spring bonnet, with the intention of turning it into this year's one. Lambert is reading the evening paper. He looks up.

"It says here that 'Mr Fitzwarren' also known as Lawyer Jacob Jarvis was a misapplied genius," Lambert pulls a disgusted face. "I quote: *'He is a member of an honourable profession whose talents have taken so perverted and mistaken a direction.'* There! What do you think of that, sister?"

"I think London is well rid of such geniuses, then, and so are we," Helena says tartly.

Lambert reads on. "At the time of his arrest he was defrauding four law firms, two banks and was drawing considerable sums of money from the London and Westminster Bank under a false name and using forged cheques. He used the money to gamble with. It is quite unbelievable!"

"It is quite believable, if you recall the way he defrauded your bank. Does it mention your name?"

Lambert scans the article. "No. Only the detectives who arrested him. But I am glad of it, for I should not like my future to be tainted with the shadow of the past. Nor yours, dearest sister. Let us now put all this behind us. Jarvis is safely behind bars awaiting trial, and my name has been completely cleared of all wrongdoing. I start my new employment on Monday, and most importantly, we are together again at last."

Helena beams at him. "Yes, that is the most important thing of all."

"Tell me again, what were the names of the boy and girl who helped you?" Lambert asks, as he folds up the paper.

"Pin and Muggly," Helena says. "Such funny names. And I know exactly what you're going to say, brother: that we owe them a debt of gratitude. We do, and their reward is already on its way."

Indeed it is. And here, in a part of the city that you will never visit, is the boy Muggly himself, his arm still hanging at an awkward angle, making his way along a series of backstreets, his boots clomping on the damp evening cobbles. He goes round a street corner, sidles down a narrow alley and raps upon the unpainted door of an insignificant house that you would never notice.

The door is opened immediately by Pin, almost beside herself with excitement.

"Oh Muggly!" she exclaims, hauling him over the threshold. "You are here at last. Such a wonder! It has just been brought in. Come and see!"

Muggly follows her up the stairs to the small attic space that doubles as workroom, dining room, living room and Pin's bedroom, and his eyes widen in astonishment. There, on the table, is a great pie. It is covered in a rich golden-brown pastry crust, with a funnel of steam rising from the middle. The whole room smells of steak and onions and heat and happiness.

The two friends gaze at the pie, growing dizzy in their contemplation of its enormous magnificence. And then Pin's sister steps into the room, carrying three tin plates, and a selection of mismatched spoons.

Finis

Thank you for reading this novel. If you have enjoyed it why not leave a review on Amazon and recommend it to others. All reviews, however long or short help writers like me to continue doing what we love.

Printed in Great Britain
by Amazon

40088641R00155